Lifetime Library

Favorite Stories For Young Readers

LORNA DOONE

LORNA DOONE

by R. D. Blackmore

ILLUSTRATED BY PAULINE BAYNES
ABRIDGED BY OLIVE JONES

General Editor: Grace Hogarth

Published simultaneously in the United States and the United Kingdom by

American Education Publications
MIDDLETOWN CONNECTICUT

and

Everyweek Educational Press Limited
RICKMANSWORTH HERTFORDSHIRE

Library of Congress Catalog number 77-106510

Printed in Great Britain by W. S. Cowell Ltd
at their press in the Butter Market, Ipswich

Contents

Editor's Note to Young Readers

THE exciting and haunting story of *Lorna Doone* was first published in 1869. A best seller in England and America, it was translated into many languages and, three different times, made into a film.

One of these movies was recently described this way in the television section of an American newspaper: "Farmers rebel against the terror tactics of the ruthless Doone family. Farmers' leader falls in love with outlaw's niece."

From such a brief description, you might be prepared to watch a typical TV Western. Yet *Lorna Doone* takes place 300 years ago, long before outlaws and feuds appeared in America.

"Doone Country" is Exmoor, a beautiful part of England in the southwestern counties of Devon and Somerset. The rushing rivers and waterfalls, the bare uplands and wooded valleys of Exmoor are much the same today as they were when the Doones were riding high long ago.

Were the Doones real? Did a John Ridd help to bring them to justice? Anyone who has read *Lorna Doone* wants to answer "yes" to these questions because the story seems so real. Yet only part of it can be proved by history books. The rest is built from legend and the imagination of an inspired author.

BLACKMORE'S FINEST WORK

Richard Blackmore wrote many novels during his lifetime (1825–1900). He was puzzled and even upset because none of his other books ever won the same popular acclaim as *Lorna Doone*. Why is this one story still read and loved, long after the author's other novels have been all but forgotten? Perhaps because there is so much of Blackmore's boyhood imagination and experience in this work.

He grew up in Exmoor. He knew the countryside and its people. And, as a boy, he must have believed the legends told in Exmoor about the Doone family. He described the stories as "nurse-tales of childhood—the savage deeds of the outlaw Doones in the depth of Bagworthy Forest."

Blackmore's descriptions of Exmoor, of the Doones, and of John Ridd's country life are vivid and clear. What may not be equally clear to today's readers are the parts of the story based on historical events. To understand these scenes, you should know a little about England 300 years ago.

ENGLAND IN THE SEVENTEENTH CENTURY

The 1600's were years full of religious wars and intolerance. Catholics and Protestants feared each other in many countries, including England. There, in 1649, King Charles I was overthrown in a revolution led by a stern Protestant, Oliver Cromwell. After Cromwell's death, England accepted as its king the Protestant son of Charles I. Charles II ruled until his death in 1685. Then his brother, a Catholic, became King James II.

Like John Ridd's cousin, Tom Faggus, many Protestants feared and hated James II. So they supported the cause and claims of the Duke of Monmouth, a son of Charles II. Monmouth had tried to prove that his mother and father were legally married and that he was therefore the king's legal heir. He failed in this attempt, so later tried to take the throne by force. He gathered an army to march against the forces of James II. At the Battle of Sedgemoor, Monmouth was defeated, taken prisoner, and executed.

Sedgemoor is the battle described when John Ridd becomes the prisoner of Jeremy Stickles. James II is the king whom John meets in London. As you read John's story, you will discover for yourself what it felt like to be living in the seventeenth century.

1. The War-path of the Doones

If anybody cares to read a simple tale told simply, I, John Ridd, of the parish of Oare, in the county of Somerset, yeoman and churchwarden, have seen and had a share in some doings of this neighbourhood, which I will try to set down in order, God sparing my life and memory. And they who light upon this book should bear in mind that I am nothing more than a plain unlettered man, not read in foreign languages, as a gentleman might be, nor gifted with long words save what I may have won from the Bible, or Master William Shakespeare, whom I do value highly. In short, I am an ignoramus, but pretty well for a yeoman.

My father being of good substance, at least as we reckon in Exmoor, and seized in his own right of the best and largest of the three farms into which our parish is divided, he, being a great admirer of learning, and well able to write his name, sent me his only son to be schooled at Tiverton, in the county of Devon. For the chief boast of that ancient town (next to its woollenstaple) is a worthy grammar-school, founded and handsomely endowed in the year 1604, by Master Peter Blundell.

Here, by the time I was twelve years old, I had risen into the

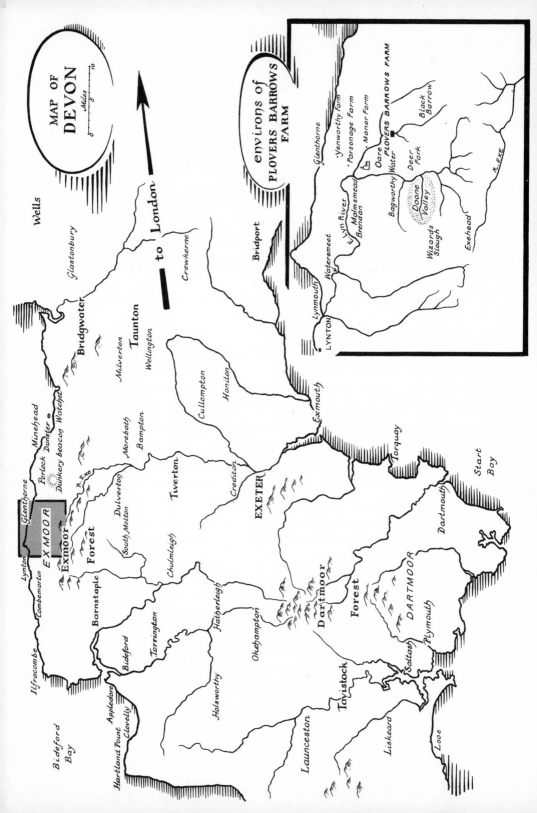

MAP OF
DEVON

Miles
0   5   10

environs of
PLOVERS BARROWS
FARM

PLOVERS BARROWS FARM

Black
Barrow

Glenthorne

Yenworthy Farm

Parsonage Farm

Manor Farm

R. EXE

Deer
Park

Oare

Malmsmead
Brendan

Bagworthy Water

Doone
Valley

Lyn River

Watersmeet

Wizards
Slough

Exehead

Lynmouth

LYNTON

Wells

Glastonbury

to London

Crewkerne

Bridport

Taunton

Milverton

Bridgwater

Wellington

Minehead

Porlock Dunster

Dunkery beacon Watchet

Morebath

Bampton

Cullompton

Honiton

Exmouth

R. Exe

Glenthorne

Lynton

EXMOOR

Combemartin

Exmoor

Forest

South Molton

Dulverton

Tiverton

Crediton

EXETER

Torquay

Start
Bay

Ilfracombe

Barnstaple

Chulmleigh

Hatherleigh

Dartmoor

Forest

Dartmouth

Bideford
Bay

Bideford

Torrington

Okehampton

Dartmoor

DARTMOOR

Plymouth

Hartland Point
Clovelly

Appledore

Holsworthy

Tavistock

Saltash

Liskeard

Looe

Launceston

upper school, and could make bold with Eutropius and Caesar—
by aid of an English version—and as much as six lines of Ovid.
Some even said that I might, before manhood, rise almost to the
third form, being of a persevering nature; albeit, by full consent of all (except my mother), thick-headed. It came to pass,
by the grace of God, that I was called away from learning, whilst
sitting at the desk of the junior first in the upper school. But if
you doubt of my having been there go and see my name graven
on that very form. Forsooth, from the time I was strong enough
to open a knife and to spell my name, I began to grave it in the
oak, and there my grandson reads it now, at this present time
of writing, and hath fought a boy for scoffing at it—"John Ridd
his name."

Now the cause of my leaving Tiverton school, and the way of it,
were as follows. On the 29th day of November, in the year of
our Lord 1673, the very day when I was twelve years old, we
came out of school at five o'clock, as the rule is upon Tuesdays.
According to custom, we drove the day-boys in brave rout down
the causeway, from the school-porch even to the gate. Suddenly
there came from the side of Lowman bridge a very small string
of horses, only two indeed, and a red-faced man on the bigger nag,
Peggy.

"Plaise ye, worshipful masters," he said, "carn'e tull whur our
Jan Ridd be?" The other little chaps pointed at me.

"Oh, John, John," I cried; "what's the use of your coming
now, and Peggy over the moors, too, and it is so cruel cold for
her? The holidays don't begin till Wednesday fortnight, John.
To think of your not knowing that!"

John Fry leaned forward in the saddle, and turned his eyes
away from me.

I pushed the boys right and left as I said, "John, is father up in
town? He always used to come for me."

"Vayther'll be at the crooked post, t'other side o' telling-
house. Her coodn't lave 'ouze by raison of the Christmas bakkon
comin' on, and zome o' the cider welted."

3

He looked at the nag's ears as he said it; and, being up to John Fry's ways, I knew that it was a lie. And my heart fell, like a lump of lead.

From Tiverton town to the town of Oare is a very long and painful road, for the way is still unmade, at least, on this side of Dulverton, although there is less danger now than in the time of my schooling. It is to the credit of this age, that now we have laid down rods and fagots, so that a man in good daylight need not sink, if he be quite sober. There is nothing I have striven at more than doing my duty, way-warden over Exmoor. But in those days, when I came from school, it was a sad and sorry business to find where lay the highway.

We left the town very early in the morning, after lying one day to rest, as was demanded by the nags, sore of foot and foundered. It was high noon before we were got to Dulverton that day. My mother had an uncle living there, but we were not to visit his house this time, at which I was somewhat astonished, since we needs must stop for at least two hours, to bait our horses thorough well, before coming to the black bogway.

Now, at Dulverton, we dined upon the rarest and choicest victuals that ever I did taste. Hot mutton pasty was a thing I had often heard of from very wealthy boys and men; and to hear them talk of it made my lips smack, and my ribs come inwards. And now John Fry strode into the hostel, with the air and grace of a short-legged man, and shouted as loud as if he was calling sheep upon Exmoor, "Hot mootton pasty for twoo trarv'lers, at number vaive, in vaive minnits! Dish un up in the tin with the grahvy, zame as I hardered last Tuesday."

Of course it did not come in five minutes, nor yet in ten or twenty; but that made it all the better when it came to the real presence. Fifty years have passed me quicker than the taste of that gravy. When the mutton pasty was done, and the horses, Peggy and Smiler, had dined well also, out I went to wash at the pump, being a lover of soap and water.

Then a lady's-maid came out. With a long Italian glass in her

4

fingers very daintily, she came up to the pump in the middle of the yard, where I was running the water off all my head and shoulders, and arms, and some of my breast even, and it gave me quite a turn to see her. But she looked at me, no whit abashed, and she said to me, while I was shrinking behind the pump, and craving to get my shirt on, "Good leetle boy, come hither to me. Fine heaven! how blue your eyes are, and your skin like snow. Oh, leetle boy, let me feel it. There now, and you shall love me."

All this time she was touching my breast very lightly, with her delicate brown fingers, and I understood from her voice and manner that she was a foreigner. And then I was not so shy of her, because I could talk better English than she; and yet I longed for my jerkin, but liked not to be rude to her.

"If you please, madam, I must go."

"There, there, you shall go, leetle dear, and perhaps I will go after you. I have taken much love of you. But the Baroness is hard to me. Make the pump to flow, my dear, and give me the good water. The Baroness will not touch, unless a nebule be formed outside the glass."

I did not know what she meant by that; yet I pumped for her very heartily, and marvelled to see her for fifty times throw the water away in the trough, as if it was not good enough. At last the water suited her, with a likeness of fog outside the glass, and the gleam of a crystal under it, and then she made a courtesy to me, in a sort of mocking manner, holding the long glass by the foot, not to take the cloud off; and then she wanted to kiss me; but I have always been shy of that work.

Now, up to the end of Dulverton town, on the northward side of it, the Oare folk and the Watchett folk must trudge on together, until we come to a broken cross, where a murdered man lies buried. Peggy and Smiler went up the hill, as if nothing could be too much for them, after the beans they had eaten, and suddenly we happened upon a great coach and six horses labouring very heavily. John Fry rode on with his hat in his hand, as became him towards the quality; but I was amazed to that degree that I left my cap on my head, and drew bridle without knowing it. For in the front seat of the coach sate the foreign lady, who had met me at the pump. By her side was a little girl, dark-haired and very wonderful, with a wealthy softness on her. But in the honourable place sate a handsome lady. And close to her was a lively child, two or it may be three years old, bearing a white cockade in his hat, and staring at all and everybody. Then I took off my cap to the beautiful lady, without asking wherefore; and she put up her hand and kissed it to me.

I overtook John Fry, and asked him all about them. But John would never talk much till after a gallon of cider; and all that I could win out of him was that they were "murdering Papishers".

We saw no more of them after that, but turned into the side-way. The road got worse and worse, until there was none at all. But we pushed on as best we might. The fog came down upon the moors as thick as ever I saw it: and there was no sound of any sort, nor a breath of wind to guide us. John Fry was bowing forward with sleep upon his saddle, and now I could no longer see the frizzle of wet upon his beard—for he had a very brave one, of a bright-red colour, and trimmed into a whale-oil knot, because he was newly-married.

"Mercy of God! Where be us now?" said John Fry, waking suddenly; "us ought to have passed hold hash, Jan. Zeen it on the road, have 'ee?"

"No indeed, John; no old ash. Nor nothing else to my knowing; nor heard nothing, save thee snoring."

"Watt a vule thee must be then, Jan; and me myzell no better. Harken, lad, harken!"

We drew our horses up and listened, through the thickness of the air, and with our hands laid to our ears. At first there was nothing to hear, except the panting of the horses and the soft sounds of the lonely night. Then there came a mellow noise, very low and mournsome. Three times it came and went again; and then I touched John Fry to know that there was something near me.

6

"Doon't 'e be a vule, Jan! Vaine moozick as iver I 'eer. God bless the man as made un doo it."

"Have they hanged one of the Doones then, John?"

"Hush, lad; never talk laike o' thiccy. Hang a Doone! God knoweth, the King would hang pretty quick, if her did."

"Then who is it in the chains, John?"

"It be nawbody," said John, "vor as to make a fush about. Belong to t'other zide o' the moor, and come staling shape to our zide. Red Jem Hannaford his name. Thank God for him to be hanged, lad; and good cess to his soul, for craikin' zo."

So the sound of the quiet swinging led us even as far as the foot of the gibbet where the four cross-ways are. John Fry shook his bridle-arm, and smote upon Smiler merrily, as he jogged into the homeward track. But I was sorry for Red Jem, and wanted to know more about him, and whether he might not have avoided this miserable end. But John would talk no more about it.

"Hould thee tongue, lad," he said sharply; "us be naigh the Doone-track now, two mile from Dunkery Beacon hill, the haighest place of Hexmoor. So happen they be abroad to-naight us must crawl on our belly-places, boy."

I knew at once what he meant—those bloody Doones of Bagworthy, the awe of all Devon and Somerset, outlaws, traitors, murderers. My little legs began to tremble to and fro upon Peggy's sides, as I heard the dead robber in chains behind us, and thought of the live ones still in front.

We were come to a long deep "goyal," as they call it on Exmoor—to wit, a long trough among wild hills, falling towards the plain country. We rode very carefully down our side, and through the soft grass at the bottom, and all the while we listened as if the air was a speaking-trumpet. Then gladly we breasted our nags to the rise, when I heard something, and caught John's arm. It was the sound of horses' feet, knocking up through splashy ground, as if the bottom sucked them. Then a grunting of weary men, and the lifting noise of stirrups, and sometimes the clank of iron and the blowing of hairy nostrils.

"God's sake, Jack, slip round her belly, and let her go where she wull."

As John Fry whispered, so I did, for he was off Smiler by this time; but our two pads were too fagged to go far, and began to nose about and crop, sniffing more than they need have done. I crept to John's side very softly, with the bridle on my arm.

"Let goo braidle; let goo, lad. Plaise God they take them for forest-ponies, or they'll zend a bullet through us."

I saw what he meant, and let go the bridle; for now the mist was rolling off, and we were against the sky-line to the dark cavalcade below us. John lay on the ground by a barrow of heather, and I crept to him, afraid of the noise I made in dragging my legs along, and the creak of my cord breeches. John bleated like a sheep to cover it—a sheep very cold and trembling. Then just as the foremost horseman passed, scarce twenty yards below us, a puff of wind came up the glen, and the fog rolled off before it. And suddenly a strong red light spread like fingers over the moor-land, and hung on the steel of the riders.

"Dunkery Beacon," whispered John, so close into my ear, that I felt his lips and teeth ashake; "dursn't fire it now, no more than to show the Doones way home again, since the naight as they went up, and throwed the watchman atop of it. Why, wutt be 'bout, lad? God's sake——"

For I could keep still no longer, but wriggled away from his arm, until I was under a grey patch of stone; there I lay, scarce twenty feet above the heads of the riders, and I feared to draw my breath. For now the beacon was rushing up, in a fiery storm to heaven. All around it was hung with red, and a giant beard of fire streamed throughout the darkness.

But most of all, the flinging fire leaped into the rocky mouth of the glen below me, where the horsemen passed in silence, scarcely deigning to look round. Heavy men, and large of stature, reckless how they bore their guns, with leathern jerkins, and long boots, and iron plates on breast and head, plunder heaped behind their saddles, and flagons slung in front of them; more than thirty went along, like clouds upon red sunset. Some had carcases of sheep swinging with their skins on, others had deer, and one had a child flung across his saddle-bow. Whether the child were dead, or alive, was beyond my vision, only it hung head downwards there. They had got the child, a very young one, for the sake of the dress, no doubt, which they could not stop to pull off from it; for the dress shone bright, where the fire struck it, as if with gold and jewels. I longed in my heart to know most sadly, what they would do with the little thing, and whether they would eat it.

It touched me so to see that child, a prey among those vultures, that in my foolish rage and burning I stood up, and shouted to them, leaping on a rock, and raving out of all possession. Two of them turned round, and one set his carbine at me, but the other said it was but a pixie, and bade him keep his powder.

John Fry now came up to me, danger being over, cross, and stiff, and aching sorely from his wet couch of heather. "Small thanks to thee, Jan, as my new waife bain't a widder. And who be you to zupport of her, and her son, if she have one? Zarve thee right, if I was to chuck thee down into the Doone-track."

However, I answered nothing at all, except to be ashamed of myself; and soon we found Peggy and Smiler victualling where the grass was good.

My father never came to meet us, although the dogs kept such a noise that he must have heard us. All at once my heart went down, and all my breast was hollow. There was not even the lanthorn light on the peg against the cow's house, and nobody said "Hold your noise!" to the dogs.

Woe is me! I cannot tell. How I knew I know not now—only that I slunk away, without a tear, or thought of weeping, and hid me in a saw-pit. All I wanted was to hide, and none to tell me anything. By and by, a noise came down, as of women's weeping; and there my mother and sister were, choking and holding together. Although they were my dearest loves, I could not bear to look at them.

2. A rash Visit

My dear father had been killed by the Doones of Bagworthy, while riding home from Porlock market, on the Saturday evening. With him were six brother-farmers. These seven farmers were jogging along, when suddenly a horseman stopped in the starlight full across them.

By dress and arms they knew him well, and by his size and stature; and though he seemed one man to seven, it was in truth one man to one. Of the six there was not one but pulled out his money, and sang small beer to a Doone.

But father set his staff above his head, and rode at the Doone robber. With a trick of his horse, the wild man escaped the sudden onset; although it must have amazed him sadly, that any durst resist him. Then when Smiler was carried away with the dash and the weight of my father the outlaw plundered the rest of the yeomen. But father, drawing at Smiler's head, to try to come back and help them, was in the midst of a dozen men, who seemed to come out of a turf-rick, some a-horse, and some a-foot.

Nevertheless, he smote lustily so far as he could see; and being of great size and strength they had no easy job with him.

But a man beyond the range of staff was crouching by the peat-stack, with a long gun set to his shoulder, and he got poor father against the sky, and I cannot tell the rest of it. Smiler came home, with blood upon his withers, and father was found in the morning dead on the moor.

It was more of woe than wonder, being such days of violence, that mother knew herself a widow, and her children fatherless. Of children there were only three. I was the eldest, and felt it a heavy thing on me; next came sister Annie, with about two years between us; and then the little Eliza.

Now, before I got home and found my sad loss—and no boy ever loved his father better than I loved mine—mother had done a most wondrous thing. Upon the Monday morning, while her husband lay unburied, she gathered a black cloak round her, and set off on foot for the Doone-gate.

In early afternoon she came to the hollow and barren entrance. No gun was fired at her, only her eyes were covered over, and somebody led her by the hand. A very rough road was all that she remembered. At the end of this road they delivered her eyes, and she could scarce believe them.

For she stood at the head of a deep green valley, carved from out the mountains in a perfect oval, with a fence of sheer rock standing round it, eighty feet or a hundred high; from whose brink black wooded hills swept up to the sky-line. By her side a little river glided out from underground with a soft dark babble. Further down, on either bank, were covered houses, built of stone, square and roughly cornered, set as if the brook were meant to be the street between them. Only one room high they were, and not placed opposite each other, but in and out as skittles are; only that the first of all, which proved to be the captain's, was a sort of double house, or rather two houses joined together by a plank-bridge over the river.

Two men led my mother down a steep and gliddery stair-way,

and thence, as far as the house of the captain. And there at the door, they left her trembling, strung as she was, to speak her mind. Now, after all, what right had she, a common farmer's widow, to take it amiss that men of birth thought fit to kill her husband? And the Doones were of very high birth, as well we clods of Exmoor knew; and we had enough of good teaching now to feel that all we had belonged of right to those above us.

A tall man, Sir Ensor Doone, came out with a bill-hook in his hand, and hedger's gloves going up his arms, as if he were no better than a labourer at ditch-work.

"Good woman, you are none of us. Who has brought you hither? Young men must be young—but I have had too much of this work."

And he scowled at my mother, for her comeliness; and yet looked under his eyelids, as if he liked her for it. But as for her, in the flash she spoke. "What you mean, I know not. Traitors! cut-throats! cowards! I am here to ask for my husband."

"Madam," said Sir Ensor Doone, "I crave pardon of you. My eyes are old, or I might have known. Now, if we have your husband prisoner, he shall go free without ransom, because I have insulted you."

"Loth would I be," said mother, sobbing, "loth indeed, Sir Ensor Doone, to accuse any one unfairly. But I have lost the very best husband God ever gave to a woman."

Here mother burst out crying again.

"This matter must be seen to at once," the old man answered. "Madam, if any wrong has been done, trust the honour of a Doone; I will redress it to my utmost. Come inside and rest yourself. What was your good husband's name, and when and where fell this mishap?"

"Deary me," said mother, as he sat a chair for her very polite, but she would not sit upon it; "Saturday morning I was a wife, sir; and Saturday night I was a widow, and my children fatherless. My husband's name was John Ridd, sir, as everybody knows; and there was not a finer or better man, in Somerset or Devon.

He was coming home from Porlock market, and a new gown for me on the crupper, and a shell to put my hair up,—oh, John, how good you were to me!"

"Madam, this is a serious thing," Sir Ensor Doone said graciously, and showing grave concern; "my boys are a little wild, I know. And yet I cannot think that they would willingly harm any one. Send Counsellor to me," he shouted, from the door of his house; and down the valley went the call.

Counsellor Doone came in, ere yet my mother was herself again. A square-built man of enormous strength, but a foot below the Doone stature (which I shall describe hereafter), he carried a long grey beard descending to the leather of his belt. Great eyebrows overhung his face.

"Counsellor," said Sir Ensor Doone, standing back in his height from him, "here is a lady of good repute in this part of the country, who charges the Doones with having slain her husband—"

"Murdered him! murdered him!" cried my mother; "if ever there was a murder. Oh, sir! oh, sir! you know it."

"Put the case," said the Counsellor.

"The case is this," replied Sir Ensor. "This lady's worthy husband was slain, it seems, upon his return from the market at Porlock last Saturday night."

"Cite his name," said the Counsellor.

"Master John Ridd, as I understand. Counsellor, we have heard of him often; a worthy man and a peaceful one, who meddled not with our duties. Now, if any of our boys have been rough, they shall answer it dearly. And yet I can scarce believe it."

The square man with the long grey beard spoke, and his voice was like a fall of stones in the bottom of a mine.

"Few words will be enow for this. Four or five of our best-behaved and most peaceful gentlemen went to the little market at Porlock, with a lump of money. They bought some household stores and comforts at a very high price, and pricked upon the homeward road. When they drew bridle to rest their horses, a robber of great size and strength rode into the midst of them, thinking to kill or terrify. His arrogance, and hardihood, amazed them. He had smitten three of them senseless, for the power of his arm was terrible; whereupon the last man tried to ward his blow with a pistol. Carver, sir, it was, our brave and noble Carver, who saved the lives of his brethren and his own; and glad enow they were to escape. Notwithstanding, we hoped it might be only a flesh-wound, and not to speed him in his sins."

At this atrocious tale of lies mother was too much amazed to do any more than look at him, as if the earth must open. She turned suddenly on Sir Ensor, and caught a smile on his lips.

"All the Doones are gentlemen," answered the old man, gravely. "We are always glad to explain, madam, any mistake which the rustic people may fall upon about us; and we wish you clearly to conceive, that we do not charge your poor husband with any set purpose of robbery; neither will we bring suit for any attainder of his property. Is is not so, Counsellor?"

"Without doubt his land is attainted; unless in mercy you forbear, sir."

"Counsellor, we will forbear. Madam, we will forgive him. The waters are strong at Porlock, and even an honest man may use his staff unjustly, in this uncharted age of violence and rapine."

The Doones to talk of rapine! Mother's head went round so, that she courtesied to them both, scarcely knowing where she was, but calling to mind her manners. With that, she dried her tears in haste, and went, for fear of speaking mischief.

But when she was on the homeward road, and the sentinels had charge of her, blinding her eyes, as if she were not blind enough with weeping, some one came in haste behind her, and thrust a heavy leathern bag into the limp weight of her hand.

"Captain sends you this," he whispered; "take it to the little ones."

But mother let it fall in a heap; and then for the first time crouched before God, that even the Doones should pity her.

Good folk, who dwell in a lawful land, if any such there be, may judge our neighbourhood harshly, unless the whole truth is set before them. Many of us ask leave to explain how, and why, the robbers came to that head in the midst of us. In or about the year of our Lord 1640, great estates in the north country were suddenly confiscated, through some feud of families, and strong influence at Court, and the owners were turned upon the world. These estates were in co-heirship, so that if either tenant died all would come to the live one, in spite of any testament.

One of the joint owners was Sir Ensor Doone, and the other owner was his cousin, the Earl of Lorne and Dykemont. Lord Lorne was some years the elder of his cousin Ensor Doone, and was making suit to gain severance of the cumbersome joint-tenancy, by any fair apportionment, when suddenly this blow fell on them, by wiles and women's meddling; and instead of dividing the land, they were divided from it.

The nobleman was still well-to-do, though crippled in his expenditure, but as for the cousin, he was left a beggar. He thought that the other had wronged him. Many friends advised him to make interest at Court, for, being a good Catholic, which Lord Lorne was not, he would be sure to find hearing there. But he, like a very hot-brained man, although he had long been married to the daughter of his cousin (whom he liked none the more for that), drove away with his wife and sons, and the relics of his money, swearing hard at everybody.

Some say that, in the bitterness of that wrong he slew a gentleman of the Court. One thing, at any rate, is sure—Sir Ensor was made a felon outlaw, through some violent deed ensuing upon his dispossession.

In great despair at last, he resolved to settle in some outlandish part, where none could be found to know him; and so, in an evil day for us, he came to the West of England. And here, when he had discovered a place which seemed almost to be made for him, so withdrawn, so self-defended, and uneasy of access, some of the country-folk around brought him little offerings—a side of bacon, a keg of cider, hung mutton, or a brisket of venison; so that for a little while he was very honest. But when the newness of his coming began to wear away, and our good folk were apt to think, that even a gentleman ought to work, or pay other men for doing it, and all cried out to one another, how unfair it was that owning such a fertile valley, young men would not spade or plough by reason of noble lineage—then the young Doones, growing up, took things they would not ask for.

There was not more than a dozen of them, counting a few retainers, who still held by Sir Ensor; but soon they grew and multiplied in a manner surprising to think of. Whether it was the venison, or whether it was the Exmoor mutton, or the keen soft air of the moorlands, anyhow the Doones increased much faster than their honesty.

There was not one among the Doones but was a mighty man, straight and tall, and wide, and fit to lift four hundred-weight. If son or grandson of old Doone, or one of the northern retainers, failed at the age of twenty, while standing on his naked feet, to touch with his forehead the lintel of Sir Ensor's door, and to fill the door-frame with his shoulders from sidepost even to sidepost, he was led away to the narrow pass, which made their valley so desperate, and thrust from the crown with ignominy, to get his own living honestly. Now, the measure of that doorway is, or rather was, I ought to say, six feet and one inch lengthwise, and two feet all but two inches taken crossways in the clear.

Not that I think anything great of a standard the like of that; for if they had set me in that door-frame at the age of twenty, it is like enough that I should have walked away with it on my shoulders, though I was not come to my full strength then.

Now, after all this which I have written, you will understand the Doones far better than I did; and therefore none will doubt, when I tell them that our good justitiaries feared to make an ado, or hold any public enquiry about my dear father's death. They would all have had to ride home at night and who could say what might betide them?

So we buried him quietly—all except my mother, indeed, for she could not keep silence—in the little churchyard of Oare.

3. Hard it is to Climb

ABOUT the rest of all that winter I remember very little, being only a young boy then, and missing my father most out of doors; as when it came to the bird-catching, or the tracking of hares in the snow, or the training of a sheep-dog. Oftentimes I looked at his gun, an ancient piece found in the sea.

After a little while, it came to me as a natural thing to practise shooting with that great gun. Gradually I won such skill, that I sent nearly all the lead gutter from the north porch of our little church, a thing which has often repented me since, especially as churchwarden, and made me pardon many bad boys.

Almost everybody knows, in our part of the world at least, how pleasant and soft the fall of the land is round about Plover's Barrows farm. All above it is strong dark mountain, spread with heath, and desolate, but near our house are trees, and bright green grass, and orchards full of contentment, and a man may scarce espy the brook, although he hears it everywhere. And indeed a stout good piece of it comes through our farm-yard, and swells sometimes to a rush of waves.

But about two miles below our farm, the Bagworthy water runs into the Lynn, and makes a real river of it. Thence it hurries away, to rocks and woods again, where the stream is covered over, and dark, heavy pools delay it. There are plenty of fish all down this way, and the further you go the bigger they be; and sometimes in the summer months, when mother could spare me off the farm, I came down here, with Annie to help (because it was so lonely), and caught well-nigh a basketful of little trout and minnows, with a hook and a bit of worm on it. For of all the things I learned at Blundell's, only two abode with me, and one of these was the knack of fishing, and the other the art of swimming. And indeed they have a very rude manner of teaching children to swim there; for the big boys take the little boys, and put them through a certain process, which they grimly call "sheep-washing."

As for me, they had no need to throw me more than once, because I jumped in of my own accord. Nevertheless, I learnt to swim there, as all the other boys did. I loved the water naturally, and could not long be out of it.

But now, although my sister Annie came to keep me company, it happened that neither of us had been up the Bagworthy water. We knew that it brought a good stream down, as full of fish as of pebbles. But whether we were afraid or not, I cannot tell, because it is so long ago; but I think that had something to do with it. For Bagworthy water ran out of Doone valley, a mile or so from the mouth of it.

But when I was turned fourteen years old, and put into good small-clothes, buckled at the knee, and strong blue worsted hosen, knitted by my mother, it happened to me without choice, I may say, to explore the Bagworthy water.

My mother had long been ailing, and not well able to eat much; and there is nothing that frightens us so much as for people to have no love of their victuals. Now I chanced to remember, that once I had brought dear mother from Tiverton a jar of pickled loaches, caught by myself in the Lowman river, and baked in the kitchen oven, with vinegar, a few leaves of bay, and about a dozen pepper-corns. And mother had said that, in all her life, she had never tasted anything fit to be compared with them. Being resolved to catch some loaches, I set forth without a word to anyone, in the forenoon of St. Valentine's day, 1675-6. The winter had been long, and snow lay here and there.

I never could forget that day, and how bitter cold the water was. For I doffed my shoes and hose, and put them into a bag about my neck, and tied my shirt-sleeves back to my shoulders. Then I took a three-pronged fork firmly bound to a rod with cord, and a piece of canvas kerchief, with a lump of bread inside it; and so went into the pebbly water, trying to think how warm it was. For more than a mile all down the Lynn stream, scarcely a stone I left unturned, being thoroughly skilled in the tricks of the loach, and knowing how he hides himself.

When I had travelled two miles or so, conquered now and then with cold, and coming out to rub my legs into a lively friction, suddenly, in an open space I found a good stream flowing softly into the body of our brook. And it brought a larger power of water than the Lynn itself had, gliding smoothly and forcibly, as if upon some set purpose. Hereupon I drew up, and having skipped about awhile on the bank, was kindly inclined to eat.

Now all the turn of all my life hung upon that moment. But as I sat there munching a crust of Betty Muxworthy's sweet brown bread, and a bit of cold bacon along with it, it seemed a frightful thing, knowing what I did of it, to venture where no grown man durst, up the Bagworthy water.

However, as I ate more and more, my spirit arose within me. So I put the bag round my neck again, and buckled my breeches far up from the knee, expecting deeper water, and crossing the Lynn, went stoutly up under the branches which hang so dark on the Bagworthy river. Here I had very comely sport of loaches, trout, and minnows, forking some, and tickling some, and driving others to shallow nooks, when I could bail them ashore. Now, if you have ever been fishing, you will not wonder that I was led on, forgetting all about any danger, and taking no heed of the time.

The place grew thicker and thicker, and the covert grew darker above me. For now the day was falling fast behind the brown of the hill-tops. And every moment, as the sky was clearing up for a white frost, the cold of the water got worse and worse, until I was fit to cry with it. And so, in a sorry plight, I came to an opening in the bushes, where a great black pool lay in front of me.

Now, though I could swim with great ease and comfort, and feared no depth of water, yet I had no desire to go over head and ears into this great pool, being so cramped and weary. And the look of this black pit was enough to stop one from diving into it, even on a hot summer's day with sunshine on the water.

But soon I saw the reason of the stir and depth of that great pit, as well as of the roaring sound which long had made me wonder. For skirting round one side, with very little comfort, because the rocks were high and steep, and the ledge at the foot so narrow, I came to a sudden sight and marvel, such as I never dreamed of. For, lo! I stood at the foot of a long pale slide of water, coming smoothly to me, without any break or hindrance, for a hundred yards or more, and fenced on either side with cliff, sheer, and straight, and shining. The water neither ran nor fell, nor leaped with any spouting, but made one even slope of it, looking like a plank of deal laid down a deep black staircase. The look of this place had a sad effect, scaring me very greatly, and making me feel that I would give something, only to be at home again, with Annie cooking my supper, and our dog, Watch, sniffing upward.

I would risk a great deal to know, what made the water come down like that, and what there was at the top of it. Therefore, seeing hard strife before me, I girt up my breeches anew. Then I bestowed my fish around my neck more tightly, and not stopping to look much, for fear of fear, crawled along over the fork of rocks, where the water had scooped the stone out; and softly I let my feet into the dip and rush of the torrent.

The green wave came down, and my legs were gone off in a moment, and I had not time to cry out with wonder, only to knock my head very sadly. But before I knew aught, with a roar of water upon me, my fork, praise God, stuck fast in the rock, and I was borne up upon it. I felt nothing. But presently the dash of the water upon my face revived me.

Therefore I gathered my legs back slowly. And in this manner I won a footing, leaning well forward like a draught-horse, with the ashen stake set behind me. Then I said to myself, "John Ridd, the sooner you get yourself out by the way you came, the better it will be for you." But to my great dismay and affright I saw that no choice was left me now, except that I must climb somehow up that hill of water, or else be washed down into the pool, and whirl around till it drowned me. For there was no chance of fetching back, by the way I had gone down into it; and further up was a hedge of rock on either side of the water-way, rising a hundred yards in height, and for all I could tell five hundred, and no place to set a foot in.

I grasped the good loach-stick under a knot, and so with a sigh of despair began my course up the fearful torrent-way. To me it seemed half-a-mile at least of sliding water above me, but in truth it was little more than a furlong, as I came to know afterwards. It would have been a hard ascent, even without the slippery slime, and the force of the river over it, and I had scanty hope indeed of ever winning the summit. Nevertheless my terror left me, now I was face to face with it, and had to meet the worst.

The water was only six inches deep, or from that to nine at the utmost, and all the way up I could see my feet looking white in the gloom of the hollow, and here and there I found resting-place, to hold on by the cliff and pant awhile. And gradually as I went on, a warmth of courage breathed in me, to think that perhaps no other had dared to try that pass before me. How I went carefully, step by step, keeping my arms in front of me, and never daring to straighten my knees, is more than I can tell clearly. The greatest danger of all was just where I saw no jeopardy, but ran up a patch of black ooze-weed in a very boastful manner, being now not far from the summit.

Here I fell very piteously. But the fright of that brought me to again, and my elbow caught in a rock-hole; and so I managed to start again. Now being in the most dreadful fright, because I was so near the top, I laboured hard with both legs and arms, going like a mill, and grunting. At last the rush of forked water, where first it came over the lips of the fall, drove me into the middle, and I stuck awhile with my toe-balls on the slippery links of the pop-weed, and the world was green and gliddery, and I durst not look behind me. Then I made up my mind to die at last; for so my legs would ache no more, and my breath not pain my heart so; only it did seem such a pity, after fighting so long, to give in, and the light was coming upon me, and again I fought towards it; then suddenly I felt fresh air, and fell into it headlong.

When I came to myself again, my hands were full of young grass and mould; and a little girl kneeling at my side was rubbing my forehead tenderly, with a dock-leaf and a handkerchief.

"Oh, I am so glad," she whispered softly, as I opened my eyes and looked at her; "now you will try to be better, won't you?"

I had never heard so sweet a sound as came from between her bright red lips, while there she knelt and gazed at me. And then, my nature being slow, I wandered with my hazy eyes down the black shower of her hair; and where it fell on the turf, among it was the first primrose of the season. And since that day, I think of her when I see an early primrose.

Thereupon I sate upright, with my little trident still in one hand, and was much afraid to speak to her.

"What is your name?" she said, as if she had every right to ask me; "and how did you come here, and what are these wet things in this great bag?"

"You had better let them alone," I said; "they are loaches for my mother. But I will give you some, if you like."

"Dear me, how much you think of them! Why, they are only fish. But how your feet are bleeding! oh, I must tie them up for you. And no shoes nor stockings! Is your mother very poor, poor boy?"

"No," I said, being vexed at this; "we are rich enough to buy all this great meadow, if we chose; and here my shoes and stockings be."

"Why, they are quite as wet as your feet; and I cannot bear to see your feet. Oh, please to let me manage them."

"Oh, I don't think much of that," I replied; "I shall put some goose-grease to them. But how you are looking at me! I never saw any one like you before. My name is John Ridd. What is your name?"

"Lorna Doone," she answered, in a low voice, as if afraid of it, and hanging her head; "and I thought you must have known it."

Then I stood up, and touched her hand, and tried to make her look at me; but her blushes turned into tears, and her tears to long, low sobs.

"Don't cry," I said, "whatever you do. I will give you all my fish, Lorna, and catch some more for mother; only don't be angry with me."

She flung her little soft arms up, and looked at me so piteously that what did I do but kiss her. It seemed to be a very odd thing, because I hated kissing so, as all honest boys must do. But she touched my heart with a sudden delight. Then I felt my cheeks grow burning red, and I gazed at my legs and was sorry.

Here was I, a yeoman's boy, and there was she, a lady born, and thoroughly aware of it. For though her hair was fallen down, by reason of her wildness, and some of her frock was touched with wet, where she had tended me so, behold her dress was pretty enough for the queen of all the angels! The colours were bright and rich indeed, and the substance very sumptuous.

Now, seeing how I heeded her, and feeling that I had kissed her, although she was such a little girl, eight years old or thereabouts, she turned to the stream in a bashful manner, and rubbed one leg against the other.

I for my part took up all my things to go, and made a fuss about it; to let her know I was going. But she did not call me back at all, as I had made sure she would do; moreover, I knew that to try the descent was almost certain death to me, and it looked as dark as pitch; and so at the mouth I turned round again, and came back to her, and said, "Lorna."

"Oh, I thought you were gone," she answered; "why did you ever come here? Do you know what they would do to us, if they found you here with me? They would kill us both outright, and bury us here by the water."

"But what should they kill me for?"

"Because you have found the way up here, and they never could believe it. Now, please to go; oh please to go. They will kill us both in a moment. I like you very much. I will call you John Ridd, if you like; only please to go, John. And when your feet are well, you know, you can come and tell me how they are."

"But I tell you, Lorna, I like you very much indeed. And I never saw any one like you; and I must come back again to-morrow, and so must you, to see me; and I will bring you such a maun of things—there are apples still, and a thrush I caught with only one leg broken, and our dog has just had puppies"—

"Oh dear, they won't let me have a dog. There is not a dog in the valley. They say they are such noisy things— Hush!" A shout came down the valley and Lorna's face was altered from pleasant play to terror. She shrank to me, and looked up at me, with such a power of weakness, that I at once made up my mind to save her, or to die with her.

"Come with me down the waterfall. I can carry you easily; and mother will take care of you."

"No, no," she cried, as I took her up: "I will tell you what to do. They are only looking for me. You see that hole there?"

She pointed to a little niche in the rock, which verged the meadow, about fifty yards away from us. "There is a way out from the top of it; they would kill me if I told it. Oh, here they come; I can see them."

The little maid turned as white as the snow which hung on the rocks above her. And then she began to sob aloud. But I drew her behind the withy-bushes, and close down to the water. Here they could not see either of us from the upper valley. Luckily I had picked up my fish, and taken my three-pronged fork away.

Crouching in that hollow nest, I saw a dozen fierce men come down, on the other side of the water, but looking lax and jovial, as if they were come from riding. "Queen, queen!" they were shouting, "where the pest is our little queen gone?"

"They always call me 'queen,' and I am to be queen by and by," Lorna whispered to me. "Oh, they are crossing by the timber there, and then they are sure to see us."

"Stop," said I; "now I see what to do. I must get into the water and you must go to sleep."

"To be sure, yes, away in the meadow there. But how bitter cold it will be for you!"

She saw in a moment the way to do it, sooner than I could tell her; and there was no time to lose.

"Now mind you never come again," she whispered over her shoulder, as she crept away, "only I shall come sometimes."

Daring scarce to peep, I crept into the water, and lay down bodily in it, with my head between two blocks of stone, and some flood-drift combing over me. The dusk was deepening between the hills, and a white mist lay on the river. There seemed to be no chance at all, but that the men must find me. For all this time, they were shouting and keeping such a hallabaloo, that the rocks all round the valley rang; and my heart quaked.

Neither in truth did I try to stop it, being now so desperate, till I caught a glimpse of the little maid. And then I knew that for her sake I was bound to be brave, and hide myself. She was lying beneath a rock, thirty or forty yards from me, feigning to be fast asleep, with her dress spread beautifully.

Presently one of the great rough men came round a corner upon her; and there he stopped, and gazed awhile at her fairness and her innocence. Then he caught her up in his arms, and kissed her so that I heard him; and if I had only brought my gun, I would have tried to shoot him.

"Here our queen is! Here's the queen!" he shouted to his

27

comrades; "fast asleep, by God, and hearty! Now I have first claim to her; and no one else shall touch the child. Back to the bottle, all of you!"

He set her dainty little form upon his great square shoulder, and her narrow feet in one broad hand; and so in triumph marched away. Going up that darkened glen, little Lorna turned and put up a hand to me; and I put up a hand to her, in the thick of the mist and the willows.

I crept into a bush for warmth, and rubbed my shivering legs on bark. Then, as daylight sank below the forget-me-not of stars, I knew that now must be my time to get away.

Therefore, wringing my sodden breeches, I managed to crawl from the bank to the niche in the cliff, which Lorna had shown me. Through the dusk, I had trouble to see the mouth; nevertheless I entered well, and held on by some dead fern-stems, and did hope that no one would shoot me. But while I was hugging myself like this, my joy was like to have ended in sad grief. For hearing a noise in front of me, and like a coward afraid to turn round or think of it, I felt myself going down some deep passage, into a pit of darkness. It was no good to catch the sides, for the whole thing seemed to go with me. Then, without knowing how, I was leaning over a night of water.

This water was of black radiance, spanned across with vaults of rock. With that chill and dread upon me, and the sheer rock all around, I must have lost my wits, and gone to the bottom.

But suddenly a robin sang in the brown fern and ivy behind me. Gathering quick warm comfort, I sprang up the steep way towards the star-light. Climbing back, I heard the cold greedy wave go lapping, like a blind black dog, into the distance of arches, and hollow depths of darkness. I scrambled back to the mouth of that pit, as if the evil one had been after me. And sorely I repented now of all my foolish folly in venturing into that accursed valley. Before very long the moon appeared, over the edge of the mountain, and then I espied rough steps, and rocky, made as if with a sledge-hammer, narrow, steep, and far asunder, scooped here and there in the side of the entrance, and then round a bulge of the cliff, like the marks upon a great brown loaf, where a hungry child has picked at it. And higher up, there seemed to be a rude broken track.

Herein was small encouragement; and at first I was minded to lie down and die; but it seemed to come amiss to me. Moreover, I saw a movement of lights at the head of the valley, as if lanthorns were coming after me. Straightway, I set foot in the lowest stirrup (as I might almost call it), and clung to the rock with my nails, and worked to make a jump into the second stirrup. But the third step-hole was the hardest of all, and the rock swelled out on me over my breast, and there seemed to be no attempting it, until I espied a good stout rope hanging in a groove of shadow, and just managed to reach the end of it.

How I clomb up, and across the clearing, and found my way home through the Bagworthy forest, is more than I can remember now, for I took all the rest of it then as a dream, by reason of perfect weariness.

I deserved a good beating that night, after making such a fool of myself, and grinding good fustian to pieces. But when I got home, all the supper was in, and the men sitting at the white table, and mother, and Annie, and Lizzie near by, all eager and offering to begin, and by the fire was Betty Muxworthy, scolding, and cooking, and tasting her work, all in a breath, as a man would say. Betty being wronged in the matter of marriage, a generation or two agone, by a man who came hedging and ditching, had now no mercy, except to believe that men from cradle to grave are liars, and women fools to look at them. I looked through the door from the dark by the woodstack, and was half of a mind to stay out, like a dog, for fear of the rating and reckoning; but the way my dear mother was looking about, and the browning of the sausages, got the better of me.

But nobody could get out of me, where I had spent all the day and evening; although they worried me never so much, and longed to shake me to pieces. I just held my tongue, and ate my supper rarely, and let them try their taunts and jibes, and drove them almost wild after supper, by smiling exceeding knowingly.

The result of my adventure in the Doone Glen was to make me dream a good deal of nights, which I had never done much before, and to drive me, with tenfold zeal and purpose, to the practice of bullet-shooting.

I could hit the barn-door now capitally well, with the Spanish match-lock, and even with John Fry's blunderbuss, at ten good landyards distance. I worked hard at the gun, and began to long for a better tool, that would make less noise and throw straighter. But the sheep-shearing came, and the hay season next, and then the harvest of small corn, and the digging of the root called "batata" (a new but good thing in our neighbourhood, which our folk have turned into "taties"), and then the sweating of the apples, and the turning of the cider-press, and the stacking of the fire-wood, and netting of the woodcocks.

How the year went by, I know not; only that I was abroad all day, shooting, or fishing, or minding the farm, or riding after some stray beast. The fright I had taken that night, in Glen Doone, satisfied me for a long time thereafter; and I took good care not to venture even in the fields and woods of the outer farm, without John Fry for company. Betwixt the desire to vaunt, and the longing to talk things over, I gradually laid bare to him nearly all that had befallen me; except, indeed, about Lorna. Not that I did not think of her, but of course I was only a boy as yet, and therefore inclined to despise young girls.

And yet my sister Annie was, in truth, a great deal more to me than all the boys of the parish put together: Annie was of a pleasing face and very gentle manner, almost like a lady, some people said. And afterwards she grew up to be a very comely maiden, tall, and with a well-built neck, and very fair white shoulders, under a bright cloud of curling hair.

4. A Man justly Popular

IT happened upon a November evening (when I was about fifteen years old, and out-growing my strength very rapidly, my sister Annie being turned thirteen, and a deal of rain having fallen, and all the troughs in the yard being flooded) that the ducks in the court made a terrible quacking. Thereupon Annie and I ran out, to see what might be the sense of it.

Annie began to cry "dilly, dilly, einy, einy, ducksey," but they only quacked three times as hard, and ran round, till we were giddy. I knew at once that there must be something or other amiss in the duck-world. Sister Annie perceived it too, for she counted them like a good duck-wife, and could only tell thirteen of them, when she knew there ought to be fourteen.

And so we began to search about, and found good reason for the urgence of the duck-birds. Lo! the old white drake, the father of all, was now in a sad predicament, yet quacking very stoutly. For the brook was now coming down in a great brown flood.

There is always a hurdle, swung by a chain at either end from an oak laid across the channel. And the use of this hurdle is to keep our kine at milking time from straying away there drinking. But now the torrent came down so vehemently that the chains at full stretch were creaking, and the hurdle was going sea-saw with a sulky splash on the dirty red comb of the waters. But saddest to see was between two bars our venerable mallard, jammed in.

Annie was crying, and wringing her hands, and I was about to rush into the water, when a man on horseback came suddenly round the corner of the ash-hedge on the other side of the stream.

"Ho, there," he cried; "get thee back, boy. The flood will carry thee down like a straw. I will do it for thee, and no trouble."

With that he leaned forward, and spoke to his mare—she was just of the tint of a strawberry, a young thing, very beautiful—and she arched up her neck, as misliking the job; yet, trusting him, would attempt it. She entered the flood, with her dainty fore-legs sloped further and further in front of her, and her delicate ears pricked forward; but he kept her straight in the turbid rush, by the pressure of his knee on her. Then he leaned from his saddle, and caught up old Tom with his left hand, and set him between his holsters.

They landed, some thirty or forty yards lower, in the midst of our kitchen-garden; but though Annie and I were full of our thanks, he would answer us never a word, until he had spoken in full to the mare, as if explaining the whole to her.

"Sweetheart, I know thou couldst have leaped it," he said, as he patted her cheek, "but I had good reason, Winnie dear, for making thee go through it."

She sniffed at him very lovingly, and they understood one another. Then he took from his waistcoat two pepper-corns, and made the old drake swallow them, and tried him softly upon his legs. Old Tom stood up quite bravely, and clapped his wings; and then away into the court-yard.

Having watched the end of that adventure, the gentleman turned round to us, with a pleasant smile; and we came up and looked at him. He was rather short, but very strongly built and springy, his legs were bowed with much riding, and he looked as if he lived on horseback. He was not more than four-and-twenty, fresh and ruddy-looking, with a short nose, and keen blue eyes, and a merry waggish jerk about him.

"Well, young uns, what be gaping at?" He gave pretty Annie a chuck on the chin.

"Your mare," said I, standing stoutly up, being a tall boy now; "I never saw such a beauty, sir. Will you let me have a ride of her?"

"Think thou couldst ride her, lad? Thou couldst never ride her. Tut! I would be loth to kill thee."

"Ride her!" I cried with the bravest scorn, for she looked so kind and gentle; "there never was horse upon Exmoor foaled, but I could tackle in half-an-hour. Only I never ride upon saddle. Take them leathers off of her. Do you think I am a fool, good sir? Only trust me with her, and I will not over-ride her."

"For that I will go bail, my son. She is liker to over-ride thee. But the ground is soft to fall upon, after all this rain. Now come out into the yard, young man, for the sake of your mother's cabbages. And the mellow straw-bed will be softer for thee, since pride must have its fall. I am thy mother's cousin, boy. Tom Faggus is my name; and this is my young mare, Winnie."

What a fool I must have been not to know it at once! Tom Faggus, the great highwayman, and his young blood-mare, the strawberry!

Mr. Faggus gave his mare a wink, and she walked demurely after him, a bright young thing, flowing over with life.

"Up for it still, boy, be ye?" Tom Faggus stopped, and the mare stopped there; and they looked at me provokingly.

"Is she able to leap, sir? There is good take-off on this side of the brook."

"Good tumble-off, you mean, my boy. Well, there can be small harm to thee. I am akin to thy family, and know the substance of their skulls."

"Let me get up," said I, waxing wroth. Then Mr. Faggus was up on his mettle. He spoke very softly to the filly.

"Not too hard, my dear," he said; "let him gently down on

the mixen. That will be quite enough." Then he turned the saddle off, and I was up in a moment. She began at first so easily, and minced about as if pleased to find so light a weight on her, that I thought she knew I could ride a little and feared to show any capers. "Gee wugg, Polly!" cried I, for all the men were now looking on. With that I plugged my heels into her.

First she reared upright in the air, and struck me full on the nose with her comb, and then down with her fore-feet deep in the straw, and her hind-feet going to heaven. Finding me stick to her still like wax, away she flew with me. She drove full-head at the cobwall, then she turned like light, and ground my left knee against it. "Mux me;" I cried, for my breeches were broken, "if you kill me, you shall die with me." Then she took the court-yard gate at a leap, and away for the water-meadows, while I lay on her neck, and wished I had never been born.

Then in her fury at feeling me still, she leaped the wide water-trough sideways across, to and fro, till no breath was left in me. The hazel-boughs took me too hard in the face, and the tall dog-briars got hold of me, till I longed to give up. But there came a shrill whistle from up the home-hill, where the people had hurried to watch us; and the mare stopped as if with a bullet; then set off for home with the speed of a swallow, and going as smoothly and silently. At last, as she rose at our gate like a bird, I tumbled off into the mixen.

"Well done, lad," Mr. Faggus said, good naturedly; for all were now gathered round me, as I rose from the ground some-what tottering, and miry, and crestfallen, but otherwise none the worse. "Not at all bad work, my boy; we may teach you to ride by and by, I see; I thought not to see you stick on so long"—

"Foul shame to thee then, Tom Faggus," cried mother, coming up suddenly, and speaking so that all were amazed, having never seen her wrathful; "to put my boy, my boy, across her, as if his life were no more than thine! The only son of his father, an honest man, and a quiet man, not a roystering drunken robber!"

Everybody looked at mother, to hear her talk like that, knowing

34

how quiet she was, day by day. And the men began to shoulder their shovels, both so as to be away from her, and to go and tell their wives of it. Winnie too was looking at her. And then she came to me, and trembled, and stooped her head, and asked my pardon, if she had been too proud with me.

"Winnie shall stop here to-night," said I, for Tom Faggus still said never a word all the while; but began to buckle his things on. "Mother, I tell you, Winnie shall stop; else I will go away with her. I never knew what it was till now, to ride a horse worth riding."

"Young man," said Tom Faggus, still preparing sternly to depart, "you know more about a horse than any man on Exmoor. Your mother may well be proud of you, but she need have had no fear. Good-bye, John; I hoped to have done you pleasure. But though not a crust I have tasted since this time yesterday, having given my meat to a widow, I will go and starve on the moor, far sooner than eat the best supper that ever was cooked, in a place that has forgotten me." With that he fetched a heavy sigh, as if for my father; and feebly got upon Winnie's back.

But before he was truly gone out of our yard, my mother came softly after him, with her afternoon apron across her eyes, and one hand ready to offer him. "Stop, Cousin Tom," my mother said, "a word with you, before you go."

"Why, bless my heart!" Tom Faggus cried, with the form of his countenance so changed, that I verily thought another man must have leaped into his clothes—"do I see my Cousin Sarah? I thought every one was ashamed of me, and afraid to offer me shelter, since I lost my best cousin, John Ridd. 'Come here,' he used to say, 'Tom, come here, when you are worried, and my wife shall take good care of you.' I am nothing now, since the day I lost Cousin Ridd." And with that he began to push on again; but mother would not have it so.

"Cousin Tom," said mother, "it would be a sad and unkinlike thing, for you to despise our dwelling-house."

Tom Faggus stopped to sup that night with us, and took a little of everything; a few oysters first, and then dried salmon, and then ham and eggs, done in small curled rashers, and then a few collops of venison toasted, and next to that a little cold roast-pig, and a wood-cock on toast to finish with, before the Schiedam.

Tom Faggus was a jovial soul, if ever there has been one. There was about him such a love of genuine human nature, that if a traveller said a good thing, he would give him back his purse again. It is true that he took people's money, more by force than fraud; and the law (being used to the other course) was bitterly moved against him. These things I do not understand; having seen so much of robbery (some legal, some illegal), that I scarcely know, as here we say, one crow's foot from the other. After all, I could not see (until I grew much older, and came to have some property) why Tom Faggus, working hard, was called a robber; while the King, doing nothing at all (as became his dignity), was liege-lord, and paramount owner.

After supper, Tom Faggus kept us very merry, sitting in the great chimney-corner, and making us play games with him. And all the while, he was smoking tobacco, in a manner I never had seen before, having it rolled in little sticks, about as long as my finger, blunt at one end, and sharp at the other. The sharp end he would put in his mouth, and lay a brand of wood to the other, and then draw a white cloud of curling smoke.

Cousin Tom set to, and told us whole pages of stories, not about his own doings at all; but strangely enough they seemed to concern almost every one else we had ever heard of. He spoke with the voices of twenty people, giving each person the proper manner, and the proper place to speak from; so that Annie and Lizzie ran all about, and searched the clock and the linen-press. And he changed his face every moment so, and with such power of mimicry, he made even mother laugh so that she broke her new tenpenny waist-band; and as for us children, we rolled on the floor, and Betty Muxworthy roared in the wash up.

Now although Mr. Faggus was so clever, and generous, and celebrated, I know not whether, upon the whole, we were rather proud of him as a member of our family, or inclined to be ashamed of him. Our place was to comfort rather than condemn him, though our ways in the world were so different, knowing as we did his story. By trade he had been a blacksmith, in the town of Northmolton, in Devonshire. Not only could he read and write, but he had solid substance; a piece of land worth a hundred pounds, and right of common for two hundred sheep, and a score-and-a-half of beasts. And being left an orphan he began to work right early. He loved a maid of Southmolton. Her name was Betsy Paramore, and her father had given consent, when suddenly, like a thunderbolt, a lawyer's writ fell upon him.

This was the beginning of a lawsuit with Sir Robert Bampfylde, a gentleman of the neighbourhood. And by that suit of law poor Tom was ruined altogether. But he saddled his horse, before they could catch him, and rode away to Southmolten, looking like a madman. But when he arrived there, they showed him the face of the door alone; for the news of his loss was before him.

All this was very sore upon Tom; and he took it to heart so grievously, that he said, "The world hath preyed on me, like a wolf. God help me now to prey on the world."

And in sooth it did seem, for a while, as if Providence were with him; for he took rare toll on the highway, and his name was soon as good as gold anywhere this side of Bristowe. Let it be known in any township that Mr. Faggus was taking his leisure at the inn, and straightway all the men flocked thither to drink his health without outlay, while the children were set at the cross-roads to give warning of any officers.

He came again, about three months afterwards, in the beginning of the spring-time, and brought me a beautiful new carbine. And he taught me how to ride bright Winnie, who was grown since I had seen her, but remembered me most kindly.

Now I feel that of those boyish days I have little more to tell. I began to work at the farm in earnest, and tried to help my mother and when I remembered Lorna Doone, it seemed no more than the thought of a dream.

I grew four inches longer in every year of my farming, and a matter of two inches wider; until there was no man of my size to be seen elsewhere upon Exmoor. There is no Doone's door at Plover's Barrows, and if there were I could never go through it. They vexed me so much about my size that I grew shame-faced, and feared to encounter a looking-glass. But mother was very proud, and said she never could have too much of me.

The worst of all to make me ashamed of bearing my head so high was our little Eliza, who never could come to a size herself. Her wit was full of corners, and uncomfortable. You never could tell what she might say next: and I like not that kind of woman.

As for the Doones, they were thriving still, and no one to come against them. Complaints were made from time to time, both in high and low quarters and once or twice in the highest of all, to wit, King Charles the Second himself. But His Majesty made a good joke about it, and was so much pleased with himself thereupon that he quite forgave the mischief. Moreover, the main authorities were a long way off; and the Chancellor had no cattle on Exmoor. Therefore, the Doones went on as they listed, and none saw fit to meddle with them.

Now a strange thing came to pass that winter, when I was twenty-one years old. The weather was very mild and open, and scarcely any snow fell. But the nights were wonderfully dark, and all day long the mists were rolling upon the hills, as if the whole land were a wash-house. The moorland was full of snipes and teal, and curlews flying and crying, and lapwings flapping heavily, and ravens hovering round dead sheep. But that which made us crouch in by the fire, or draw the bed-clothes over us, and try to think of something else, was a strange mysterious sound.

At grey of night, when the sun was gone, and no red in the west remained, suddenly a wailing voice rose along the valleys, and a sound in the air, as of people running. And then there was rushing of something by, and melancholy laughter, and the hair of a man would stand on end, before he could reason properly. When I had heard that sound three times, I was loth to go abroad by night, even so far as the stables.

5. Master Huckaback comes in

MR. REUBEN HUCKABACK was my mother's uncle, being indeed her mother's brother. He owned the very best shop in Dulverton and did a fine trade in soft ware. And we being now his only kindred (except indeed his grand-daughter, little Ruth Huckaback), mother beheld it a Christian duty to keep as well as could be with him, both for love of a nice old man, and for the sake of her children. And truly, the Dulverton people said that he was the richest man in their town.

Now this old gentleman must needs come away to spend the New Year-tide with us. He saddled his horse, and rode off towards Oare, with a warm stout coat upon him, leaving Ruth and his headman plenty to do, and little to eat, until they should see him again.

It had been settled between us, that we should expect him soon after noon, on the last day of December. We had put off our dinner till one o'clock (which to me was a sad foregoing), and there was to be a brave supper at six o'clock, upon New Year's-eve.

Nicholas Snowe was to come in the evening, with his three tall comely daughters, strapping girls, and well skilled in the dairy; and the story was all over the parish that I should have been in love with all three, if there had been but one of them.

Now when I came in, before one o'clock, after seeing to the cattle, I fully expected to find Uncle Ben sitting in the fireplace, lifting one cover and then another, as his favourite manner was, and making sweet mouths over them; for he loved our bacon rarely.

"Oh Johnny, Johnny," my mother cried, running out of the grand show-parlour, where the case of stuffed birds was, and peacock-feathers, and the white hare killed by grandfather: "I am so glad you are come at last. There is something sadly amiss, Johnny."

"Well, mother, what is the matter, then?"

"I only hope it is nothing to grieve about, but what would you say if the people there"—she never would call them "Doones"— "had gotten your poor Uncle Reuben, horse and all?"

"Why, mother, I should be sorry for them. He would set up a shop by the river-side, and come away with all their money. But let us have our dinner. You know we promised not to wait for him after one o'clock; and you only make us hungry. After that I will go to seek for him in the thick of the fog, like a needle in a hay-band."

So we made a very good dinner indeed, though wishing that he could have some of it, and wondering how much to leave for him; and then I set out with my gun to look for him.

I followed the track on the side of the hill, from the farm-yard, where the sledd-marks are—for we have no wheels upon Exmoor yet, nor ever shall, I suppose. After that I went down to the Lynn-stream, and leaped it, and so up the hill and the moor beyond. The fog hung close all around me there.

After that I kept on the track, trudging very stoutly, for nigh upon three miles, and my beard (now beginning to grow at some length) was full of great drops and prickly, whereat I was very proud. We called all this part "Gibbet-moor," but though there were gibbets enough upon it, most part of the bodies was gone, for the value of the chains, they said, and the teaching of young chirurgeons. But of all this I had little fear, being no more a school-boy now, but a youth well acquaint with Exmoor. My carbine was loaded and freshly primed, and I knew myself to be even now a match in strength for any two men of the size around our neighbourhood, except in the Glen Doone. "Girt Jan Ridd," I was called already, and folk grew feared to wrestle with me.

No sooner was I come to the crossways by the black pool in the hole, but I heard a rough low sound, very close in the fog, as of a hobbled sheep a-coughing. A dry short wheezing sound it was, barred with coughs, but thus I made the meaning of it.

"Lord have mercy upon me! An' if I cheated Sam Hicks last week, Lord knowest how well he deserved it, and lied in every stocking's mouth—oh Lord, where be I a-going?"

These words, with many jogs between them, came to me through the darkness, and then a long groan, and a choking. I made towards the sound, and presently was met, point-blank, by the head of a mountain-pony. Upon its back lay a man, bound down, with his feet on the neck and his head to the tail, and his arms falling like stirrups. The wild little nag was scared of its life by the unaccustomed burden, and had been tossing and rolling hard, in desire to get ease of it.

Before the little horse could turn, I caught him, jaded as he was, by his wet and grizzled forelock.

"Good and worthy sir," I said to the man who was riding so roughly; "fear nothing: no harm shall come to thee."

"Help, good friend, whoever thou art," he gasped.

"What, Uncle Ben!" I cried. "Uncle Ben here in this plight! What, Mr. Reuben Hackaback!"

"An honest hosier and draper, serge and long-cloth ware-houseman"—he groaned from rib to rib—"at the sign of the Gartered Kitten, in the loyal town of Dulverton. For God's sake, let me down, good fellow; but take notice that the horse is mine, no less than the nag they robbed from me."

"What, Uncle Ben, dost thou not know me, thy dutiful nephew, John Ridd?"

Not to make a long story of it, I cut the thongs that bound him, and set him astride on the little horse; but he was too weak to stay so. Therefore I mounted him on my back, and leading the pony by the cords set out for Plover's Barrows. Uncle Ben went fast asleep on my back, being jaded and shaken beyond his strength, for a man of three-score and five.

Now as soon as ever I brought him in, we set him up in the chimney-corner, and then he fell asleep again.

"He shall marry Ruth," he said by-and-by, to himself and not to me; "he shall marry Ruth for this, and have my little savings, soon as they be worth the having. Very little as yet, and ever so much gone to-day, along of them rascal robbers."

My mother made a dreadful stir, to see Uncle Ben in such a sorry plight as this; so I left him to her care and Annie's; and soon they fed him rarely, while I went out to look to the comfort of the captured pony. And in truth he was worth the catching, and served us very well afterwards; though Uncle Ben was inclined to claim him. "But," I said, "you shall have him, sir, and welcome, if you will only ride him home, as first I found you riding him." And with that he dropped it.

Of course, the Doones, and nobody else, had robbed good Uncle Reuben; and then they grew sportive, and took his horse, an especially sober nag, and bound the master upon the wild one, for a little change as they told him. For two or three hours they had fine enjoyment, chasing him through the fog, and making much sport of his groanings; and then waxing hungry they went their way, and left him. Now Mr. Huckaback, growing able to walk in a few days' time, became thereupon impatient and could not be brought to understand why he should have been robbed.

"I have never deserved it," he said to himself; "I have never deserved it, and will not stand it; in the name of our lord the King, not I! Nephew Jack, because you have no gift of talking, I think that I may trust you. Now; mark my words, this villain job shall not have ending here. I have another card to play. I will go to King Charles the Second himself, or a man who is bigger than the King, and to whom I have ready access. I will not tell thee his name at present." The man he meant was Judge Jeffreys.

"And when are you likely to see him, sir?"

"May be in the spring, may be not until summer. Now, I have been in this lonely hole, far longer than I intended, by reason of this rage; yet I will stay here one day more, upon a certain condition: that you shall guide me to-morrow, without a word to any one, to a place where I may well descry the dwelling of these scoundrel Doones, and learn the best way to get at them, when the time shall come. Can you do this for me? I will pay you well, boy."

I promised very readily to do my best to serve him; but vowed I would take no money for it. Accordingly, on the day following, with Uncle Reuben mounted on my ancient Peggy, I made foot for the westward, directly after breakfast. Uncle Ben refused to go, unless I would take a loaded gun. There was very little said between us, along the lane and across the hill, although the day was pleasant. I could see that he was not so full of security as an elderly man should keep himself. Therefore, out I spake and said, "Uncle Reuben, have no fear. I know every inch of the ground, sir; and there is no danger nigh us."

"Fear, boy! Who ever thought of fear! 'Tis the last thing would come across me. Pretty things they primroses."

At once I thought of Lorna Doone, the little maid of so many years back, and how my fancy went with her.

My uncle interrupted me, misliking so much silence now, with the naked woods falling over us. For we were come to Bagworthy forest, the blackest and the loneliest place of all that keep the sun out. However, we saw nothing there, until we came to the bank of the hill, where the pony could not climb it. Uncle Ben was very loth to get off, but I persuaded him that now he must go to the end of it. Therefore we made Peggy fast and speaking cheerfully he took his staff, and I my gun, to climb the thick ascent.

There was no path of any kind. And we knew that we could not go astray, so long as we breasted the hill before us; inasmuch as it formed the rampart, or side-fence of Glen Doone. At last, though very loth to do it, I was forced to leave my gun behind, because I required one hand to drag myself up the difficulty, and one to help Uncle Reuben. And so at last we gained the top.

The chine of highland, whereon we stood, curved to the right and left of us, crowned with trees and brushwood. At about half a mile in front of us, another crest, just like our own, bowed around to meet it; but failed, by reason of two narrow clefts, of which we could only see the brink. One of these clefts was the Doone-gate, with a portcullis of rock above it; and the other was the chasm, by which I had once made entrance. Betwixt them lay a bright green valley, rimmed with sheer black rock, and seeming to have sunken bodily from the black rough heights above. It looked as if no frost could enter, neither winds go ruffling. But for all that, Uncle Reuben was none the worse nor better. He looked down into Glen Doone first, and sniffed as if he were smelling it, like a sample of goods from a wholesale house; and then he looked at the hills over yonder, and then he stared at me.

"See you not, how this great Doone valley may be taken in half-an-hour?"

"Yes, to be sure I do, uncle; if they like to give it up, I mean."

"Three culverins on yonder hill, and three on the top of this one—and we have them under a pestle."

But I was not attending to him. For I had long ago descried that little opening in the cliff, through which I made my exit, as before related, on the other side of the valley. Now gazing at it, I saw a little figure come, and pause, and pass into it. Something very light and white, gone almost before I knew that any-one had been there. And yet my heart come to my ribs, and all my blood was in my face, for though seven years were gone, and she must have forgotten me, at that moment, I felt that I was face to face with fate, weal or woe, in Lorna Doone.

45

6. John is Bewitched

Now Master Reuben Huckaback being gone, my spirit began to burn for something to go on with; and nothing showed a braver hope of adventure, than a lonely visit to Glen Doone, by way of the perilous passage discovered in my boyhood. Therefore I waited for nothing more than the slow arrival of new small-clothes, made by a good tailor at Porlock, for it seemed a pure duty to look my best; and when they were come and approved, I started, regardless of the expense, and forgetting (like a fool) how badly they would take the water.

I chose a seven-foot staff of ash, and fixed a loach-fork in it, to look as I had looked before; and out of the back door I went, and so through the little orchard, and down the brawling Lynn-brook. Not being now so much afraid, I struck across the thicket land between the meeting waters, and came upon the Bagworthy stream near the great black whirlpool. Nothing amazed me so much as to find how shallow the stream now looked to me, although the pool was still as black, and greedy, as it used to be. And still the great rocky slide was dark, and difficult to climb; though the water, which once had taken my knees, was satisfied now with my ankles. After some labour, I reached the top; and halted to look about me well, before trusting to broad daylight.

The winter had been a very mild one; and now the spring was toward. The valley into which I gazed was fair with early promise, having shelter from the wind, and taking all the sunshine.

While I was letting my thoughts go wild to sounds and sights of nature, a sweeter note than thrush ever wooed a mate in, floated on the valley breeze, at the quiet turn of sundown. The words were of an ancient song, fit to cry or laugh at.

> "Love, an if there be one,
>   Come my love to be,
> My love is for the one
>   Loving unto me."

All this I took in with great eagerness. But all the time, I kept myself in a black niche of the rock, where the fall of the water began. But presently I ventured to look forth, where a bush was; and then I beheld the loveliest sight.

By the side of the stream, she was coming to me, even among the primroses, as if she loved them all. I could not see what her face was, my heart so awoke and trembled; only that her hair was flowing from a wreath of white violets, and the grace of her coming was like the appearance of the first wind-flower. Scarcely knowing what I did, I came from the dark mouth of the chasm; and stood, afraid to look at her. She was turning to fly, not knowing me, and frightened, perhaps, at my stature; when I fell on the grass (as I fell before her seven years agone that day), and I just said, "Lorna Doone!"

"Oh, indeed," she cried, with a feint of anger; "oh, if you please, who are you, sir, and how do you know my name?"

"I am John Ridd," I answered; "the boy who gave you those beautiful fish, when you were only a little thing, seven years ago to-day. And do you remember how kind you were, and saved my life by your quickness, and went away riding upon a great man's shoulder, as if you had never seen me, and yet looked back through the willow-trees?"

"Oh, yes, I remember everything; because it was so rare to see any, except—I mean, because I happen to remember. But I think, Master Ridd, you cannot know," she said, with her eyes taken from me, "what the dangers of this place are, and the nature of the people." She was trembling, from real fear of violence. And, to tell the truth, I grew afraid.

Therefore, without more ado, it struck me that I had better go. So would she look the more for me, and think the more about me. For, of course, I knew what a churl I was, compared to her birth and appearance; but meanwhile I might improve myself, and learn a musical instrument.

"Mistress Lorna, I will depart"—mark you, I thought that a powerful word—"in fear of causing disquiet. If any rogue shot me, it would grieve you; I make bold to say it; and it would be the death of mother. Few mothers have such a son as me. Try to think of me, now and then; and I will bring you some new-laid eggs, for our young blue hen is beginning."

"I thank you heartily," said Lorna; "but you need not come to see me. You can put them in my little bower, where I am almost always—I mean whither daily I repair; to think, and to be away from them."

"Only show me where it is. Thrice a day, I will come—"

"Nay, Master Ridd, I would never show thee—never, because of peril—only that so happens it, thou hast found the way already."

And she smiled. So I touched her white hand softly, when she gave it to me; and then, for the rest of the homeward road, was mad with every man in the world, who would dare to think of looking at her.

In the early part of March, there came a change of weather. All the young growth was arrested by a dry wind from the east, which made both faces and fingers burn, when a man was doing ditching. In all things there is comfort, and now I had much satisfaction, in my uncouth state, from labouring, by the hour together, at the hedging and the ditching, meeting the bitter wind face to face, feeling my strength increase. In the rustling rush of

48

every gust, in the graceful bend of every tree, in all of these, and many others, there was aching ecstasy, delicious pang of Lorna.

When the weather changed in earnest, and the south-west wind blew softly, and the lambs were at play with the daisies, it was more than I could do to keep from thought of Lorna. And if one stood beneath an elm, all the sprays above were rasped and trembling with a redness. And so I stopped beneath the tree, and carved L. D. upon it.

The upshot of it all was this, that as no Lorna came to me, except in dreams or fancy, and as my life was not worth living without constant sign of her, forth I must again to find her.

In good sooth, I had to spring ere ever I got to the top of the rift leading into Doone-glade. For the stream was rushing down in strength; a mort of rain having fallen last night, and no wind come to wipe it. However, I reached the head ere dark, with more difficulty than danger. Hereupon I grew so happy, at being on dry land again, and come to look for Lorna, with pretty trees around me, that what did I do but fall asleep with my best coat sunk in a bed of moss, among wetness and wood-sorrel.

There was a little runnel, going softly down beside me, falling from the upper rock. This was very pleasant to me, now and then, to gaze at; blinking as the water blinked, and falling back to sleep again. Suddenly my sleep was broken by a shade cast over me; between me and the low sunlight, Lorna Doone was standing.

"Master Ridd, are you mad?" she said, and took my hand to move me. "Come away, if you care for life. The patrol will be here directly. Be quick, Master Ridd, let me hide thee."

Without another word, she led me, though with many timid glances towards the upper valley, to, and into, her little bower. I spoke before of a certain deep and perilous pit, in which I was like to drown myself, through hurry and fright of boyhood. But now it was clear the entrance to the pit was only to be found by seeking it. Inside the niche of native stone, the plainest thing of all to see, at any rate by day-light, was the stairway hewn from rock, and leading up the mountain, by means of which I had escaped. To the right side of this was the mouth of the pit, still looking very formidable; though Lorna laughed at my fear of it, for she drew her water thence. But on the left was a narrow crevice, very difficult to espy, and having a sweep of grey ivy laid over it.

Lorna raised the screen for me, but I had much ado to pass, on account of bulk and stature. However, I got through at last, and broke into the pleasant room, the lone retreat of Lorna. The chamber was of unhewn rock, round, as near as might be, eighteen or twenty feet across, and gay with rich variety of fern, and moss, and lichen. Overhead there was no ceiling but the sky itself, flaked with little clouds of April whitely wandering over it. The floor was made of soft, low grass, mixed with moss and primroses. In the midst a tiny spring arose.

While I was gazing at all these things, with wonder and some sadness, Lorna said, "Where are the new-laid eggs, Master Ridd? Or hath blue hen ceased laying?"

I did not altogether like the way in which she said it, with a sort of a dialect, as if my speech could be laughed at.

"Here be some," I answered, speaking as if in spite of her. "I would have brought thee twice as many, but that I feared to crush them in the narrow ways, Mistress Lorna."

And so I laid her out two dozen upon the moss of the rock ledge, unwinding the wisp of hay from each, as it came safe out of my pocket. Lorna looked with growing wonder, and to my amazement what did she do but burst into a flood of tears!

"What have I done?" I asked, with shame, scarce daring even to look at her, "oh, what have I done to vex you so?"

"It is nothing done by you, Master Ridd," she answered; "it is only something that comes upon me, with the scent of the pure true clover-hay. Moreover, you have been too kind; and I am not used to kindness."

Some sort of awkwardness was on me, at her words and weeping. Therefore I abstained from speech. And as it happened, this was the way to make her tell me more about it.

Lorna liked me all the better for my good forbearance; and told me all about everything I wished to know, every little thing she knew, except indeed, how Master Ridd stood with her.

"There are but two in the world, who ever listen and try to help me; one of them is my grandfather, and the other is a man of wisdom, whom we call the Counsellor. My grandfather, Sir Ensor Doone, is very old and harsh of manner (except indeed to me); he seems to know what is right and wrong, but not to want to think of it. And among the women, there are none with whom I can hold converse, since my Great-Aunt Sabina died, who took such pains to teach me. She was a lady of high repute, and lofty ways, and learning, but grieved and harassed more and more, by the coarseness, and the violence, and the ignorance, around her. Very often she used to say that I was her only comfort, and I am sure she was my only one; and when she died, it was more to me than if I had lost a mother.

"For I have no remembrance now of father, or of mother; although they say that my father was the eldest son of Sir Ensor Doone, and the bravest, and the best of them. And so they call me heiress to this little realm of violence; and in sorry sport sometimes, I am their Princess or their Queen.

"Many people living here, as I am forced to do, would perhaps be very happy, and perhaps I ought to be so. We have a beauteous valley, sheltered from the cold of winter, although I must acknowledge that it is apt to rain too often.

"All around me is violence and robbery, coarse delight and savage pain, reckless joke and hopeless death. Young as I am, I live beneath a curse that lasts for ever."

Here Lorna broke down for awhile, and cried so very piteously, that doubting of my right or power to comfort, I did my best to hold my peace, and tried to look very cheerful. Then thinking that might be bad manners, I went to wipe her eyes for her.

"Master Ridd," she began again, "I am both ashamed and vexed, at my own childish folly. But you, who have a mother, who thinks (you say) so much of you, and sisters, and a quiet home; you cannot tell what a lonely nature is. It does not happen many times, that I give way like this. Sometimes I am so full of anger, that I dare not trust to speech, at things they cannot hide from me. They used to boast to Great-Aunt Sabina of pillage, and of cruelty, on purpose to enrage her; but they never boast to me. It even makes me smile sometimes, to see how awkwardly they come, and offer for temptation to me shining packets of ornaments, and finery, of jewels lately belonging to other people.

"We should not be so quiet here, and safe from interruption, but that I have begged one privilege. This was, that this narrowing of the valley, where it is most hard to come at, might be looked upon as mine, except for purposes of guard. Therefore none, beside the sentries, ever trespass on me here, unless it be my grandfather, or the Counsellor, or Carver.

"You must be tired of this story, and the time I take to think, and the weakness of my telling; but my life from day to day shows so little variance. Neither of the old men is there, whom I can revere or love (except alone my grandfather, whom I love with trembling); neither of the women any whom I like to deal with, unless it be a little maiden, whom I saved from starving.

"A little Cornish girl she is, not so very much less in width, than if you take her lengthwise. Her father seems to have been a miner, a Cornishman of more than average excellence. Very few things can have been beyond his power of performance; and yet he left his daughter to starve upon a peat-rick. His name was Simon Carfax. Gwenny Carfax, my young maid, well remembers how her father was brought up from Cornwall. Her mother had been buried, just a week or so before; and he was sad about it, and had been off his work, and was ready for another job. Then people came to him by night, and said that he must want a change. So what with grief and the inside of a square bottle, Gwenny says they brought him off. The last she saw of him was this, that he went down a ladder somewhere on the wilds of Exmoor, leaving her with bread and cheese, and his travelling-hat to see to. And from that day to this, he never came above the ground again.

"But Gwenny, holding to his hat, and having eaten the bread and cheese, dwelt three days near the mouth of the hole; and then it was closed over, the while that she was sleeping. With weakness, and with want of food, she lost herself distressfully, and went away, for miles or more, and lay upon a peat-rick to die.

"That very day, I chanced to return from Great-Aunt Sabina's dying place. Returning very sorrowful, I found this little stray thing lying, with not a sign of life, except the way that she was biting. Black root-stuff was in her mouth, and a piece of dirty sheep's wool.

"I tried to raise her, but she was too square and heavy for me; and so I put food in her mouth. The victuals were very choice and rare, being what I had taken over, to tempt poor Great-Aunt Sabina. Gwenny ate them without delay, and then was ready to eat the basket, and the ware that had contained them.

"Gwenny took me for an angel and she followed me. I brought her home with me, so far as this can be a home; and she made herself my sole attendant. She has beaten two or three other girls, who used to wait upon me, until they are afraid to come near the house of my grandfather. She seems to have no kind of fear even of our roughest men. As for the wickedness, and theft, and revelry around her, she says it is no concern of hers, and they know their own business best. By this way of regarding men, she has won upon our riders, so that she is almost free from all control of place and season, and is allowed to pass where none even of the youths may go. She sets me good example of a patience and contentment, hard for me to imitate. Oftentimes, I am so vexed that I am at the point of flying from this dreadful valley, and risking all that can betide me, in the unknown outer world. If it were not for my grandfather, I would have done so long ago; but I cannot bear that he should die, with no gentle hand to comfort him.

"Once, indeed, I had the offer of escape, and kinsman's aid, and high place in the gay, bright world. And it ended so dreadfully, that I even shrink from telling you about it; for that one terror changed my life, at a blow, from childhood to a sense of death and darkness. Be content now, Master Ridd; ask me nothing more about it, so your sleep be sounder."

But I, Joh Ridd, being young and rash, had no more of manners than to urge poor Lorna onward. Therefore she went on again.

"It is scarce a twelvemonth yet, although it seems ten years agone, since I blew the downy globe to learn the time of day, or made a captive of myself with dandelion fetters; for then I had not very much to trouble me in earnest.

"But now, at the time I speak of, one evening of last summer, a horrible thing befell, which took all play of childhood from me. I had been long by the waterside, at this lower end of the valley, plaiting a little crown of woodbine to please my grandfather, who likes to see me gay at supper-time. Being proud of my tiara, I set it on my head at once, and ventured by a path not often trod. For I must be home at the supper-time, or grandfather would be exceeding wroth.

"Therefore I made short cut through the ash-trees covert. At a sudden turn of the narrow path, a man leaped out from behind a tree, and seized hold of me. I tried to shriek, but my voice was still; and I could only hear my heart.

"'Now, Cousin Lorna, my good cousin,' he said, with ease, and calmness; 'your voice is very sweet, no doubt, from all that I can see of you. But I pray you keep it still, unless you would give to dusty death your very best cousin, and trusty guardian, Alan Brandir of Loch Awe.'

"'You my guardian!' I said, for the idea was too ludicrous.

"'I have in truth that honour, madam,' he answered with a bow; 'unless I err in taking you for Mistress Lorna Doone.'

"'You have not mistaken me. My name is Lorna Doone.'

"'Then I am your faithful guardian, Alan Brandir of Loch Awe; called Lord Alan Brandir, son of a worthy peer of Scotland. Now will you confide in me?'

"'I confide in you!' I cried, looking at him with amazement; 'why you are not older than I am!'

"'Yes I am, three years at least. You, my ward, are not sixteen. I, your worshipful guardian, am almost nineteen years of age!'

"Upon hearing this I looked at him, for that seemed then a venerable age; but the more I looked, the more I doubted.

"'Now am I to your liking, cousin?' he asked.

"'Truly I know not,' I said; 'but you seem good-natured, and to have no harm in you. Do they trust you with a sword?'

"For in my usage among men of stature, and strong presence, this pretty youth, so tricked and slender, seemed nothing but a doll to me. Although he scared me in the wood, now that I saw him in good twilight, lo! he was but little greater than my little self; and so tasselled, and so ruffled with a mint of bravery, and a green coat barred with red, and a slim sword hanging under him, it was the utmost I could do, to look at him half-gravely.

"'I fear that my presence hath scarce enough of ferocity about it.' He gave a jerk to his sword as he spoke.

"'Hush!' I said; 'talk not so loudly.'

"'I pray be you not vexed with me,' he answered in a softer voice; 'for I have travelled far and sorely, for the sake of seeing you. I know right well among whom I am, and that their hospitality is more of the knife than the salt-stand.'

"'Worshipful guardian,' I said. 'Only tell me, how I am akin and under wardship to thee, and what purpose brings thee here.'

"'In order, cousin—all things in order, even with fair ladies. First, my father is thy grandmother's brother. For my father, being a leading lord in the councils of King Charles the Second, appointed me to learn the law. But first, your leave, young Mistress Lorna; I cannot lay down legal maxims, without aid of smoke.'

"He leaned against a willow-tree, and drawing from a gilded box a little dark thing like a stick, placed it between his lips, and then striking a flint on steel, made fire, and caught it upon touchwood. With this he kindled the tip of the stick, until it glowed with a ring of red, and then he breathed forth curls of smoke, blue, and smelling on the air, like spice. I had never seen this done before, though acquainted with tobacco-pipes; and it made me laugh, until I thought of the peril that must follow it.

"'Cousin, have no fear,' he said; 'this makes me all the safer: they will take me for a glow-worm, and thee for the flower it shines upon. But to return—of law I learned but little. All I care for is adventure. Nevertheless, for amusement's sake, as I must needs be at my desk an hour or so in the afternoon, I took to the sporting branch of the law, the pitfalls, and the ambuscades; and of all the traps to be laid therein, pedigrees are the rarest. And so I struck our own escutcheon, and it sounded hollow. Enough that I followed up the quarry, and I am come to this at last—we, even we, the lords of Loch Awe, have an outlaw for our cousin; and I would we had more, if they be like you.'

"'Sir,' I answered, being amused by his manner, 'surely you count it no disgrace, to be of kin to Sir Ensor Doone, and all his honest family! But tell me, sir, how you are my guardian?'

"'That I will do. You are my ward, because you were my father's ward, under the Scottish law; and now I have succeeded to that right—at least in my own opinion—under which claim I am here but to lead you away from scenes and deeds, which are not the best for young gentlewomen.'

"'But,' said I, 'good cousin Alan (if I may so call you), it is not meet for young gentlewomen, to go away with young gentlemen, though fifty times their guardians. But if you will only come with me, and explain your tale to my grandfather, he will listen to you quietly, and take no advantage of you.'

"'I thank you much, kind Mistress Lorna, to lead the goose into the fox's den! Now, come with your faithful guardian, child. I will pledge my honour against all harm, and to bear you safe to London. Come; you shall set the mode at Court, instead of pining here, and weaving coronals of daisies.'

"'I cannot go, I will not go with you, Lord Alan Brandir,' I answered. 'You are not grave enough for me, you are not old enough for me. My Aunt Sabina would not have wished it; nor would I leave my grandfather, without his full permission.'

"'Fair cousin, you will grieve for this; you will mourn, when you cannot mend it. I would my mother had been here; soon would she have persuaded you. Now adieu, fair cousin Lorna, I see you are in haste to-night; but I am right proud of my guardianship. Adieu, fair cousin, trust me well, I will soon be here again.'

"'That thou never shalt, sir,' cried a voice as loud as a culverin; and Carver Doone had Alan Brandir, as a spider hath a fly. The boy made a little shriek at first, with the sudden shock and the terror; then very bravely he strove, and struggled, to free one arm, and to grasp his sword; but as well might an infant buried alive attempt to lift his gravestone. Carver Doone, with his great arms wrapped around the slim gay body, smiled at the poor young face turned up to him; then he lifted the youth from his feet, and bore him away into the darkness.

"I was young then. I am older now: older by ten years, in thought, although it is not a twelvemonth since. I am now at home with violence; and no dark death surprises me.

"But, being as I was that night, the horror overcame me. My breath went from me, and I knew not where I was, or who.

"Yet hearkening, I heard a sharp sound as of iron, and a fall of heavy wood. No unmanly shriek came with it, neither cry for mercy. Carver Doone knows what it was; and so did Alan Brandir."

Here Lorna Doone could tell no more, being overcome with weeping. Only through her tears she whispered, as a thing too bad to tell, that she had seen that giant Carver, in a few days afterwards, smoking a little round brown stick, like those of her poor cousin. I could not press her any more with questions, although I longed very much to know, whether she had spoken of it, to her grandfather, or the Counsellor. As it grew towards the dusk, I was not best pleased to be there; for some of Lorna's fright stayed with me, as I talked it away from her.

7. John has Hope of Lorna

AFTER hearing that tale from Lorna, I went home in sorry spirits, having added fear for her, and misery about her, to all my other ailments. But the worst of all was this, that in my great dismay and anguish to see Lorna weeping so, I had promised not to cause her any further trouble from anxiety and fear of harm. And this meant that I was not to show myself within the precincts of Glen Doone, for at least another month—unless indeed anything should happen to increase her present trouble and every day's uneasiness. In that case, she was to throw a dark mantle over a large white stone, which hung within the entrance to her retreat, which, though unseen from the valley itself, was conspicuous from the height where I had stood with Uncle Reuben.

Meanwhile the work of the farm was toward, and every day gave us more ado to dispose of what itself was doing. For after the long dry skeltering wind of March and part of April, there had been a fortnight of soft wet; and when the sun came forth again, hill and valley, wood and meadow, could not make enough of him. Many a spring have I seen since then, but never yet two springs alike, and never one so beautiful. Or was it that my love came forth and touched the world with beauty?

But all this made it much harder for us, plying the hoe and harrow, to keep the fields with room upon them for the corn to tiller. The winter wheat was well enough, being sturdy and strong-sided; but the spring wheat, and the barley, and oats were over-run by ill weeds growing faster.

When we met together in the evening round the kitchen chimney-place, my mother, and Eliza, would do their very utmost to learn what I was thinking of. At these times, Annie would never ask me any crafty questions (as Eliza did), but would sit with her hair untwined, and one hand underneath her chin, sometimes looking softly at me, as much as to say that she knew it all, and I was no worse off than she. But, strange to say, my mother dreamed not, even for an instant, that it was possible for Annie to be thinking of such a thing. She was so very good and quiet, and careful of the linen, and clever about the cookery, and fowls, and bacon-curing, that people used to laugh, and say she would never look at a bachelor, until her mother ordered her.

Often I was much inclined to put her on her guard against the approaches of Tom Faggus; but I feared to make a breach between us. And our cousin Tom, by this time, was living a quiet and godly life; having retired almost from the trade.

Perhaps it is needless for me to say, that all this time, while my month was running—or rather crawling, for never month went so slow as that with me—neither weed, nor seed, nor cattle, nor my own mother's anxiety, kept me from looking once every day, and even twice on a Sunday, for any sign of Lorna.

Sure enough at last I saw that the white stone had been covered over with a cloth or mantle,—the sign that something had arisen to make Lorna want me. For a moment, I stood amazed. Then off I set, with small respect either for my knees or neck, to make the round of the outer cliffs, and come up my old access. Nothing could stop me; it was not long before I stood in the niche of rock at the head of the watercourse, and gazed into the quiet glen.

60

Many birds came twittering round me; many trees showed twinkling beauty, as the sun went lower; and the lines of water fell, from wrinkles into dimples. Little heeding, there I crouched. At last, a little figure came, looking very light and slender in the moving shadows. I went towards her. Lorna ran to me. Then she held out both hands to me; and I took and looked at them.

"Come away from this bright place," she whispered, very softly; "I am watched of late. Come beneath the shadows, John."

She stole across the silent grass; but I strode hotly after her. She led me to her own rich bower, and if in spring it were a sight, what was it in summer glory?

"Darling, do you love me?" was all that I could say to her.

"Yes, I like you very much," she answered.

"But do you love me, Lorna, Lorna; do you love me more than all the world?"

"Not by any means," said Lorna; "no; I like you very much, when you do not talk so wildly; and I like to see you come as if you would fill our valley up, and I like to think that even Carver would be nothing in your hands."

"Did they want you to marry Carver? Tell me the truth."

"Not yet, not yet. They are not half so impetuous as you are, John. I am only just seventeen, you know, and who is to think of marrying? But it seems that something frightened them. There is a youth named Charleworth Doone, every one calls him 'Charlie'; a headstrong and gay young man, very gallant in his looks and manner; and my uncle, the Councillor, chose to fancy that Charlie looked at me too much, coming by my grandfather's cottage. That was why I gave the token that I wished to see you, Master Ridd. And now I am watched, and spied, and followed, and half my little liberty seems to be taken from me. I could not be here speaking with you even in my own nook and refuge, but for the aid, and courage of dear little Gwenny Carfax."

She let the gentle tears flow fast, and came and sat so close beside me, that I trembled like a folded sheep at the bleating of her lamb. But recovering comfort quickly, without more ado,

I raised her left hand. And then, before she could say a word, or guess what I was up to, on her finger was my ring—a ring of pearls with a sapphire in the midst of them, as pretty as could well be found, a thing the price of which had quite frightened me, till the shop-keeper said it was nothing at all, and that no young man, with a lady to love him, could dare to offer her rubbish.

"Oh, you crafty Master Ridd!" said Lorna, looking up at me, and blushing now a far brighter blush than when she spoke of Charlie; "I thought that you were much too simple ever to do this sort of thing. No wonder you can catch the fish."

"Have I caught you, little fish? Or must all my life be spent in hopeless angling for you?"

"Neither one, nor the other, John! You have not caught me yet altogether, though I like you dearly, John. As for hopeless angling, John—that all others shall have until I tell you otherwise."

With the large tears in her eyes she drew my ring from off her finger, and held it out to me; and then, seeing how my face was falling, thrice she touched it with her lips, and sweetly gave it back to me. "John, I dare not take it now; else I should be cheating you. I will try to love you dearly, even as you deserve and wish. Keep it for me just till then."

"Dearest darling, love of my life," I whispered through her clouds of hair; "how long must I wait to know, how long must I linger doubting whether you can ever stoop from your birth and wondrous beauty to an ignorant unlettered yeoman"—

"I will not have you revile yourself," said Lorna, very tenderly—just as I had meant to make her. "You are not rude and unlettered, John. You know a great deal more than I do: you have learned both Greek and Latin, and you have been at the very best school in the West of England. None of us but my grandfather, and the Counsellor (who is a great scholar), can compare with you in this. And though I have laughed at your manner of speech, I only laughed in fun, John; I never meant to vex you by it, nor knew that I had done so. Now, John, if you please, it is high time for you to go home to your mother. I love your mother very much, from what you have told me about her, and I will not have her cheated."

"If you truly love my mother," said I, very craftily, "the only way to show it is by truly loving me."

Upon that, she laughed at me in the sweetest manner, and with such provoking ways, and such come-and-go of glances, that I knew quite well, while all my heart was burning hot within me, that Lorna Doone had now begun, and would go on, to love me.

Although I was under interdict for two months from my darling, lighter heart was not on Exmoor than I bore for half the time, and even for three-quarters. For she was safe; I knew that daily by a mode of signals, well-contrived between us now, on the strength of our experience.

Then the golden harvest came. A wealth of harvest, such as never gladdened all our country-side since my father ceased to reap, and his sickle hung to rust. There had not been a man on Exmoor fit to work that reaping-hook, since the time its owner fell, in the prime of life and strength, before a sterner reaper. But now I took it from the wall, where mother proudly stored it.

All the parish was assembled in our upper courtyard; for we were to open the harvest that year, as had been settled with Farmer Nicholas, and with Jasper Kebby, who held the third or little farm. We started in proper order: first, the parson, Josiah Bowden, wearing his gown and cassock, with the parish Bible in his hand, and a sickle strapped behind him. All our family came next, I leading mother with one hand, in the other bearing my father's hook and with a loaf of our own bread and a keg of cider upon my back. Behind us Annie and Lizzie walked, wearing wreaths of corn-flowers, set out very prettily. After us, the maidens came, milkmaids and the rest of them, with Betty Muxworthy at their head, scolding even now. Then the Snowes came trooping forward, Farmer Nicholas in the middle.

After the Snowes, came Jasper Kebby, with his wife new-married. After these the men came. And after these men and their wives came all the children toddling, picking flowers by the way. There must have been three-score of us, and the lane was full of people. When we were come to the big field-gate, Parson Bowden heaved up the rail; and he said that everybody might hear him, though his breath was short, "In the name of the Lord, Amen!"

Then Parson Bowden read some verses from the parish Bible; and then he laid the Bible down on the square head of the gate-post, and despite his gown and cassock, three good swipes he cut of corn, and laid them right end onwards. When he had stowed the corn like that, mother entered, leaning on me, and we both said, "Thank the Lord for all His mercies, and these the first fruits of His hand!" And then the clerk gave out a psalm verse by verse. And when the psalm was sung, parson took a stoop of cider and we fell to at reaping.

Whish, the wheat falls! In truth we did reap well and fairly, through the whole of that afternoon, I not only keeping lead, but keeping the men up to it. We got through a matter of ten acres, ere the sun hung his red cloak on the clouds, and fell into grey slumber. Seeing this we wiped our sickles, and our breasts and foreheads, and soon were on the homeward road.

Of course all the reapers came at night to the harvest-supper, and Parson Bowden to say the grace, as well as to help to carve for us. And some help was needed there, I can well assure you; for the reapers had brave appetites, and most of their wives having babies were forced to eat as a duty. Neither failed they of this duty; and I had no time to ask questions, but help meat and ladle gravy. All the while our darling Annie, with her sleeves tucked up, and her comely figure panting, was running about with a bucket of taties mashed with lard and cabbage. Even Lizzie had left her books, and was serving out beer.

And in truth it was a noble harvest. For we had more land in wheat, that year, than ever we had before, and twice the crop to the acre; and I could not help now and then remembering, in the midst of the merriment, how my father in the churchyard yonder would have gloried to behold it. Presently therefore I slipped away from the noise, and mirth, and crossing the court-yard in the moonlight, I went as far as my father's tombstone.

I had long outgrown unwholesome feeling as to my father's death; and so had Annie. Therefore I was surprised (and indeed, startled) to see our Annie sitting there as motionless as the tomb-stone, and with all her best fal-lals upon her.

"What are you doing here, Annie?" I inquired rather sternly.

"Nothing at all," said our Annie shortly.

I was taken so aback with this that I turned round to march away. But she jumped up, and threw herself upon my bosom, with her face all wet with tears.

"Oh John, I will tell you. I will tell you. Only don't be angry."

"Angry! no indeed," said I; "what right have I to be angry with you, because you have your secrets?"

"And you have none of your own, John; of course you have none of your own? All your going out at night—Oh John, I will tell you everything, if you will look at me kindly, and promise to forgive me. Oh, I am so miserable!"

Now this moved me much towards her. Therefore I allowed her to kiss me, and to lead me away a little, as far as the old yew-tree. But even in the shadow there, she was very long before beginning, and seemed to have two minds about it, or rather perhaps a dozen; and she laid her cheek against the tree, and sobbed till it was pitiful.

"Now will you stop?" I said at last, for I knew that she would go on all night, if any one encouraged her.

"Yes, I will stop," said Annie, panting; "you are very hard on me, John; but I know you mean it for the best. If somebody else had been taken so with a pain all round the heart, John, perhaps you would have kissed her, and come a little nearer, and made opportunity to be very loving."

"From your knowledge of these things, Annie, you must have had them done to you. I demand to know this very moment who has taken such liberties."

"Then, John, you shall never know, if you ask in that manner.

Besides it was no liberty in the least at all. Cousins have a right to do things . . ." Here Annie stopped quite suddenly, having so betrayed herself.

"Alas, I feared it would come to this," I answered very sadly; "I know he has been here many a time, without showing himself to me. There is nothing meaner than for a man to sneak, and steal a young maid's heart, without her people knowing it."

"You are not doing anything of that sort yourself, then, dear John, are you?"

"Only a common highwayman!" I answered, without heeding her; "a man without an acre of his own, and liable to hang upon any common, and no other right of common over it"—

"John," said my sister, "are the Doones privileged not to be hanged upon common land?"

At this I was so thunderstruck, that I rushed across the yard, and back into the kitchen.

Meanwhile the reapers were mostly gone, to be up betimes in the morning; and some were led by their wives; and some had to lead their wives themselves; according to the capacity of man and wife respectively.

Now it began to occur to me that although dear Annie had behaved so very badly and rudely, yet it was not kind of me to leave her out there at that time of night, all alone, and in such distress. Moreover, it was only right that I should learn, for Lorna's sake, how far Annie had penetrated our secret.

Therefore I went forth at once. Poor Annie was gone back again to our father's grave; and there she sat, sobbing very gently. So I raised her tenderly, and made much of her.

"My poor Annie, have you really promised him to be his wife?"

"I to marry before my brother, and leave him with none to take care of him! Who can do him a red deer collop, as I can? Come home, dear, at once, and I will do one for you; for you never ate a morsel of supper, with all the people you had to attend upon."

This was true enough; and I allowed her to lead me home, with the thoughts of the collop uppermost. But the young hussy stopped at the farmyard gate, she looked me full in the face by the moonlight, and jerked out quite suddenly, "Can your love do a collop, John?"

"No, I should hope not," I answered rashly; "she is not a mere cook-maid, I should hope."

"She is not half so pretty as Sally Snowe; I will answer for that."

"She is ten thousand times as pretty as ten thousand Sally Snowes," I replied with great indignation.

"Oh, but look at Sally's eyes!" cried my sister rapturously.

"Look at Lorna Doone's," said I; "and you would never look again at Sally's."

"Oh, Lorna Doone, Lorna Doone!" exclaimed our Annie, clapping her hands with triumph, at having found me out so: "Lorna Doone is the lovely maiden, who has stolen poor somebody's heart so. Ah, I shall remember it; because it is so queer a name."

"I have a great mind to lend you a box on the ear," I answered her in my vexation; "and I would, if you had not been crying so, you sly good-for-nothing baggage. As it is, I shall keep it for Master Faggus, and add interest for keeping."

"Oh no, John; oh no, John," she begged me earnestly, being sobered in a moment. "Promise me, dear John, that you will not strike him; and I will promise you faithfully to keep your secret, even from mother, and even from Cousin Tom himself."

"Well," I replied, "it is no use crying over spilt milk, Annie. You have my secret, and I have yours; and I scarcely know which of the two is likely to have the worst time of it, when it comes to mother's ears."

We entered the house. And then Annie said to me very slyly, between a smile and a blush, "Don't you wish Lorna Doone was here, John, in the parlour along with mother; instead of those two fashionable milkmaids, as Uncle Ben will call them. But now you go into the parlour, dear, while I do your collop. Faith

Snowe is not come, but Polly and Sally. Sally has made up her mind to conquer you this very blessed evening, John."

And so dear Annie, having grown quite brave, gave me a little push into the parlour, where I was quite abashed to enter, after all I had heard about Sally. Behind the curtain drawn across the window-seat, no less a man than Uncle Ben was sitting half asleep and weary; and by his side a little girl, very quiet and very watchful. My mother led me to Uncle Ben, and he took my hand without rising, muttering something not over-polite, about my being bigger than ever. I asked him heartily how he was, and he said, "Well enough, for that matter; but none the better for the noise you great clods have been making. Now (if you can see so small a thing, after emptying flagons much larger) this is my granddaughter, and my heiress"— here he glanced at mother— "my heiress, little Ruth Huckaback."

"I am very glad to see you, Ruth," I answered, offering her my hand, which she seemed afraid to take; "welcome to Plover's Barrows, my good cousin Ruth."

However, my good cousin Ruth only arose, and made me a courtesy, and lifted her great brown eyes at me, more in fear, as I thought, than kinship.

"Come out to the kitchen, dear, and let me chuck you to the ceiling," I said, just to encourage her; "I always do it to little girls; and then they can see the hams and bacon." But Uncle Reuben burst out laughing; and Ruth turned away with a deep rich colour.

"Do you know how old she is, you numskull?" said Uncle Ben, in his dryest drawl; "she was seventeen last July, sir."

Here mother came up to my rescue, and said, "If my son may not dance Miss Ruth, at any rate he may dance with her. We have only been waiting for you, dear John, to have a little harvest dance, with the kitchen door thrown open."

8. John Fry's Errand

Now many people may wish to know, as indeed I myself did very greatly, what had brought Master Huckaback over from Dulverton, and yet more surprising it seemed to me, that he should have brought his granddaughter also, instead of the troops of dragoons, without which he had vowed he would never come here again.

He seemed in no hurry to take his departure, and presently Lizzie, who was the sharpest among us, said in my hearing that she believed he had purposely timed his visit so that he might have liberty to pursue his own object, whatsoever it were, without interruption from us. Now how could we look into it, without watching Uncle Reuben, whenever he went abroad? To my mind it was not clear, whether it would be fair-play at all, to follow a visitor, even at a distance from home and clear of our premises; except for the purpose of fetching him back.

For his mode was directly after breakfast to go forth upon Dolly, our Annie's pony, with a bag of good victuals hung behind him, and two great cavalry pistols in front. And he always wore his meanest clothes, as if expecting to be robbed, or to disarm the temptation thereto; and he never took his golden chronometer, neither his bag of money. He never returned until dark or more. And then Dolly always seemed very weary, and stained with a muck from beyond our parish.

But I refused to follow him, not only for the loss of a day's work to myself but chiefly because I could not think it would be upright and manly.

What was my astonishment the very next day to perceive that instead of fourteen reapers, we were only thirteen left.

"Who has been and left his scythe?" I asked; "and here's a tin cup never handled!"

"Whoy, dudn't ee knaw, Maister Jan," said Bill Dadds, looking at me queerly, "as Jan Vry wur gane avore braxvass?"

"Oh, very well," I answered, "John knows what he is doing." For John Fry was a kind of foreman now, and it would not do to say anything that might lessen his authority. But when I came home in the evening, late and almost weary, there was no Annie cooking my supper. Upon this, I went to the girls' room, not in the very best of tempers; and there I found all three of them eagerly listening to John Fry telling some great adventure.

"What does all this nonsense mean?" I said, in a voice which frightened them, as I could see by the light of our own mutton candles; "John Fry, you be off to your wife at once, or you shall have what I owe you now, instead of to-morrow morning."

John made no answer, but scratched his head, and looked at the maidens to take his part. Upon this Annie said very gently, "Now, John, sit down, and you shall know all that we have done, though I doubt whether you will approve of it. You must know, dear John, that we have been extremely curious, ever since Uncle Reuben came, to know what he was come for, especially at this time of year, when he is at his busiest. Well, we might have put up with it, if it had not been for his taking Dolly, my own pet Dolly, away every morning and keeping her out until close upon dark, and then bringing her home in a frightful condition. When we came to consider it, Ruth was the cleverest of us all; for she

70

said that surely we must have some man we could trust, about the farm, to go on a little errand; and then I remembered that old John Fry would do anything for money. And so Lizzie ran for John Fry at once, and we gave him full directions. He was to travel all up the black combe, by the track Uncle Reuben had taken; and up at the top to look forward carefully, and so to trace him without being seen."

"Well, and what did you see, John?" I asked.

"John was just at the very point of it," Lizzie answered me sharply, "when you chose to come in and stop him."

"Then let him begin again," said I.

But as he could not tell a tale in the manner of my Lorna I will take it from his mouth altogether, and state in brief what happened. When John, upon his forest pony, was come to the top of the long black combe, two miles or more from Plover's Barrows, he stopped his little nag short of the crest, and got off, and looked ahead of him. It was a long flat sweep of moorland over which he was gazing, with a few bogs here and there. John Fry knew the place well enough, but he liked it none the more for that; and, indeed, all the neighbourhood of Black Barrow Down lay under grave imputation of having been enchanted with a very evil spell.

Therefore it was very bold in John to venture across that moor alone, even with a fast pony under him, and some whiskey by his side. The truth was that he could not resist his own great curiosity. For, carefully spying across the moor, he thought he saw a figure moving in the furthest distance upon Black Barrow Down. John knew that the man who was riding there could be none but Uncle Reuben, for none of the Doones ever passed that way, and the shepherds were afraid of it. John so throbbed with hope to find some wealthy secret, that he resolved to go to the end of the matter. Therefore he only waited awhile, for fear of being discovered, till Master Huckaback turned to the left, and entered a little gully. Then John remounted, and picked his way among the morasses, as fast as ever he dared to go; until, in about half an hour, he drew nigh the entrance of the gully.

But he soon perceived that the gully was empty, and with that he hastened into it, though his heart was not working easily. Some yellow sand lay here and there between the starving grasses, and this he examined narrowly for a trace of Master Huckaback. At last he saw that the man he was pursuing had taken the course which led down hill; and down the hill he must follow him. And this John did with deep misgivings. For now he knew not where he was, and scarcely dared to ask himself, having heard of a horrible hole, somewhere in this neighbourhood, called the "Wizard's Slough". Therefore John rode down the slope, with great caution. Suddenly he turned a corner, and saw a scene which stopped him.

For there was the Wizard's Slough itself, as black as death, and bubbling, with a few scant yellow reeds in a ring around it. Outside these, bright watergrass of the liveliest green was creeping, tempting any unwary foot to step, and plunge, and founder. Of this horrible quagmire, the worst upon all Exmoor, John had heard from his grandfather. And now he proved how well it is to be wary and wide-awake, even in lonesome places. For at the other side of the Slough, where the ground was less noisome, he had observed a felled tree lying over a great hole in the earth, with staves of wood, and slabs of stone, and some yellow gravel around it. He could not make out the meaning of it, except that it probably was witchcraft. Yet Dolly seemed not to be harmed by it; for there she was, as large as life, tied to a stump not far beyond.

While John was trembling within himself, suddenly to his great amazement something white arose out of the hole. Seeing this his blood went back within him. However, the white thing itself was not so very awful, being nothing more than a long-coned night-cap with a tassel on the top, such as criminals wear at hanging-time. But when John saw a man's face under it, and a man's neck and shoulders slowly rising out of the pit, he could not doubt that this was the place where the murderers come to life again, according to the Exmoor story. Therefore he could bear no more, but climbed on his horse, and rode away at full gallop.

When John Fry had finished his story at last, I said to him very sternly, "Now, John, you have dreamed half this, my man. You know what a liar you are, John."

"This here be no lai, Maister Jan," said John, looking at me very honestly. "I wush to God it wor, boy; a maight slape this neight the better."

"I believe you speak the truth, John; and I ask your pardon. Now not a word to any one, about this strange affair. There is mischief brewing, I can see; and it is my place to attend to it."

The story told by John Fry that night made me very uneasy. We knew for certain that at Taunton, Bridgwater, and even Dulverton, there was much disaffection towards the King, and regret for the days of the Puritans.

But now we heard of arms being landed at Lynmouth, in the dead of the night, and of the tramp of men having reached some one's ears. For it must be plain to any conspirator that for the secret muster of men, and the stowing of unlawful arms, and communication by beacon lights, scarcely a fitter place could be found than the wilds of Exmoor, with deep ravines running far inland from an unwatched and mostly a sheltered sea.

But even supposing it probable that something against King Charles the Second were now in preparation amongst us, was it likely that Master Huckaback, a wealthy man, and a careful one, would have anything to do with it? That he hated the Papists, I knew full well; also that he had followed the march of Oliver Cromwell's army, but more as a suttler (people said) than as a real soldier; and that he would risk a great deal of money, to have his revenge on the Doones.

But how was it likely to be, as to the Doones themselves? Which side would they probably take in the coming movement, if movement indeed it would be? So far as they had any religion at all, by birth they were Roman Catholics—so much I knew from Lorna. Before I could quite make up my mind how to act in this difficulty, Uncle Ben went away, as suddenly as he first had come to us, giving no reason for his departure, and indeed leaving something behind him of great value to my mother. For he begged her to see to his young grand-daughter, until he could find opportunity of fetching her safely to Dulverton.

By this time, the harvest being done, and the thatching of the ricks made sure against south-western tempests, I began to burn in spirit for the sight of Lorna. I had begged my sister Annie to let Sally Snowe know, once for all, that it was not in my power to have anything more to do with her. And Annie did this uncommonly well, as she herself told me afterwards, having taken Sally in the sweetest manner into her pure confidence, and opened half her bosom to her, about my very sad love affair. Sally changed colour a little at this, and then went on about a red cow which had passed seven needles at milking time.

Upon the very day when the eight weeks were expiring, forth I went in search of Lorna, taking the pearl ring hopefully, and all the new-laid eggs I could find, and a dozen and a half of small trout from our brook. But alas, I was utterly disappointed; for although I waited and waited for hours, no Lorna ever appeared at all. And another thing occurred as well, which vexed me. And this was that my little offering of the trout, and the new-laid eggs, was carried off in the coolest manner by that vile Carver Doone. For thinking to keep them the fresher and nicer, I laid them in a little bed of reeds by the side of the water, and placed some dog-leaves over them. And when I was watching from my hiding-place beneath the willow-tree I became aware of a great man coming leisurely down the valley. He might have seemed a good man, but for the cold and cruel hankering of his steel-blue eyes.

As he marched along the margin of the stream, he espied my little hoard, covered up with dog-leaves. He saw that the leaves were upside down, and this of course drew his attention. I saw him stoop, and lay bare the fish, and the eggs set a little way from them. To my surprise, he seemed well-pleased; and his harsh short laughter came to me without echo. "Ha, ha! Charlie boy! Fisherman Charlie, have I caught thee setting bait for Lorna? Now I understand thy fishings, and the robbing of Counsellor's hen roost. May I never have good roasting, if I have it not to-night, and roast thee, Charlie, afterwards!"

With this he calmly packed up my fish, and all the best of dear Annie's eggs; and went away chuckling. As I hastened sadly homeward, the wind of early autumn moaned across the moorland.

One night I noticed Betty Muxworthy going on most strangely. She made the queerest signs to me, and laid her fingers on her lips, and pointed over her shoulder. But I took little heed of her. But presently she poked me, and passing close to my ear whispered, so that none else could hear her, "Larna Doo-un."

By these words I was so startled, that I turned round and stared at her; but she pretended not to know it, and began with all her might to scour an empty crock with a besom. Favouring me with another wink, Betty went and fetched the lanthorn from the hook inside the door. Then when she had kindled it, she went outside, and pointed to the great bock of wash, and riddlings, and brown hulkage (for we ground our own corn always), and said to me quietly, "Jan Ridd, carr thic thing for me."

So I carried it for her, without any words. Then she turned upon me suddenly and saw that I had the bock by one hand very easily.

"Jan Ridd," she said, "there be no other man in England cud a'dood it. Now thee shalt have Larna."

While I was wondering how my chance of having Lorna could depend upon my power to carry pig's-wash, Betty set me to feed the pigs, while she held the lanthorn; and I saw that she would not tell me another word, until the pigs were served.

"Come now, Betty," I said, when all the pigs were at it, sucking, swilling, munching, guzzling, thrusting, and spilling the food upon the backs of their brethren (as great men do with their charity), "come now, Betty, how much longer am I to wait for your message? Surely I am as good as a pig."

"Dunno as thee be, Jan. No strakiness in thy bakkon. Now, tak my advice, Jan; thee marry Zally Snowe."

"Not with all England for her dowry. Oh Betty, you know better."

75

"Ah's me! I know much worse, Jan. Break thy poor mother's heart it will. Dost love Larna now so much?"

"With all the strength of my heart and soul. I will have her, or I will die, Betty."

"And do her love thee too, Jan?"

"I hope she does, Betty. I hope she does."

"Ah, then I may hold my tongue to it. Now, Jan, I will tell thee one thing, can't bear to zee thee vretting so. Hould thee head down, same as they pegs do."

So I bent my head quite close to her; and she whispered in my ear, "Goo of a marning, thee girt soft. Her can't get out of an avening now, her hath zent word to me, to tull'ee."

In the glory of my delight at this, I bestowed upon Betty a chaste salute, with all the pigs for witnesses. Of course I was up the very next morning before the October sunrise, and away through the wild and the woodland towards the Bagworthy water, at the foot of the long cascade. The rising of the sun was noble in the cold and warmth of it. Now, as I stood with scanty breath at the top of the long defile, and the bottom of the mountain gorge, my discontent fell away into wonder and rapture.

Much abashed with joy was I, when I saw my Lorna coming.

"At last then, you are come, John. I thought you had forgotten me. I could not make you understand—they have kept me prisoner every evening: but come into my house; you are in danger here."

Meanwhile I could not answer, being overcome with joy; but followed to her little grotto, where I had been twice before. I knew that the crowning moment of my life was coming—that Lorna would own her love for me.

"You know what I am come to ask," I whispered very softly.

"If you are come on purpose to ask anything, why do you delay so?" She turned away, but I saw that her lips were trembling.

"I delay so long, because I fear; because my whole life hangs in balance on a single word. I have loved you long and long," I pursued, being reckless now; "when you were a little child, as a boy I worshipped you; now that you are a full-grown maiden,—I love you, more than tongue can tell."

"You have been very faithful, John," she murmured to the fern and moss; "I suppose I must reward you."

"That will not do for me," I said; "I must have your heart of hearts; even as you have mine, Lorna."

While I spoke, she glanced up shyly, flung both arms around my neck, and answered with her heart on mine, "Darling, you have won it all. I shall never be my own again. I am yours, my own one, for ever and for ever."

I am sure I know not what I did, or what I said thereafter, being overcome with transport by her words and at her gaze. I had taken one sweet hand; and then I slipped my little ring upon the wedding finger; and this time Lorna kept it, and clung to me with a flood of tears.

"It can never, never be," she murmured to herself alone. "Who am I, to dream of it?"

There was, however, no possibility of depressing me at such a time. Therefore, at her own entreaty taking a very quick adieu, and by her own invitation an exceeding kind one, I hurried home with deep exulting, yet some sad misgivings, for Lorna had made me promise now to tell my mother everything.

Unluckily for my designs, who should be sitting down at breakfast with my mother and the rest but Squire Faggus, as everybody now began to entitle him? I noticed something odd about him, something uncomfortable in his manner. He took his breakfast as it came, without a single joke about it, or preference of this to that; but with sly soft looks at Annie, who seemed unable to sit quiet, or to look at any one steadfastly. I feared in my heart what was coming on, and felt truly sorry for poor mother. Being resolved to allow him fair field to himself, I carried my dinner upon my back, and spent the whole day with the furrows.

When I returned, Squire Faggus was gone. And Lizzie came running to meet me, at the bottom of the woodrick, and cried, "Oh John, there is such a business. Mother is in such a state of mind, and Annie crying her eyes out. What do you think? You never would guess; though I have suspected it, ever so long."

"No need for me to guess," I replied, as though with some indifference; "I knew all about it long ago."

Mother sent at once for me, while I was trying to console my darling sister Annie.

"Oh, John! speak one good word for me," she cried, with her tearful eyes looking up at me.

"Not one, my pet, but a hundred," I answered; "have no fear, little sister; I am going to make your case so bright, by comparison I mean, that mother will send for you in five minutes, and call you her best, her most dutiful child, and praise Cousin Tom to the skies."

"Oh John, dear John, you won't tell her about Lorna—oh not to-day, dear. I am sure she could not bear it, after this great shock already."

"She will bear it all the better," said I; "the one will drive the other out."

I would regret to write down what mother said about Lorna, in her first surprise and tribulation. However, by the afternoon, when the sun began to go down upon us, our mother sat on the garden bench, with her head on my great otter-skin waistcoat (which was waterproof), and her right arm round our Annie's waist, and scarcely knowing which of us she ought to make the most of, or which deserved most pity. Not that she had forgiven yet the rivals to her love—Tom Faggus, I mean, and Lorna—but that she was beginning to think a little better of them now.

After this, for another month, nothing worthy of notice happened, except perhaps that I found it needful to visit Lorna, immediately after my discourse with mother, and to tell her all about it. My beauty gave me one sweet kiss with all her heart, and I begged for one more to take to our mother, and before leaving, I obtained it. When I told her how my mother and Annie, as well as myself, longed to have her at Plover's Barrows, she only answered with a bright blush, that while her grandfather was living she would never leave him; and asked how long I would wait for her.

"Not a day if I had my will," I answered very warmly; "but all my life," I went on to say, "if my fortune is so ill. And how long would you wait for me, Lorna?"

"Till I could get you," she answered slyly, with a smile which was brighter to me than the brightest wit could be. "And now," she continued, "you bound me, John, with a very beautiful ring to you, and when I dare not wear it, I carry it always on my heart. But I will bind you to me, you dearest, with the very poorest and plainest thing that ever you set eyes on. Look at it, what a queer old thing! There are some ancient marks upon it, very grotesque and wonderful; it looks like a cat in a tree almost. This old ring must have been a giant's; therefore it will fit you perhaps, you enormous John. It has been on the front of my old glass necklace (which my grandfather found them taking away, and very soon made them give back again) ever since I can remember; and long before that, as some woman told me. Now you seem very greatly amazed; pray what thinks my lord of it?"

"That it is worth fifty of the pearl thing which I gave you, you darling. This is not the ring of any giant. It is nothing more nor less than a very ancient thumb-ring. I will accept it, my own one love; and it shall go to my grave with me." And so it shall, unless there be villains who would dare to rob the dead.

Now I have spoken about this ring because it holds an important part in the history of my Lorna. I asked her where the glass necklace was, which she had worn in her childhood, and she answered that she hardly knew, but remembered that her grandfather had begged her to give it up to him, when she was ten years old or so, and had promised to keep it for her; at the same time giving her back the ring, and fastening it from her pretty neck, and telling her to be proud of it. And so she always had been, and it became John Ridd's delight.

9. A very Desperate Venture

Now November was upon us, and we had kept Allhallowmass, with roasting of skewered apples; and then while we were at wheat-sowing, another visitor arrived.

This was Master Jeremy Stickles. A coarse-grained, hard-faced man he was, some forty years of age or so, and of middle height and stature. He made our farmhouse his headquarters, and kept us quite at his beck and call, going out at any time of the evening, and coming back at any time of the morning, and always expecting us to be ready, whether with horse, or man, or fire, or provisions. We knew that he was employed somehow upon the service of the King, and had at different stations certain troopers and orderlies, quite at his disposal; also we knew that he never went out, without heavy fire-arms well loaded; and that he held a great commission, under royal signet. Now Master Jeremy Stickles, after awhile, perceiving that I could be relied upon, took me aside and told me nearly everything; having bound me first by oath, not to impart to any one, until all was over.

"John," he said solemnly, and with much importance, "there

be some people fit to plot, and others to be plotted against, and others to unravel plots, which is the highest gift of all. This last hath fallen to my share, and a very thankless gift it is. Much of peril too attends it; daring courage and great coolness are as needful for the work as ready wit and spotless honour. Therefore His Majesty's advisers have chosen me for this high task, and they could not have chosen a better man. Now, heard you much about the Duke of Monmouth?"

"Not so very much," I answered; "only that he was a hearty man, and a very handsome one, and now was banished by the Tories."

"There is much disaffection everywhere, and it must grow to an outbreak. The King hath many troops in London, and meaneth to bring more from Tangier; but he cannot command these country places. Now, do you understand me, John?"

"In truth, not I. I see not what Tangier hath to do with Exmoor; nor the Duke of Monmouth with Jeremy Stickles."

"Thou great clod, put it the other way. Jeremy Stickles may have much to do about the Duke of Monmouth. Now, in ten words I am here to watch the gathering of a secret plot, not so much against the King as against the due succession."

"Now I understand at last. But, Master Stickles, you might have said all that an hour ago almost."

But then my own affairs were thrown into such disorder, that I could think of nothing else. For suddenly all my Lorna's signals ceased, which I had been wont to watch for daily. The first time I stood on the wooded crest, and found no change from yesterday, I thought at least that it must be some great mistake on the part of my love. Three times I went, and waited long at the bottom of the valley, where now the stream was brown and angry with the rains of autumn. But though I waited at every hour of day and far into the night, no light footstep came to meet me.

Once I sought far up the valley, where I had never been before. Following up the river channel, in the shelter of the evening fog, I gained a corner within stone's throw of the last outlying cot.

This was a gloomy, low, square house, roughly built of wood and stone, as I saw when I drew nearer. For knowing it to be Carver's dwelling (or at least suspecting so, from some words of Lorna's), I was led by curiosity, and perhaps by jealousy to have a closer look at it. Nevertheless, I went warily, being now almost among this nest of cockatrices. The back of Carver's house abutted on the waves of the rushing stream; and seeing a loop-hole, vacant for muskets, I looked in, but all was quiet. So far as I could judge by listening, there was no one now inside, and my heart for a moment leaped with joy, for I had feared to find Lorna there. Then I took a careful survey of the dwelling, and its windows, and its door, and aspect.

I was much inclined to go further up, and understand all the village. But a bar of red light across the river, some forty yards on above me, prevented me. In that second house there was a gathering of loud and merry outlaws, making as much noise as if they had the law upon their side. Before I betook myself home that night, I had resolved to penetrate Glen Doone from the upper end, and learn all about my Lorna.

Here was every sort of trouble gathering upon me; here was Jeremy Stickles stealing upon every one in the dark; here was Uncle Reuben plotting, Satan only could tell what; here was a white night-capped man coming bodily from the grave; here was my own sister Annie committed to a highway-man, and mother in distraction; most of all, was my Lorna, stolen, dungeoned, perhaps outraged. Rudely rolling these ideas in my heavy head and brain, I resolved to let the morrow put them into form and order.

The journey was a great deal longer to fetch around the Southern hills, and enter by the Doone-gate, than to cross the lower land, and steal in by the water-slide. However, I durst not take a horse but started betimes in the evening. And thus I came to the robbers' highway. Although it was now well on towards dark, I could see the robbers' road before me, in a trough of the winding hills. I thought it safer to wait a little, as twilight melted into night; and then I crept down and stood upon the Doone-track.

As the road approached the entrance, it became more straight and strong, like a channel cut from rock, with the water brawling darkly along the naked side of it. Not a tree or bush was left, to shelter a man from bullets: all was stern, and stiff, and rugged, as I could not help perceiving, even through the darkness. And here I was particularly unlucky; for as I drew near the very entrance warily, the moon broke upon me, filling all the open spaces with the play of wavering light. I shrank back into the shadow on the right side of the road; and gloomily employed myself to watch the triple entrance, on which the moonlight fell.

All across and before the three rude and beetling archways hung a felled oak overhead, black, and thick, and threatening. This, as I heard before, could be let fall in a moment, so as to crush a score of men, and bar the approach of horses. Behind this tree, the rocky mouth was spanned with brushwood and piled timber, all upon a ledge of stone, where thirty men might lurk unseen, and fire at any invader. From that rampart it would be impossible to dislodge them, because the rock fell sheer below them twenty feet, while overhead it towered three hundred, and so jutted over that nothing could be cast upon them. And the access to this place was through certain rocky chambers known to the tenants only. But the cleverest of their devices was that, instead of one mouth only, there were three to choose from, with nothing to betoken which was the proper access.

Now I could see those three rough arches, jagged, black, and terrible; and I knew that only one of them could lead me to the valley. Therefore, without more hesitation, I plunged into the middle way, holding a long ash staff before me, shodden at the end with iron. Presently I was in black darkness, groping along the wall. Then I stumbled over something hard, and sharp, and very cold, moreover so grievous to my legs, that it needed my very best humour to forbear from swearing. But when I arose, and felt it, and knew it to be a culverin, I was somewhat reassured thereby, inasmuch as it was not likely that they would plant this engine, except in the real and true entrance. Therefore I went on again, more painfully and wearily and presently found it to be good that I had received that knock, for otherwise I might have blundered full upon the sentries, and been shot without more ado. As it was, I had barely time to draw back, as I turned a corner upon them.

There seemed to be only two of them, of size indeed and stature as all the Doones must be. It was plain, however, that each had a long and heavy carbine standing close beside him. The two villains looked very happy. They were sitting in a niche of rock, with the lanthorn in the corner, quaffing something from glass measures, and playing at push-pin or some trivial game of that sort. Each was smoking a long clay pipe. One was sitting with his knees up, and left hand on his thigh. The other leaned more against the rock, wearing leathern overalls, as if newly come from riding. I could see his face quite clearly by the light of the open lanthorn, and a handsomer or a bolder face I had seldom, if ever, set eyes upon; insomuch that it made me very unhappy to think of his being so near my Lorna.

"How long am I to stay crouching here?" I asked of myself at last, being tired of hearing them cry, "score one," "score two," "No, by—, Charlie," "By—I say it is, Phelps." Presently, as I made up my mind to steal along towards them (for the cavern was pretty wide, just there), Charlie, or Charleworth Doone, the younger man, reached to seize the money, which he swore he had won that time. The other jerked his arm, whereupon Charlie flung at his face the contents of the glass he was sipping, but missed him and hit the candle, which spluttered and then went out completely. At this, and before they had settled what to do, I was past them and round the corner.

And then, like a giddy fool as I was, I needs must give them a startler—the whoop of an owl, done so exactly, as John Fry had taught me, and echoed by the roof so fearfully, that one of them dropped the tinder box. I heard one say to the other, "Curse it,

Charlie, what was that? It scared me so, I have dropped my box; my flint is gone, and everything. Will the brimstone catch from your pipe, my lad?"

"My pipe is out, Phelps, ever so long. Damn it, I am not afraid of an owl, man. Give me the lanthorn, and stay here. I'm not half done with you yet, my friend."

"Well said, my boy, well said! Go straight to Carver's, mind you. No dallying now under Captain's window. Queen will have nought to say to you."

And so after some rude jests, and laughter, and a few more oaths, I heard Charlie coming towards me, with a loose and not too sober footfall. As he reeled a little in his gait, his leathern gaiters brushed my knee. If he had noticed it, he would have been a dead men in a moment; but his drunkenness saved him. So I let him reel on unharmed; and thereupon it occurred to me that I could have no better guide, passing as he would exactly where I wished to be; that is to say under Lorna's window. Therefore I followed him. Down a steep and winding path, with a handrail at the corners Master Charlie tripped along and after him walked I. So he led me very kindly to the top of the meadow land, where the stream from underground broke forth. Hence I had fair view and outline of the robbers' township.

I knew that the Captain's house was first, from what Lorna had said of it. I marked the position of the houses and the beauty of the village. For the stream, in lieu of any street, passing between the houses, and the snugness of the position, walled with rock, and spread with herbage, made it look, in the quiet moonlight, like a little paradise.

Master Charlie went down the village, and I followed him carefully. As I passed Sir Ensor's house, my heart leaped up, for I spied a window, higher than the rest above the ground, and with a faint light moving. This could hardly fail to be the room wherein my darling lay; for here that impudent young fellow had gazed. My heart was in my mouth when I stood in the shade by Lorna's window, and whispered her name gently. The house was of one storey only, as the others were, and only two rough windows upon that western side of it, and perhaps both of them were Lorna's.

Lorna drew back the curtain timidly. Then she opened the rough lattice; and then she sighed very sadly.

"Oh Lorna, don't you know me?" I whispered.

"John!" she cried, yet with sense enough not to speak aloud. "Oh, you must be mad, John."

"As mad as a March hare," said I, "without any news of my darling. You knew I would come: of course you did."

"Well, I thought, perhaps—you know: now, John, you need not eat my hand. Do you see they have put iron bars across?"

"Now tell me," I said; "what means all this? Why are you so pent up here? Why have you given me no token?"

"My poor grandfather is very ill: I fear that he will not live long. The Counsellor and his son are now the masters of the valley; and I dare not venture forth, for fear of anything they might do to me. Little Gwenny is no longer allowed to leave the valley; so that I could send no message. The tyrants now make sure of me. You must watch this house, both night and day, if you wish to save me. There is nothing they would shrink from, if my poor grandfather—oh, I cannot bear to think of myself, when I ought to think of him only; dying without a son to tend him or a daughter to shed a tear."

"But surely he has sons enough; and a deal too many," I was going to say, but stopped myself in time: "Why do none of them come to him?"

"I know not. I cannot tell. He is a very strange old man; and few have ever loved him. He was black with wrath at the Counsellor, this very afternoon—but I must not keep you here."

"I will not stay long; you tremble so: and yet for that very reason, how can I leave you, Lorna?"

"You must—you must," she answered; "I shall die if they hurt you. I hear the old nurse moving. Grandfather is sure to send for me. Keep back from the window."

However, it was only Gwenny Carfax, Lorna's little hand-maid: my darling brought her to the window, and presented her to me, almost laughing through her grief.

"Oh, I am so glad, John; Gwenny, I am so glad you came. I have wanted long to introduce you to my 'young man,' as you call him. It is rather dark, but you can see him. I wish you to know him again, Gwenny."

"I shall knoo thee again, young man; no fear of that," she answered, nodding with an air of patronage. "Now, missis, gae on coortin', and I will gae outside and watch for 'ee."

"She is the best little thing in the world," said Lorna, softly laughing; "and the queerest, and the truest. Nothing will bribe her against me. Go, do go, kind, dear, darling John."

"How can I go, without settling anything?" I asked, very sensibly. "How shall I know of your danger now?"

"I have been thinking long of something," Lorna answered rapidly. "You see that tree with the seven rooks' nests, bright against the cliffs there? Can you count them, from above, do you think? Gwenny can climb like any cat. If you see but six rooks' nests, I am in peril, and want you. If you see but five, I am carried off by Carver."

"Good God no!" said I in a tone which frightened Lorna.

"Fear not, John," she whispered sadly, and my blood grew cold at it: "I have means to stop him; or at least to save myself. If you can come within one day of that man's getting hold of me, you will find me quite unharmed."

I said, "God bless you, darling!" and she said the same to me, in a very low sad voice. And then I stole below Carver's house, in the shadow from the eastern cliff; and knowing enough of the village now to satisfy all necessity, betook myself to my well-known track in returning from the valley.

One day, Squire Faggus had dropped in upon us, just in time for dinner, and very soon he and King's messenger were as thick as need be. Tom had brought his beloved mare, to show her off to Annie, and he mounted his pretty sweetheart upon her, after giving Winnie notice to be on her very best behaviour. The squire was in great spirits, having just accomplished a purchase of land which was worth ten times what he gave for it; and this he did by a merry trick upon old Sir Roger Bassett. The whole thing was done on a bumper of claret, in a tavern where they met; and the old knight, having once pledged his word, no lawyers could hold him back from it. They could only say that Master Faggus, being attained of felony, was not a capable grantee. "I will soon cure that," quoth Tom, "my pardon has been ready for months and months, so soon as I care to sue it." And now he was telling our Annie, who listened very rosily, that he would go to London at once, and sue out his pardon.

Stickles took me aside the next day, and opened all his business to me, whether I would or not. Now what he said lay in no great compass, and may be summed in smaller still. Disaffection to the King, or rather dislike to his brother, James, and fear of Roman ascendancy, had existed now for several years, and of late were spreading rapidly; partly through the corruption of justice, and confiscation of ancient rights and charters; and partly through jealousy of the French king, and his potent voice in our affairs. Taunton, Bridgwater, Minehead, and Dulverton took the lead of the other towns in utterance of their discontent, and threats of what they meant to do, if ever a Papist dared to climb the Protestant throne of England. And as a Tory watchman, Jeremy Stickles was now among us; and his duty was threefold.

First, and most ostensibly, to see to the levying of poundage in the little haven of Lynmouth, which was now becoming a place of resort for smugglers.

Second, his duty was (though only the Doones had discovered it) to watch those outlaws, narrowly, and report of their doings and politics, whether true to the King and the Pope, or otherwise.

Jeremy Stickles' third business was entirely political; to learn the temper of our people and the gentle families, to discover any collecting of arms and drilling of man among us; in a word, to observe and forestall the enemy.

Now in providing for this last-mentioned service, the Government had made a great mistake. For all the disposable force at their emissary's command amounted to no more than a score of musketeers.

"So you see, John," he said, in conclusion, "I have more work than tools to do it with. I am heartily sorry I ever accepted such a mixed and meagre commission. Because I am not a Colonel, forsooth, or a Captain in His Majesty's service, it would never do to trust me with a company of soldiers! The only thing that I can do, with any chance of success, is to rout out these vile Doone fellows, and burn their houses over their heads. Now what think you of that, John Ridd?"

"Destroy the town of the Doones," I said, "and all the Doones inside it! Surely, Jeremy, you would never think of such a cruel act as that!"

I was thinking, of course, about the troubles that might ensue to my own beloved Lorna. If an attack of Glen Doone were made by savage soldiers and rude train-bands, what might happen, to my delicate, innocent darling? Therefore, when Jeremy Stickles again placed the matter before me, commending my strength and courage, and finished by saying that I would be worth at least four common men to him, I cut him short as follows:—

"Master Stickles, once for all, I will have nought to do with it. The reason why is no odds of thine, nor in any way disloyal. Only in thy plans remember, that I will not strike a blow, neither give any counsel, neither guard any prisoners."

"Not strike a blow," cried Jeremy, "against thy father's murderers, John!"

"Not a single blow, Jeremy; unless I knew the man who did it, and he gloried in his sin. It was a foul and dastard deed, yet not done in cold blood; neither in cold blood will I take the Lord's task of avenging it."

I made bold however to ask Master Stickles, at what time he intended to carry out this great and hazardous attempt. He answered that he had several things requiring first to be set in order, and that he must make an inland journey, even as far as Tiverton, and perhaps Crediton and Exeter, to collect his forces and ammunition for them. For he meant to have some of the yeomanry, as well as of the trained bands, so that if the Doones should sally forth on horseback, cavalry might be there to meet them, and cut them off from returning.

All this made me very uncomfortable, for many and many reasons, the chief and foremost being of course my anxiety about Lorna. If the attack succeeded, what was to become of her? Who would rescue her from the brutal soldiers, even supposing that she escaped from the hands of her own people, during the danger and ferocity? And in smaller ways, I was much put out; for instance, who would ensure our corn-ricks, sheep, and cattle, ay and even our fat pigs, now coming on for bacon, against the spreading all over the country of unlicensed marauders? Among all these troubles, there was however, or seemed to be, one comfort. Tom Faggus returned from London very proudly and very happily, with a royal pardon in black and white, which everybody admired the more, because no one could read a word of it. The Squire himself acknowledged cheerfully that he could sooner take fifty purses than read a single line of it.

And now a thing came to pass which tested my adoration pretty sharply, inasmuch as I would far liefer have faced Carver Doone and his father, nay even the roaring lion himself, with his hoofs and flaming nostrils, than have met, in cold blood, Sir Ensor Doone, the fear of the very fiercest. But that I was forced to do in the manner following. When I went up one morning to look for my seven rooks' nests, behold there were but six to be seen. I looked, and looked, and rubbed my eyes; the signal was made for me to come, because my love was in danger. For me to enter the valley now, during the broad daylight, could have brought only harm to the maiden, and certain death to myself. Therefore I ran to the nearest place where I could remain unseen, and watched the glen from the wooded height, for hours and hours. There was nothing to do, except blow on my fingers, and long for more wit.

For a frost was beginning, which made a great difference to Lorna and to myself, I trow; as well as to all the five million people who dwell in this island of England; such a frost as never I saw before, neither hope ever to see again; a time when it was impossible to milk a cow for icicles, or for a man to shave some of his beard (as I liked to do for Lorna's sake, because she was so smooth) without blunting his razor on hard grey ice.

When it grew towards dark, I was just beginning to prepare for my circuit around the hills; but suddenly Watch, our very best sheep-dog, gave a long low growl; I kept myself close as possible, and ordered the dog to be silent, and presently saw a short figure approaching from a thickly-wooded hollow on the left side of my hiding-place. It proved, to my great delight, to be the little maid Gwenny Carfax. She started a moment, at seeing me, but more with surprise than fear.

"Young man," she said, "you must come with me. I was gwain' all the way to fetch thee. Old man be dying; and her can't die, or at least her won't, without considering thee."

"Considering me!" I cried: "what can Sir Ensor Doone want with considering me? Has Mistress Lorna told him?"

"All concerning thee, and thy doings; when she knowed old man were so near his end."

Therefore, with great misgiving of myself, I sent Watch home, and followed Gwenny; who led me along very rapidly. Soon in a dark and lonely corner, she came to a narrow door, very brown and solid. This she opened without a key, by stooping down and pressing it, where the threshold met the jamb; and then she ran in very nimbly, but I was forced to be bent in two, and even so without comfort. The passage was close and difficult, and as dark as any black pitch; but it was not long. We came out soon at the other end, and were at the top of Doone valley. In the chilly dusk air it looked most untempting. As we crossed towards the Captain's house, we met a couple of great Doones lounging by the waterside. Gwenny said something to them, and although they stared very hard at me, they let me pass. When the little maid opened Sir Ensor's door, my heart thumped, quite as much with terror as with hope of Lorna's presence.

But in a moment the fear was gone, for Lorna was trembling in my arms, and my courage rose to comfort her. Lorna took me by the hand and led me into a little passage, where I could hear the river moaning and the branches rustling. At last my Lorna came back very pale, as I saw by the candle she carried, and whispered, "Now be patient, dearest. Look at him gently and steadfastly, and, if you can, with some show of reverence. Now come; walk very quietly."

She led me into a cold dark room, rough and very gloomy, although with two candles burning. I took little heed of the things in it. That which I heeded was an old man, very stern and comely, with death upon his countenance; yet not lying in his bed, but set upright in a chair, with a loose red cloak thrown over him. Upon this his white hair fell, and his pale fingers lay in a ghastly fashion, without a sign of life or movement; all rigid, calm, and relentless. Only in his great black eyes, fixed upon me solemnly, all the life of his soul was burning.

I made a low obeisance, and tried not to shiver. Only I groaned that Lorna thought it good manners to leave us two together.

"Ah," said the old man, and his voice seemed to come from a cavern of skeletons; "are you that great John Ridd?"

"John Ridd is my name, your honour," was all that I could answer; "and I hope your worship is better."

"Child, have you sense enough to know what you have been doing?"

"Yes, I know right well," I answered, "that I have set mine eyes far above my rank."

The old man's eyes, like fire, probed me whether I was jesting; then perceiving how grave I was, he took on himself to make good the deficiency with a very bitter smile.

"And know you of your own low descent, from the Ridds, of Oare?"

"Sir," I answered, being as yet unaccustomed to this style of speech, "the Ridds, of Oare, have been honest men, twice as long as the Doones have been rogues."

"I would not answer for that, John," Sir Ensor replied, very quietly, when I expected fury. "If it be so, the family is the very oldest in Europe. Now hearken to an old man's words, who has not many hours to live. There is nothing in this world to fear, nothing to revere or trust, nothing even to hope for; least of all, is there aught to love."

"I hope your worship is not quite right," I answered, with great misgivings; "else it is a sad mistake for anybody to live, sir."

"Therefore," he continued, as if I had never spoken, "though it may seem hard for a week or two, like the loss of any other toy, I forbid you ever to see that foolish child again. All marriage is a wretched farce, even when man and wife belong to the same rank of life, have temper well assorted, and about the same pittance of mind. But when they are not so matched, the farce would become a long dull tragedy. You will pledge your word in Lorna's presence, never to see or to seek her again. Now call her, for I am weary."

He kept his great eyes fixed upon me with their icy fire and then he raised one hand and pointed to the door. I made a low salute, and went straightway in search of Lorna. Lorna Doone was crying softly at a little window, and listening to the river's grief. I laid my heavy arm around her, just to comfort her. To my arm she made no answer, neither to my seeking eyes; but to my heart, once for all, she spoke with her own upon it. Not a word, nor sound between us; not even a kiss was interchanged; but man, or maid, who has ever loved hath learned our understanding.

Therefore it came to pass, that we saw fit boldly to enter Sir Ensor's room, I, for my part, fearing neither death nor hell, while she abode beside me. Old Sir Ensor looked much astonished. For forty years he had been obeyed and feared by all around him; and he knew that I had feared him vastly, before I got hold of Lorna.

"Fools you are; be fools for ever," said Sir Ensor Doone at

93

last; "it is the best thing I can wish you; boy and girl, be boy and girl, until you have grandchildren."

Partly in bitterness he spoke, and partly in pure weariness, and then he turned so as not so see us; and his white hair fell, like a shroud, around him.

It does not take a man very long to enter into another man's death, and bring his own mood to suit it. He knows that his own is sure to come. Hence it came to pass that I, after easing my mother's fears, returned (as if drawn by a polar needle) to the death-bed of Sir Ensor. There was some little confusion, people wanting to get away, and people trying to come in, and others making great to-do. But every one seemed to think, that I had a right to be there; because the women took that view of it. As for Carver and Counsellor, they were minding their own affairs, so as to win the succession; and never found it in their business to come near the dying man.

He, for his part, never asked for anyone to come near him, not even a priest, nor a monk or friar. An hour or two ere the old man died, when only we two were with him, he looked at us both very dimly and softly, as if he wished to do something for us, but had left it now too late. He let his hand drop downward, and crooked one knotted finger.

"He wants something out of the bed, dear," Lorna whispered to me; "see what it is, upon your side, there."

I followed the bent of his poor shrunken hand, and sought among the pilings; and there I felt something hard and sharp, and drew it forth and gave it to him. It flashed in the dark winter of the room. He could not take it in his hand, but let it hang, as daisies do; only making Lorna see that he meant her to have it.

"Why, it is my glass necklace!" Lorna cried, in great surprise; "my necklace he always promised me; and from which you have got the ring, John. May I have it now, dear grandfather?"

Darling Lorna wept again, because the old man could not tell her (except by one very feeble nod) that she was doing what he wished. Then she gave to me the trinket, for the sake of safety;

and I stowed it in my breast. He seemed to me to follow this, and to be well content with it.

Before Sir Ensor Doone was buried, the greatest frost of the century had set in, with its iron hand on everything. The strong men broke three good pickaxes, ere they got through the hard brown sod, where old Sir Ensor was to lie upon his back, awaiting the darkness of the Judgment-day. It was in the little chapel-yard. The ancient outlaw's funeral was a grand and moving sight; more perhaps from the sense of contrast, than from that of fitness.

After all was over, I strode across the moors very sadly; trying to keep the cold away, by virtue of quick movement. Not a flake of snow had fallen yet; all the sky was banked with darkness, hard, austere, and frowning. One thing struck me with some surprise, as I made off for our fireside, and that was how the birds were going, rather than flying as they used to fly. All the birds were set in one direction, steadily journeying westward, partly running, partly flying, partly fluttering along, silently. This movement of the birds went on, even for a week or more; every kind of thrush passed us, every kind of wild fowl, even plovers went away, and crows, and snipes, and woodcocks. And before half the frost was over, all we had in the snowy ditches were hares so tame that we could pat them; partridges that came to hand, with a dry noise in their crops; and a few poor hopping red-wings, flipping in and out the hedge, having lost the power to fly.

10. The Great Winter

IN the very night which followed old Sir Ensor's funeral, such a storm of snow began, as never have I heard nor read of, neither could have dreamed it. In the bitter morning, I arose, knowing the time from the force of habit, although the room was so dark and grey. An odd white light was on the rafters, such as I never had seen before; half the lattice was quite blocked up. With some trouble, and great care, lest the ancient frame should yield, I spread the lattice open; and saw at once that not a moment must be lost, to save our stock. All the earth was flat with snow, all the air was thick with snow; more than this no man could see, for all the world was snowing.

I shut the window, and dressed in haste; and then set forth to find John Fry, Jem Slocombe, and Bill Dadds. With spades, and shovels, and pitchforks, we four set forth to dig out the sheep.

It must have snowed most wonderfully to have made that depth of covering in about eight hours. And here it was, blocking up the doors, stopping the ways, and the watercourses, and making it very much worse to walk than in a saw-pit newly used. However we trudged along in a line; I first, and the other men after me; trying to keep my track, but finding legs and strength not up to it. Watch, like a good and faithful dog, followed us very cheerfully, leaping out of the depth, which took him over his back and ears already. However, we helped him now and then, and so after a deal of floundering, some laughter and a little swearing, we came all safe to the lower meadow, where most of our flock was hurdled.

But behold, there was no flock at all! None, I mean, to be seen anywhere; only at one corner of the field, where the snow drove in, a great white billow, as high as a barn and as broad as a house. This great drift was rolling and curling beneath the violent blast. Watch began to scratch at once, and to howl along the sides of it; he knew that his charge was buried there. We four men set to in earnest, digging with all our might and main, shovelling away at the great white pile. Each man made for himself a cave, scooping at the soft cold flux, which slid upon him at every stroke, and throwing it out behind him, in piles of castled fancy. At last we drove our tunnels in and all converging towards the middle, held our tools and listened.

I laid my head well into the chamber; and there I heard a faint "ma-a-ah," coming through some ells of snow, like a plaintive last appeal. I shouted aloud to cheer him up, for I knew what sheep it was, to wit the most valiant of all the wethers. And then we all fell to again; and very soon we hauled him out. Watch took charge of him at once, lying on his frozen fleece, and licking all his face and feet, to restore his warmth to him.

Further in, and close under the bank, where they had huddled themselves for warmth, we found all the rest of the poor sheep packed as closely as if they were in a great pie. It was strange to observe how their vapour, and breath, had scooped a coved room for them, lined with a ribbing of deep yellow snow. Also the churned snow beneath their feet was as yellow as gamboge. Two or three of the weaklier hoggets were dead, from want of air, and from pressure; but more than three-score were as lively as ever; though cramped and stiff for a little while.

97

"However shall us get 'em home?" John Fry asked in great dismay, when we had cleared about a dozen of them.

"You see to this place, John," I replied, as we leaned on our shovels a moment, and the sheep came rubbing round us: "let no more of them out for the present; they are better where they be. Watch, here boy, keep them!"

Then of the outer sheep I took the two finest and heaviest, and with one beneath my right arm, and the other beneath my left, I went straight home to the upper sheppey, and set them aside, and fastened them. Sixty-and-six I took home in that way, two at a time on each journey; and the work grew harder and harder each time, as the drifts of the snow were deepening. People talk of it to this day. Of the sheep upon the mountain, and the sheep upon the western farm, and the cattle on the upper burrows, scarcely one in ten was saved, from the pure impossibility of finding them at all. That great snow never ceased a moment for three days and nights; and then a brilliant sun broke forth.

That night, such a frost ensued as we had never dreamed of. The kettle by the fire froze; many men were killed, and cattle rigid in their head-ropes. Then I heard that fearful sound, which never I had heard before, neither since have heard, the sharp yet solemn sound of trees, burst open by the frost-blow.

We were losing half our stock, do all we could to shelter them. Even the horses in the stables (mustered all together, for the sake of breath and steaming) had long icicles from their muzzles, almost every morning. As a rule, it snowed all day, cleared up at night, and froze intensely, with the stars as bright as jewels; then in the morning snow again, before the sun could come to help.

I believe it was on Epiphany morning, when Lizzie ran into the kitchen to me, where I was thawing my goose-grease.

"What a pity you never read, John!" said my lady, as Annie and I used to call her, on account of her airs and graces.

"Much use, I should think, in reading!" I answered; "with roof coming in, and only this chimney left sticking out of the snow!"

"Now, John, this is no time to joke," she said. "Now, will you

98

listen to what I have read about climates ten times worse than this; and where none but clever men can live?"

"Impossible for me to listen now. I have hundreds of things to see to: but I will listen after breakfast to your foreign climates, child. Now attend to mother's hot coffee."

She looked a little disappointed; but when I had done my morning's work, I listened to her patiently. She told me that in the "Arctic Regions," they always had such winters as we were having now. It never ceased to freeze, she said; and it never ceased to snow; except it was too cold; and a man's skin might come off of him, before he could ask the reason. Nevertheless the people there managed to get along by a little cleverness. For seeing how the snow was spread over everything they contrived a way to glide like a flake along, with a boat on either foot, to prevent sinking.

She told me how these boats were made: very strong and very light, of ribs with skin across them; five feet long, and one foot wide; and turned up at each end, even as a canoe is. Then she told me another thing equally useful to me. And this concerned the use of sledges, and their power of gliding; all of which I could see at once, through knowledge of our own farm-sleds; which we employ in lieu of wheels, used in flatter districts. When I had heard all this from her, I looked down on her with amazement, and began to wish a little that I had given more time to books.

I fell to at once, upon that hint from Lizzie, and before very long I built myself a pair of strong and light snow-shoes, framed with ash and ribbed of withy, with half-tanned calf-skin stretched across, and an inner sole to support my feet. At first I could not walk at all, but floundered about most piteously, catching one shoe in the other, and both of them in the snow-drifts. After a while I grew more expert, but oh the aching of my ankles, when I went to bed that night. I was forced to help myself upstairs with a couple of mopsticks! And I rubbed the joints with neatsfoot oil, which comforted them greatly.

Upon the following day, I held some council with my mother;

not liking to go without her permission, yet scarcely daring to ask for it. But here she disappointed me, on the right side of disappointment; saying that she had seen my pining, and rather than watch me grieving so, I might go upon my course, and God's protection go with me!

When I started on my road across the hills and valleys (which now were pretty much alike), the utmost I could hope to do was to gain the crest of hills, and look into the Doone Glen. Through the sparkling breadth of white and past the humps of laden trees, I contrived to get along, half sliding and half walking, in places where a plain-shodden man must have sunk. At last I got to my spy-hill, although I never should have known it, but for what it looked on. For all the beautiful Glen Doone now was besnowed half up the sides, and at either end so that it was more like the white basins wherein we boil plum-pudding. Not a patch of grass was there, not a black branch of a tree; all was white; and the little river flowed beneath an arch of snow; if it managed to flow at all.

Now this was a great surprise to me; not only because I believed Glen Doone to be a place outside all frost, but also because I thought perhaps that it was quite impossible to be cold near Lorna. The snow came on again. And I set my back and elbows well against a snow-drift, hanging far adown the cliff, and saying some of the Lord's Prayer, threw myself on Providence. Before there was time to think or dream, I landed very beautifully upon a ridge of run-up snow in a quiet corner. My good shoes, or boots, preserved me from going far beneath it. Having set myself aright, I made boldly across the valley. If Lorna had looked out of the window, she would not have known me, with those boots upon my feet, and a well-cleaned sheepskin over me. The house was partly drifted up; and I crossed the little stream almost without knowing that it was under me. At first, being pretty safe against interference from the other huts, by virtue of the blinding snow, I examined all the windows; but these were coated so with ice, like ferns and flowers and dazzling stars, that no one could so much as guess what might be inside of them.

I was forced, much against my will, to venture to the door and knock, in a hesitating manner, not being sure but what my answer might be the mouth of a carbine. I heard a pattering of feet and a whispering going on, and then a shrill voice through the keyhole, asking, "Who's there?"

"Only me, John Ridd," I answered; and then the door was opened about a couple of inches, with a bar behind it still; and then the little voice went on, "Put thy finger in, young man, with the old ring on it. But mind thee, if it be the wrong one, thou shalt never draw it back again."

Laughing at Gwenny's mighty threat, I showed my finger in the opening: upon which she let me in, and barred the door again like lightning.

"What is the meaning of all this, Gwenny?" I asked, as I slipped about on the floor, for I could not stand there firmly with my great snow-shoes on.

"Maning enough, and bad maning too," the Cornish girl made answer. "Us be shut in here, and starving, and durstn't let any body in upon us. I wish thou wer't good to ate, young man: I could manage most of thee."

I was so frightened by her eyes, full of wolfish hunger, that I could only say, "Good God!" having never seen the like before. Then drew I forth a large piece of bread, which I had brought in case of accidents, and placed it in her hands. She leaped at it, as a starving dog leaps at sight of his supper, and she set her teeth in it, and then withheld it from her lips, with something very like an oath at her own vile greediness; and then away round the corner with it, no doubt for her young mistress. I meanwhile was occupied in taking my snow-shoes off, yet wondering much within myself, why Lorna did not come to me.

But presently I knew the cause; for Gwenny called me, and I ran, and found my darling quite unable to say so much as, "John, how are you?" Between hunger, and cold, and the excitement of my coming, she had fainted away, and lay back on a chair, as white as the snow around us. In betwixt her delicate lips, Gwenny was thrusting with all her strength the hard brown crust of the rye-bread, which she had snatched from me so.

"Get water, or get snow," I said; "don't you know what fainting is, you very stupid child?"

"Never heered on it, in Carnwall," she answered; "be un the same as bleeding?"

"It will be directly, if you go on squeezing away with that crust so. Eat a piece: I have got some more. Leave my darling now to me."

Hearing that I had some more, the starving girl could resist no longer, but tore it in two, and had swallowed half, before I had coaxed my Lorna back to sense, and hope, and joy, and love.

"I never expected to see you again. I had made up my mind to die, John; and to die without your knowing it."

"Eat up your bit of brown bread, Gwenny. It is not good enough for your mistress. Bless her heart, I have something here such as she never tasted the like of. Look here, Lorna; smell it first. I have had it ever since Twelfth-day, and kept it all the time for you. Annie made it."

And then I showed my great mince-pie in a bag of tissue paper, and I told them how the mince-meat was made of golden pippins finely shred, with the undercut of the sirloin, and spice and fruit accordingly and far beyond my knowledge. But Lorna would not touch a morsel, until she had thanked God for it, and put a piece in Gwenny's mouth. Lorna had as much as she could do to finish her own half of pie; whereas Gwenny Carfax ate up hers without winking, after finishing the brown load; and then I begged to know the meaning of this state of things.

"The meaning is sad enough," said Lorna; "and I see no way out of it. We are both to be starved until I let them do what they like with me."

"That is to say, until you choose to marry Carver Doone, and be slowly killed by him."

"Slowly! No, John, quickly. I hate him with such bitterness, that less than a week would kill me."

Then I spoke, with a strange tingle upon both sides of my heart, knowing that this undertaking was a serious one for all, and might burn our farm down, "If I warrant to take you safe, and without much fright or hardship, Lorna, will you come with me?"

"To be sure I will, dear," said my beauty with a smile, and a glance to follow it; "I have small alternative, to starve, or go with you, John."

"Gwenny, have you courage for it? Will you come with your young mistress?"

"Will I stay behind?" cried Gwenny, in a voice that settled it. And so we began to arrange about it; and I was much excited. It was useless now to leave it longer: if it could be done at all, it could not be too quickly done. Now while we sat, reflecting much, and talking a good deal more, in spite of all the cold, she said, in her silver voice, "Now, John, we are wasting time, dear. You have praised my hair, till it curls with pride, and my eyes till you cannot see them. Don't you think that it is high time to put on your snow-shoes, John?"

"Certainly not," I answered, "till we have settled something more. I was so cold when I came in; and now I am as warm as a cricket."

"Remember, John," said Lorna, nestling for a moment to me; "the severity of the weather makes a great difference between us. And you must never take advantage. Come to this frozen window, John, and see them light the stack-fire. They will little know who looks at them. Breathe three times, like that, and that; and then you rub it with your fingers, before it has time to freeze again."

And then I saw, far down the stream (or rather down the bed of it, for there was no stream visible), a little form of fire arising, red, and dark, and flickering. Presently it caught on something, and went upward boldly.

"Do you know what all that is, John?" asked Lorna. "The Doones are firing Dunkery beacon, to celebrate their new captain."

"But how could they bring it here, through the snow? If they have sledges, I can do nothing."

"They brought it before the snow began. The moment poor grandfather was gone, even before his funeral, the young men began at once upon it. They have often promised to bring it here for their candle; and now they have done it. Ah, now look! The tar is kindled."

I looked upon it very gravely, knowing that this heavy outrage to the feelings of the neighbourhood would cause more stir than a hundred sheep stolen, or a score of houses sacked. Not of course that the beacon was of the smallest use to any one, yet I knew that we valued it, and spoke of it as a mighty institution. The fire went up very merrily. I was astonished at its burning in such mighty depths of snow; but Gwenny said that the wicked men had been three days hard at work, clearing, as it were, a cock-pit for their fire to have its way. And now they had a mighty pile, which must have covered five landyards square, heaped up to a goodly height, and eager to take fire.

In this I saw great obstacle to what I wished to manage. For when this pyramid should be kindled thoroughly, and pouring light and blazes round, would not all the valley be like a white room full of candles? Thinking thus, I was half inclined to abide my time for another night; and then my second thoughts convinced me that I would be a fool in this. For lo, what an opportunity! All the Doones would be drunk, of course, in about three hours' time, and getting more and more in drink, as the night went on. As for the fire, it must sink in about three hours or more, and only cast uncertain shadows friendly to my purpose. And then the outlaws must cower round it, as the cold increased on them, helping the weight of the liquor; and in their jollity any noise would be cheered as a false alarm. Most of all, when these wild and reckless villains should be hot with ardent spirits, what was door, or wall, to stand betwixt them and my Lorna?

This thought quickened me so much that I told her in a few short words how I hoped to manage it. "Sweetest, in two hours' time, I shall be again with you. Have everything you care to take in a very little compass; and Gwenny must have no baggage."

Now, being homeward-bound by the shortest possible track, I slipped along between the bonfire and the boundary cliffs, where I found a caved way of snow behind a sort of avalanche: so that if the Doones had been keeping watch (which they were not doing, but revelling) they could scarcely have discovered me. And when I came to my old ascent, all my water-slide was now less a slice than path of ice. Lo, it was easy track and channel, as if for the very purpose made, down which I could guide my sledge, with Lorna sitting in it. I hastened home at my utmost speed, and told my mother to have plenty of fire blazing, and plenty of water boiling, and food enough hot for a dozen people, and the best bed aired with the warming-pan. Dear mother smiled softly at my excitement.

After this I took some brandy, both within and about me. Also I carried some other provisions, grieving much at their coldness; and then I went to the upper linhay, and took our new light pony-sledd. On the snow it ran as sweetly as if it had been made for it. I girded my own body with a dozen turns of hay-rope. I put a good piece of spare rope in the sledd, and the cross-seat with the back to it, as well as two or three fur coats: and then just as I was starting, out came Annie, in spite of the cold.

"Oh, John, here is the most wonderful thing! Mother had gotten it in a great well of cupboard, with camphor, and spirits, and lavender. Lizzie says it is a most magnificent sealskin cloak, worth fifty pounds, or a farthing."

"At any rate it is soft and warm," said I, very calmly flinging it into the bottom of the sledd. "Tell mother I will put it over Lorna's feet."

"Lorna's feet! Oh, you great fool;" cried Annie, "over her shoulders; and be proud, you very stupid John."

"It is not good enough for her feet;" I answered, with strong emphasis; "but don't tell mother I said so, Annie. Only thank her very kindly."

With that I drew my traces hard, and set my ashen staff into the snow, and struck out with my best foot foremost (the best one at snow-shoes, I mean), and the sledd came after me lightly. The full moon rose bright behind me casting on the snow long shadows. I went on quietly, and at a very tidy speed; being only too thankful that the snow had ceased, and no wind as yet arisen.

Daring not to risk my sledd by any fall from the valley-cliffs, I dragged it very carefully up the steep incline of ice, through the narrow chasm, and so to the very brink and verge where first I had seen my Lorna. I had a strong ash stake, to lay across from rock to rock, and break the speed of descending. With this I moored the sledd quite safe, at the very lip of the chasm, where all was now substantial ice, green and black in the moonlight; and then I set off up the valley, skirting along one side of it.

The stack-fire still was burning strongly, but with more of heat than blaze; and many of the younger Doones were playing on the verge of it, the children making rings of fire, and their mothers watching them. All these I passed, without the smallest risk or difficulty. And then I crossed, with more of care, and to the door of Lorna's house, and made the sign, and listened, after taking my snow-shoes off.

But no one came, neither could I espy a light. And I seemed to hear a faint low sound, like moaning. Then I set all my power at once against the door. In a moment it flew inwards, and I glided along the passage with my feet still slippery. There in Lorna's room I saw, by the moonlight flowing in, a sight which drove me beyond sense. Lorna was behind a chair, crouching in the corner, with her hands up. In the middle of the room lay Gwenny Carfax, stupid, yet with one hand clutching the ankle of a struggling man. Another man stood above my Lorna, trying to draw the chair away. In a moment I had him round the waist, and he went out of the window with a mighty crash of glass; luckily for him that window had no bars like some of them. Then I took the other man by the neck. I bore him out of the house as lightly as I would bear a baby, yet squeezing his throat a little more than I fain would do to an infant. I cast him, like a skittle, from me into a snowdrift, which closed over him. Then I looked for the

other fellow, tossed through Lorna's window; and found him lying stunned and bleeding. Charleworth Doone, if his gushing blood did not much mislead me.

It was no time to linger now: I fastened my shoes in a moment and caught up my own darling; and telling Gwenny to follow me, I ran the whole distance to my sledd. Then by the time I had set up Lorna, beautiful and smiling, with the sealskin cloak all over her, sturdy Gwenny came along, having trudged in the track of my snow-shoes, although with two bags on her back. I set her in beside her mistress, to support her, and keep warm; and then I hung behind the sledd, and launched it down the steep and dangerous way. With my staff from rock to rock, and my weight thrown backward, I broke the sledd's too rapid way. Unpursued, we skirted round the black whirling pool, and gained the meadows beyond it. Here there was hard collar work, the track being all uphill and rough; and Gwenny wanted to jump out, to lighten the sledd and to push behind. But I would not hear of it; because it was now so deadly cold, and I feared that Lorna might get frozen, without having Gwenny to keep her warm. And after all, it was the sweetest labour I had ever known in all my life, to be sure that I was pulling Lorna, and pulling her to our own farm-house.

I drew my traces tight, and set my whole strength to the business; and we slipped along at a merry pace. And so in about an hour's time, in spite of many hindrances, we came home to the old courtyard, and all the dogs saluted us. Even at this length of time, I can hardly tell it, because it moves my heart so. The sledd was at the open door. At the door were all our people; I put the others by, and fetched my mother forward.

"You shall see her first," I said; "is she not your daughter? Hold the light there, Annie."

Dear mother's hands were quick and trembling, as she opened the shining folds; and there she saw my Lorna sleeping, with her black hair all dishevelled, and she bent and kissed her forehead, and only said, "God bless her, John!" And then she was taken with violent weeping, and I was forced to hold her. They carried Lorna into the house, crowding round her, so that I thought I was not wanted among so many women. . .

Then there came a message for me, that my love was seeking all around for me.

That sight I shall not forget. For in the settle by the blazing fireplace was my Lorna, propped with pillows round her. The small hands found their way, as if by instinct, to my great protecting palms; and trembled there, and rested there. For a little while we lingered thus. And then a little sob disturbed us, and mother tried to make believe that she was only coughing. But Lorna jumped up, and ran to the old oak chair, where mother was by the clockcase pretending to be knitting, and she took the work from mother's hands, and laid them both upon her head, kneeling humbly, and looking up.

"God bless you, my fair mistress!" said mother, bending nearer and then as Lorna's gaze prevailed, "God bless you, my sweet child!"

11. A Change long Needed

JEREMY STICKLES was gone south, ere ever the frost set in; for the purpose of mustering forces to attack the Doone Glen. But now this weather had put a stop to every kind of movement. And to tell the truth, I cared not how long this weather lasted, so long as we had enough to eat, and could keep ourselves from freezing. The Doones could not come prowling after Lorna, while the snow lay piled between us, with the surface soft and dry. However, I set all hands on to thresh the corn, ere the Doones could come and burn the ricks.

I very soon persuaded Lorna that for the present she was safe, and that she was not only welcome, but as gladdening to our eyes as the flowers of May. For Lorna had so won them all, by her kind and gentle ways, and her mode of hearkening to everybody's trouble, as well as by her beauty, that I could almost wish sometimes the rest would leave her more to me. But mother could not do enough; and Annie almost worshipped her; and even Lizzie could not keep her bitterness towards her; especially when she found that Lorna knew as much of books as need be. As for John Fry, and Betty, and Molly, they were a perfect plague, when

Lorna came into the kitchen. For betwixt their curiosity to see a live Doone in the flesh, and their high respect for birth, and their admiration of a beauty, there was no getting the dinner cooked, with Lorna in the kitchen.

After a fortnight of our life, and freedom from anxiety, all her bright young wit was flashing, like a newly-awakened flame, and all her high young spirits leaped, as if dancing to its fire. And yet she never spoke a word which gave more pain than pleasure. And even in her outward look there was much of difference. Whether it was our harmless love of God, and trust in one another; or whether it were our air, and water, and the pea-fed bacon; anyhow my Lorna grew richer and more lovely every day.

Although it was the longest winter ever known in our parts (never having ceased to freeze for a single night, and scarcely for a single day, from the middle of December till the second week in March), to me it was the very shortest and the most delicious; and verily I do believe it was the same to Lorna. One leading feature of that long cold, and a thing remarked by every one, had been the hollow moaning sound ever present in the air, morning, noon, and night-time, and especially at night. But now, about the tenth of March, that miserable moaning noise died away from out the air; and we, being now so used to it, thought at first that we must be deaf. And soon a brisk south wind arose, and the blessed rain came driving. We all ran out, and filled our eyes, and filled our hearts, with gazing. True, the snow was piled up now all in mountains round us; true, the air was still so cold that our breath froze on the doorway, and the rain was turned to ice, wherever it struck anything: nevertheless it was rain.

But as the rain came down the very noblest thing of all was to hear, and see, the gratitude of the poor beasts yet remaining, and the few surviving birds. From the cowhouse lowing came. Then the horses in the stables, packed as closely as they could stick to keep the warmth in one another, began with one accord to lift up their voices, snorting, snaffling, whinnying, and neighing, and trotting to the door to know when they should have work again.

To whom, as if in answer, came the feeble bleating of the sheep.

Lorna had never seen, I dare say, anything like this before, and it was all that we could do to keep her from rushing forth, with only little lambswool shoes on. I caught her up, and carried her in. And I set her there, in her favourite place, by the sweet-scented wood-fire; and she paid me porterage, without my even asking her; and I was fain to stay with her; until our Annie came to say that my advice was wanted. That was the way they always put it, when they wanted me to work for them. And in truth, it was time for me to work. For the rain was now coming down in earnest; and threatened to flood everything. Already it was ponding up, like a tide advancing, at the threshold of the door, both because great piles of snow trended in that direction, and also that the gulley hole now was choked with lumps of ice, as big as a man's body. It was not long before I managed to drain off this threatening flood, by opening the old sluice-hole.

At first, the rain made no impression on the bulk of snow, but ran from every sloping surface, and froze on every flat one, through the coldness of the earth. After a good while, however, this state of things began to change, and a worse one to succeed it; for now the snow came thundering down from roof, and rock, and ivied tree, and floods began to roar and foam in every trough and gulley. It was now high time to work very hard; both to make up for the farm-work lost during the months of frost and snow, and also to be ready for a great and vicious attack from the Doones, who would burn us in our beds, at the earliest opportunity.

As for Lorna, she would come out. There was no keeping her in the house. She had taken up some peculiar notion that she must earn her living by the hard work of her hands. She even began upon mother's garden, before the snow was clean gone from it, and sowed a beautiful row of peas, every one of which the mice ate. But though it was very pretty to watch her working for her very life, yet I was grieved for many reasons, and so was mother also. In the first place, she was too fair and dainty for this rough, rude work. And again (which was the worst of all things), mother's garden lay exposed to a dark deceitful coppice, where a man might lurk, and watch all the fair gardener's doings. It was true that none could get at her thence, while the brook which ran between poured so great a torrent. Still the distance was but little for a gun to carry, if any one could be brutal enough to point a gun at Lorna.

Now in spite of the floods, Squire Faggus came at last, riding his famous strawberry mare. There was a great ado between him and Annie, as you may well suppose, after some four months of parting. Tom Faggus had very good news to tell, and he told it with such force of expression as made us laugh very heartily. He had taken up his purchase from old Sir Roger Bassett of a nice bit of land, to the south of the moors. When the lawyers knew thoroughly who he was, and how he had made his money, they behaved uncommonly well to him, and showed great sympathy with his pursuits. And so they made old Squire Bassett pay the bill for both sides; and all he got for three hundred acres was a hundred and twenty pounds; though Tom had paid five hundred. Now this farm of Squire Faggus (as he truly now had a right to be called) was of the very finest pasture.

Being such a hand as he was, at making the most of everything, he had actually turned to his own advantage that extraordinary weather, which had so impoverished every one around him. For he taught his Winnie to go forth in the snowy evenings and to whinny to the forest ponies, and lead them all to her master's homestead. And Winnie never came home at night without at least a score of ponies trotting shyly after her, tossing their heads and their tails in turn, and making believe to be very wild, although hard pinched by famine. Of course, Tom would get them all into his pound in about five minutes; for he himself could neigh in a manner which went to the heart of the wildest horse. And then he fed them well, and turned them into his great cattle-pen, to abide their time for breaking, when the snow and frost should be over. He had gotten more than three hundred now, in this saga- cious manner; he doubted not that they would fetch him as much as ten pounds apiece all round, being now in great demand. I told him I wished that he might get it: but as it proved, he did.

Then he pressed us both on another point, the time for his marriage to Annie. I said that we must allow the maid herself to settle, when she would leave home and all.

Upon this I went in search of Lorna, to tell her of our cousin's arrival, and to ask whether she would think fit to see him, or to dine by herself that day. But Lorna had some curiosity to know what this famous man was like. Accordingly she turned away, with one of her very sweetest smiles, saying that she must not meet a man of such fashion and renown, in her common gardening frock; but must try to look as nice as she could, if only in honour of dear Annie. And truth to tell, when she came to dinner, everything about her was the neatest, and the prettiest, that can possibly be imagined. Two things caught Squire Faggus' eyes, after he had made a most gallant bow, and received a most graceful courtesy; and he kept his bright bold gaze upon them, first on one and then on the other, until my darling was hot with blushes. The two objects of his close regard were, first, and most worthily, Lorna's face, and secondly, the ancient necklace restored to her by Sir Ensor Doone.

A very good dinner we made, I remember, and a very happy one; attending to the women first, as now in the manner of eating; except among the workmen. With them, of course, it is needful that the man (who has his hours fixed) should be served first, and make the utmost of his time for feeding; while the women may go on, as much as ever they please, afterwards. Now when the young maidens were gone—for we had quite a high dinner of fashion that day, with Betty Muxworthy waiting, and Gwenny Carfax at the gravy—and only mother, and Tom, and I remained at the white deal table, with brandy, and schnapps, and hot water jugs; Squire Faggus said quite suddenly, and perhaps on purpose to take us aback, in case of our hiding anything, "What do you know of the history of that beautiful maiden, good mother?"

"Not half so much as my son does," mother answered, with a

soft smile at me; "and when John does not choose to tell a thing, wild horses will not pull it out of him."

"Come, come," said Master Faggus, smiling very pleasantly, "you two understand each other, if any two on earth do. Ah, if I had only had a mother, how different I might have been!" And with that he sighed; and then he produced his pretty box, full of rolled tobacco, and offered me one, as I now had joined the goodly company of smokers. So I took it and watched what he did with his own, lest I might go wrong about mine. But when our cylinders were both lighted, Tom Faggus told us that he was sure he had seen my Lorna's face before, many and many years ago, when she was quite a little child, but he could not remember where it was. He could not be mistaken, he said, for he had noticed her eyes especially. I asked him if he had ever ventured in the Doone-valley; but he shook his head, and replied that he valued his life a deal too much for that. He told us clearly and candidly that we were both very foolish. For he said that we were keeping Lorna, at the risk not only of our stock, and the house above our heads, but also of our precious lives; and after all was she worth it, although so very beautiful? Upon which I told him, with indignation, that I would thank him for his opinion, when I had requested it.

"Bravo, our John Ridd!" he answered: "fools will be fools till the end of the chapter. Nevertheless, in the name of God, don't let that child go about, with a thing worth half the county on her."

"She is worth all the county herself," said I, "and all England put together; but she has nothing worth half a rick of hay upon her; for the ring I gave her cost only"—and here I stopped, for mother was looking, and I never would tell her how much it had cost me.

"Tush, the ring!" Tom Faggus cried, with a contempt that moved me; "I would never have stopped a man for that. But the necklace, you great oaf, the necklace is worth all your farm put together, and your Uncle Ben's fortune to the back of it; ay, and all the town of Dulverton."

"What," said I, "that common glass thing, which she has had from her childhood!"

"Glass indeed! They are the finest brilliants ever I set eyes on: and I have handled a good many. Trust me," answered Tom, in his loftiest manner, "trust me, good mother, and simple John, for knowing brilliants, when I see them. I would have stopped an eight-horse coach, with four carabined outriders, for such a booty as that. But alas, those days are over: those were days worth living in. How fine it was by moonlight!"

"Master Faggus," began my mother, with a manner of some dignity, "that is not the tone in which you have hitherto spoken to me about your former pursuits and life. What I mean, Master Faggus, is this: you have won my daughter's heart somehow; and you won my consent to the matter, through your honest sorrow, and manly undertaking to touch no property but your own. I will not risk my Annie's life, with a man who yearns for the highway."

Now as nothing very long abides, it cannot be expected that a women's anger should last very long. And my mother could not long retain her wrath against the Squire Faggus. But how my mother contrived to know, that because she had been too hard upon Tom, he must be right about the necklace, is a point which I never could clearly perceive. To prove herself right in that conclusion, she went herself to fetch Lorna. And then mother led her up to the light, for Tom to examine her necklace.

On the shapely curve of her neck it hung, like dewdrops upon a white hyacinth; and I was vexed that Tom should have the chance to see it there. But even as if she had read my thoughts, Lorna turned away, and softly took the jewels from the place which so much adorned them. Then she laid the glittering circlet in my mother's hands; and Tom Faggus took it eagerly, and bore it to the window.

"Don't you go out of sight," I said; "you cannot resist such things as those, if they be what you think them."

"Jack, I shall have to trounce thee yet. I am now a man of

honour, and entitled to the duello. What will you take for it, Mistress Lorna?"

"I am not accustomed to sell things, sir," replied Lorna. "What is it worth, in your opinion?"

"Do you think it is worth five pounds, now?"

"Oh no! I never had so much money as that in all my life. It is very bright and very pretty; but it cannot be worth five pounds, I am sure. But, sir, I would not sell it to you, not for twenty times five pounds. My grandfather was so kind about it; and I think it belonged to my mother."

"There are twenty-five rose diamonds in it, and twenty-five large brilliants that cannot be matched in London. How say you, Mistress Lorna, to a hundred thousand pounds?"

My darling's eyes flashed at this. And then Lorna took the necklace very quietly from the hand of Squire Faggus, who had not half done with admiring it, and she went up to my mother, with the sweetest smile I ever saw.

"Dear, kind mother, I am so glad," she said in a whisper, coaxing mother out of sight of all but me; "now you will have it, won't you, dear? And I shall be so happy; for a thousandth part of your kindness to me no jewels in the world can match."

I cannot lay before you the grace with which she did it. Mother knew not what to say. Of course she would never dream of taking such a gift as that; and yet she saw how sadly Lorna would be disappointed. Therefore mother did, from habit, what she almost always did, she called me to help her. But knowing that my eyes were full, I pretended not to hear my mother, but to see a wild cat in the dairy. Therefore I cannot tell what mother said in reply to Lorna; for when I came back behold Tom Faggus had gotten again the necklace and was delivering all around a dissertation on precious stones, and his sentiments about those in his hand. He said that the work was very ancient, but undoubtedly very good; the cutting of every line was true, and every angle was in its place. He said that of one thing he was quite certain: to wit, that a trinket of this kind never could have belonged to any ignoble family, but to one of the very highest and most wealthy in England. Tom Faggus said that the necklace was made, he would answer for it, in Amsterdam, two or three hundred years ago, long before London jewellers had begun to meddle with diamonds.

We said no more about the necklace, for a long time afterwards; neither did my darling wear it, now that she knew its value, but did not know its history. She came to me the very next day, trying to look cheerful, and begged me if I loved her to take charge of it again, as I once had done before. I told her that, having been round her neck so often, it was now a sacred thing, more than a million pounds could be. Therefore it should dwell for the present in the neighbourhood of my heart.

Tom Faggus took his good departure on the very day I am speaking of, the day after his arrival. Scarcely was Tom clean out of sight, and Annie's tears not dry yet when in came Master Jeremy Stickles, splashed with mud from head to foot, and not in the very best of humours, though happy to get back again.

"A pretty plight you may call this, for His Majesty's Commissioner to return to his headquarters in!" he cried, with a stamp which sent the water hissing from his boot among the embers; "Annie, my dear," for he was always very affable with Annie, "will you help me off with my overalls, and then turn your pretty hand to the gridiron? Not a blessed morsel have I touched for more than twenty-four hours."

"Surely than you must be quite starving, sir," my sister replied with the greatest zeal; for she did love a man with an appetite.

12. Every Man must Defend Himself

IT was only right in Jeremy Stickles that he would not tell, before our girls, what the result of his journey was. But he led me aside in the course of the evening, and told me all about it. He complained that the weather had been against him bitterly, closing all the roads around him. It had taken him eight days, he said, to get from Exeter to Plymouth; whither he found that most of the troops had been drafted off from Exeter, and their commanders had orders on no account to quit the southern coast and march inland. Neither was this the worst of it; for Jeremy made no doubt but what (if he could only get the militia to turn out in force) he might manage, with the help of his own men, to force the stronghold of the enemy; but the truth was that the officers, knowing how hard it would be to collect their men at that time of the year, and in that state of the weather, began with one accord to make every possible excuse.

And so it came to pass that the King's Commissioner returned, without any army whatever; but with promise of two hundred men when the roads should be more passable. And meanwhile what were we to do, abandoned as we were to the mercies of the

Doones, with only our own hands to help us? And herein I grieved at my own folly, in having let Tom Faggus go, whose wit and courage would have been worth at least half-a-dozen men to us. Upon this matter I held long council with my good friend Stickles; telling him all about Lorna's presence, and what I knew of her history. He agreed with me, that we could not hope to escape an attack from the outlaws. Also he praised me for my forethought, in having threshed out all our corn, and hidden the produce in such a manner that they were not likely to find it. Furthermore, he recommended that all the entrances to the house should at once be strengthened, and a watch must be maintained at night; and he thought it wiser that I should go (late as it was) to Lynmouth, if a horse could pass the valley, and fetch every one of his mounted troopers. My errand was given me, and I set forth upon it; for John Fry was afraid of the waters.

Knowing how fiercely the floods were out, I resolved to travel the higher road, by Cosgate and through Countisbury; therefore I swam my horse through the Lynn, and thence galloped up and along the hills. I could see all the inland valleys ribbon'd with broad waters. But when I descended the hill towards Lynmouth, I feared that my journey was all in vain. For the East Lynn was ramping and roaring frightfully, lashing whole trunks of trees on the rocks, and rending them, and grinding them. And into it rushed, from the opposite side, a torrent even madder, scattering wrath with fury. It was certain death to attempt the passage; and the little wooden footbridge had been carried away long ago.

I followed the bank of the flood to the beach, and there had the luck to see Will Watcombe on the opposite side, caulking an old boat. Though I could not make him hear a word, from the deafening roar of the torrent, I got him to understand at last that I wanted to cross over. Upon this he fetched another man, and the two of them launched a boat; and paddling well out to sea, fetched round the mouth of the frantic river. The other man proved to be Stickles' chief mate; and so he went back, and fetched his comrades, bringing their weapons, but leaving their horses behind. There were but four of them; however to have even these was a help; and I started again at full speed for my home; for the men must follow afoot, and cross our river high up on the moorland, so that I arrived at Plover's Barrows more than two hours before them. But they had done a sagacious thing, for by hoisting their flag upon the hill, they fetched the two watchmen from the Foreland, and added them to their number.

It was lucky that I came home so soon; for I found the house in a great commotion, and all the women trembling. When I asked what the matter was, Lorna answered that she had stolen out to the garden towards dusk, to watch some favourite hyacinths just pushing up, when she descried two glittering eyes glaring at her steadfastly, from the elder bush beyond the stream. Then Carver Doone, with his deadly smile, gloating upon her horror, lifted his long gun, and pointed full at Lorna's heart. In vain she strove to turn away; fright had stricken her stiff as stone. With no sign of pity in his face, but a well-pleased grin at all the charming palsy of his victim, Carver Doone lowered, inch by inch, the muzzle of his gun. When it pointed to the ground, between her delicate arched insteps, he pulled the trigger, and the bullet flung the mould all over her. It was a refinement of bullying, for which I swore to God that I would smite down Carver Doone.

My darling fell away on a bank of grass, and wept at her own cowardice. While she leaned there, Carver came to the brink of the flood, which alone was between them.

"I have spared you this time," he said, in his deep, calm voice, "only because it suits my plans. But unless you come back to-morrow, pure, and with all you took away, your death is here, where it has long been waiting." Although his gun was empty, he struck the breech of it with his finger; and then he turned away, and Lorna saw his giant figure striding across the meadow-land.

Now, expecting a sharp attack that night—which Jeremy Stickles the more expected, after the words of Carver, which seemed to be meant to mislead us—we prepared a great quantity of knuckles of pork, and a ham in full cut, and a fillet of hung mutton. For we would almost surrender, rather than keep our garrison hungry. Before the maidens went to bed, Lorna made a remark which seemed to me a very clever one.

"Shall I tell you what I think, John? You know how high the rivers are, higher than ever they were before. I believe that Glen Doone is flooded, and all the houses under water."

"You little witch," I answered; "what a fool I must be not to think of it! Of course it is; it must be. The torrent from all the Bagworthy forest, and all the valleys above it, and the great drifts in the glen itself, never could have outlet down my famous water-slide. The valley must be under twenty feet at least. You may take my word for it, that your pretty bower is six feet deep."

"Well, my bower has served its time," said Lorna, blushing as she remembered all that had happened there; "and my bower now is here, John. But I am so sorry to think of all the poor women flooded out of their houses, and sheltering in the snow-drifts. However, there is one good of it: they cannot send many men against us, with all this trouble upon them."

"You are right," I replied; "how clever you are! And now we shall beat them, I make no doubt, even if they come at all. And I defy them to fire the house: the thatch is too wet for burning."

˙ We sent all the women to bed quite early, except Gwenny Carfax and our old Betty. For my part, I had little fear, after what Lorna had told me, as to the result of the combat. It was not likely that the Doones could bring more than eight or ten men against us, while their homes were in such danger; and to meet these we had eight good men, including Jeremy, and myself, all well-armed and resolute, besides our three farm-servants, and the parish-clerk, and the shoemaker. Bill Dadds had a sickle, Jim Slocombe a flail, the cobbler had borrowed the constable's staff, and the parish clerk had brought his pitch-pipe, which was enough to break any man's head. But John Fry, of course, had his blunderbuss, loaded with tin-tacks and marbles, and more likely to kill the man who discharged it than any other person; but we knew that John had it only for show. Now it was my great desire, and my chiefest hope, to come across Carver Doone that night, and settle the score between us; not by any shot in the dark, but by a conflict man to man. Now at last I had found a man whose strength was not to be laughed at.

Therefore I was not content to abide within the house, or go the rounds with the troopers; but betook myself to the rickyard, knowing that the Doones were likely to begin their onset there. For they had a pleasant custom, when they visited farm-houses, of lighting themselves towards picking up anything they wanted, or stabbing the inhabitants, by first creating a blaze in the rick-yard. Now I had not been so very long waiting in our mow-yard, with my best gun ready, and a big club by me, before a heaviness of sleep began to creep upon me. So I leaned back in the clover-rick, and dozed.

It was not likely that the outlaws would attack our premises, until some time after the moon was risen; because it would be too dangerous to cross the flooded valleys in the darkness of the night. But even so, it was very foolish to abandon watch, especially in such as I, who sleep like any dormouse. Moreover I had chosen the very worst place in the world for such employment, with a goodly chance of awakening in a bed of solid fire. And so it must have been, but for Lorna's vigilance. Her light hand upon my arm awoke me, not too readily; and leaping up, I seized my club, and prepared to knock down somebody.

"Who's that?" I cried. "My darling, is it you? And breaking all your orders?"

"How could I sleep, while at any moment you might be killed beneath my window? And now is the time of real danger; for men can see to travel." I saw at once the truth of this. The moon was high, and clearly lighting all the watered valleys.

"The man on guard at the back of the house is fast asleep," she continued. "Gwenny, who came with me, has heard him snoring for two hours. I think the women ought to be the watch, because they have had no travelling. Where do you suppose little Gwenny is? She is perched in yonder tree, which commands the Barrow valley. She says that they are almost sure to cross the streamlet there; and she is sure to see them, and in good time to let us know."

"What a shame," I cried, "that the men should sleep, and the maidens be the soldiers! Now go indoors, darling, without more words."

She only said, "God keep you, love!" and then away she tripped across the yard. And thereupon I shouldered arms, and resolved to tramp till morning. But before long, a short wide figure stole towards me, and I saw that it was Gwenny herself.

"Ten on 'em crossed the watter down yonner," said Gwenny, putting her hand to her mouth, and seeming to regard it as good news rather than otherwise; "be arl craping up by hedge-row now."

"There is no time to lose, Gwenny. Run to the house, and fetch Master Stickles, and all the men; while I stay here."

The robbers rode into our yard as coolly as if they had been invited. Then they actually opened our stable-doors, and turned our honest horses out, and put their own rogues in the place of them. At this my breath was quite taken away; for we think so much of our horses. By this time I could see our troopers, waiting in the shadow of the house, and expecting the order to fire. But Jeremy Stickles very wisely kept them in readiness, until the enemy should advance upon them.

"Two of you lazy fellows go," it was the deep voice of Carver Doone, "and make us a light to cut their throats by. Only one thing, once again. If any man touches Lorna, I will stab him where he stands. She belongs to me. There are two other young damsels here, whom you may take away if you please. And the mother, I hear, is still comely. Now for our rights. We have borne too long the insolence of these yokels. Kill every man, and every child, and burn the cursed place down."

As he spoke thus blasphemously, I set my gun against his breast; and by the light buckled from his belt, I saw the little "sight" of brass gleaming alike upon either side, and the sleek round barrel glimmering. The aim was sure as death itself. If I only drew the

124

trigger (which went very lightly) Carver Doone would breathe no more. And yet—will you believe me?— I could not pull the trigger. Would to God that I had done so! For I never had taken human life. Therefore I dropped my carbine, and grasped again my club, which seemed a more straightforward implement.

Presently two young men came towards me, bearing brands of resined hemp, kindled from Carver's lamp. The foremost of them set his torch to the rick within a yard of me, the smoke concealing me from him. I struck him with a back-handed blow on the elbow, and I heard the bone of his arm break. With a roar of pain he fell on the ground, and his torch dropped there, and singed him. The other man stood amazed at this, not having yet gained sight of me; till I caught his firebrand from his hand, and struck it into his countenance. With that he leaped at me; but I caught him, in a manner learned from early wrestling, and snapped his collar-bone, as I laid him upon the top of his comrade. This little success so encouraged me, that I was half inclined to advance, and challenge Carver Doone to meet me; but I bore in mind that he would be apt to shoot me without ceremony. While I was hesitating thus a blaze of fire lit up the house, and brown smoke hung around it. Six of our men had let go at the Doones, by Jeremy Stickles' order, as the villains came swaggering down in the moonlight. Two of them fell, and the rest hung back.

Being unable any longer to contain myself, I came across the yard, expecting whether they would shoot at me. However, no one shot at me; and I went up to Carver Doone, whom I knew by his size in the moonlight, and I took him by the beard, and said, "Do you call yourself a man?"

For a moment, he was so astonished that he could not answer. And then he tried a pistol at me; but I was too quick for him.

"Now, Carver Doone, take warning," I said to him. "You are a despicable villain. Lie low in your native muck."

And with that word, I laid him flat upon his back in our straw-yard. Seeing him down the others ran, though one of them made a shot at me, and some of them got their horses, before our men came up; and some went away without them. And among these last was Captain Carver, who arose, while I was feeling myself (for I had a little wound), and strode away with a train of curses. We gained six very good horses, as well as two young prisoners, whom I had smitten by the clover-rick. And two dead Doones were left behind.

I scarcely know who made the greatest fuss about my little wound, mother, or Annie, or Lorna. Most unluckily it had been impossible to hide it. For the ball had cut along my temple, just above the eye-brow; and being fired so near at hand, the powder too had scarred me. Therefore it seemed a great deal worse than it really was; and the sponging, and the plaistering, and the sobbing, made me quite ashamed to look Master Stickles in the face.

Without waiting for any warrant, Stickles sent our prisoners off, bound and looking miserable, to the jail at Taunton. I was desirous to let them go free, if they would promise amendment; but Master Stickles said, "Not so." Both those poor fellows were executed, soon after the next assizes. Lorna had done her very best to earn another chance for them; even going down on her knees to that common Jeremy, and pleading with great tears for them. However, although much moved by her, he vowed that to set them free was more than his own life was worth; for all the country knew, by this time, that two captive Doones were roped to the cider-press at Plover's Barrows.

That day we were reinforced so strongly from the stations along the coast, even as far as Minehead, that we not only feared no further attack, but even talked of assaulting Glen Doone, without waiting for the train-bands. However, I thought that it would be mean to take advantage of the enemy in the thick of the floods and confusion; and several of the others thought so too, and not like fighting in water. Therefore it was resolved to wait, and keep a watch upon the valley, and let the floods go down again.

13. The Way to make the Cream Rise

Now the business I had most at heart was to marry Lorna as soon as might be, and then to work the farm so well, as to nourish all our family. However, my dear mother would have it that Lorna was too young, as yet, to think of being married. And another difficulty was, that as we had all been Protestants from the time of Queen Elizabeth, the maiden must be converted first, and taught to hate all Papists. Now Lorna had not the smallest idea of ever being converted. She said that she loved me truly, but wanted not to convert me; and if I loved her equally, why should I wish to convert her?

As I came in one evening, soon after dark, my sister Eliza met me at the corner of the cheese-room, and she said, "Don't go in there, John," pointing to mother's room; "until I have had a talk with you. It is something very important about Mistress Lorna Doone. Do you know a man of about Gwenny's shape, nearly as broad as he is long, but about six times the size of Gwenny, and with a length of snow-white hair?"

"I know the man from your description, although I have never seen him. Now where is my Lorna?"

"Your Lorna is with Annie, having a good cry, I believe; and Annie too glad to second her. She knows that this great man is here, and knows that he wants to see her."

I was almost sure that the man who was come must be the Counsellor himself; of whom I felt much keener fear than of his son Carver. And knowing that his visit boded ill to me and Lorna, I went and sought my dear; and led her with a heavy heart, from the maiden's room to mother's, to meet our dreadful visitor. Mother was standing by the door, making courtesies now and then, and listening to a long harangue upon the rights of state and land. My dear mother stood gazing at him, spell-bound by his eloquence. Then he advanced with zeal to Lorna; holding out both hands at once.

"My darling child, my dearest niece; how wonderfully well you look! Mistress Ridd, I give you credit. This is the country of good things. I never would have believed our Queen could have looked so Royal. This must be your son, Mistress Ridd, the great John, the wrestler. I may now be regarded, I think, as this young lady's legal guardian. Her father was the eldest son of Sir Ensor Doone; and I happened to be the second son. As Lorna's guardian, I give my full and ready consent to her marriage with your son, madam."

"O how good of you, sir, how kind! Well, I always did say, that the learnedest people were, almost always, the best and kindest."

"Madam, that is a great sentiment. What a goodly couple they will be! But while we talk of the heart, what is my niece Lorna doing, that she does not come and thank me, for my perhaps too prompt concession to her youthful fancies?"

Lorna, being challenged thus, came up and looked at her uncle, with her noble eyes fixed full upon his. "Well, uncle, I should be very grateful, if I did not know that you have something yet concealed from me."

"And my consent," said the Counsellor, "is the more liberal, frank, and candid, in the face of an existing fact, which might have appeared to weaker minds in the light of an impediment."

"What fact do you mean, sir? Is it one that I ought to know?"

"My dear child, I prolong your suspense. However, if you must have my strong realities, here they are. Your father slew dear John's father, and dear John's father slew yours."

Then feeling that I must speak first I took my darling round the waist, and led her up to the Counsellor. "Now, Sir Counsellor Doone," I said, "you know right well, that Sir Ensor Doone gave approval."

"Approval to what, good rustic John? To the slaughter so reciprocal?"

"No, sir, not to that; even if it ever happened; which I do not believe. But to the love betwixt me and Lorna; which your story shall not break, without more evidence than your word."

Then mother looked at me with wonder, being herself too amazed to speak; and the Counsellor looked, with great wrath in his eyes, which he tried to keep from burning.

"How say you then, John Ridd," he cried, "is this a thing of the sort you love? Is this what you are used to?"

"So please your worship," I answered; "no kind of violence can surprise us, since first came Doones upon Exmoor. Up to that time none heard of harm. But ever since the Doones came first, we are used to anything."

"Thou varlet," cried the Counsellor, "is this the way we are to deal with such a low-bred clod as thou? To question the doings of our people! Lorna Doone, stand forth from contact with that heir of parricide; and state in your own mellifluous voice, whether you regard this slaughter as a pleasant trifle."

"Without any failure of respect for your character, good uncle," she answered, "I decline politely to believe a word of what you have told me. And even if it were proved to me, all I can say is this, if my John will have me, I am his for ever."

This long speech was too much for her; she fell into my arms.

"You old villain," cried my mother, shaking her fist at the Counsellor. "My sweet love, my darling child," our mother went on to Lorna, "pretty pet, not a word of it is true, upon that old

130

liar's oath; and if every word were true, poor chick, you should have our John all the more for it."

I was amazed at mother's words, being so unlike her; while I loved her all the more because she forgot herself so. In another moment in ran Annie, ay and Lizzie also, knowing by some mystic sense that something was astir. And now the Counsellor beckoned to me to come away; which I, being smothered with women, was only too glad to do.

"That is the worst of them," said the old man, when I had led him to our kitchen, with an apology at every step, and given him hot schnapps and water, and a cigarro of brave Tom Faggus: "you never can say much, sir, in the way of reasoning (however gently meant and put) but what these women will fly out. Now of this business, John," he said, after getting to the bottom of the second glass, "taking you on the whole, you know, you are wonderfully good people: and instead of giving me up to the soldiers, as you might have done, you are doing your best to make me drunk."

"Not at all, sir," I answered; "not at all, your worship. Let me mix you another glass. We rarely have a great gentleman by the side of our embers and oven."

"My son," replied the Counsellor, standing across the front of the fire, to prove his strict sobriety: "I meant to come down upon you to-night; but you have turned the tables upon me. Not through any skill on your part, but through your simple way of taking me, as a man to be believed: combined with the comfort of this place, and the choice tobacco, and cordials. I have not enjoyed an evening so much: God bless me if I know when!"

That night the reverend Counsellor, not being in such state of mind as ought to go alone, kindly took our best old bedstead. I set him up so that he need but close both eyes; and in the morning, he was thankful for all that he could remember. I, for my part, scarcely knew whether he really had begun to feel good-will towards us, or whether he was merely acting. And it had struck me, several times, that he had made a great deal more of the spirit he had taken than the quantity would warrant, with a man so wise and solid. Neither did I quite understand a little story which Lorna told me, how that in the night awaking, she seemed to hear a sound in her room, as if there had been someone groping carefully among the things within her drawers or wardrobe-closet. But the noise had ceased at once, she said, when she sat up in bed and listened; and knowing how many mice we had, she took courage, and fell asleep again.

After breakfast, the Counsellor followed our Annie into the dairy, to see how we managed the clotted cream, of which he had eaten a basinful.

"Your honour must plainly understand," said Annie, being now alone with him, and spreading out her light quick hands over the pans, "that they are brought in here to cool, after being set in the basin-holes, with the wood ash under them, which I showed you in the back-kitchen. And they must have very little heat, only just to make the bubbles rise, and the scum upon the top set thick: and after that, it clots as firm—oh, as firm as my two hands be."

"Have you ever heard," asked the Counsellor, "that if you pass across the top, without breaking the surface, a string of beads, or polished glass, the cream will set three times as solid, and in thrice the quantity?"

"No, sir; I have never heard that," said Annie, staring with all her simple eyes; "what a thing it is to read books, and grow learned! But I will get my coral necklace; it will not be witchcraft, will it, sir?"

"Certainly not," the old man replied. "But coral will not do, my child, neither will anything coloured. The beads must be of plain common glass; but the brighter they are the better."

"Then I know the very thing," cried Annie; "as bright as bright can be. Dearest Lorna has a necklace of some old glass-beads. I will go for it, in a moment."

"My dear, it cannot be half so bright as your own pretty eyes.

But remember one thing, Annie, you must not say what it is for; else the charm will be broken. Bring it here, without a word; if you know where she keeps it."

"To be sure I do," she answered. "John used to keep it for her. But she took it away from him last week."

Annie found it sparkling in the little secret hole, near the head of Lorna's bed; and without a word to anyone she brought it down, and danced it in the air before the Counsellor.

"Oh, that old thing!" said the gentleman, in a tone of some contempt; "I remember that old thing well enough. However, no doubt, it will answer our purpose. Three times three, I pass it over. Crickleum, crankum, grass and clover! What are you feared of, you silly child?"

"Good sir, it is perfect witchcraft! I am sure of that, because it rhymes. Shall I ever go to heaven again? Oh, I see the cream already!"

"Now," he said, in a deep stern whisper; "not a word of this to living soul: neither must you, nor any other enter this place for three hours at least. By that time the charm will have done its work: the pan will be cream to the bottom; and you will bless me for a secret which will make your fortune. Put the bauble under this pannikin; which none must lift for a day and a night. Have no fear, my simple wench; not a breath of harm shall come to you, if you obey my orders. Go to your room, without so much as a single word to any one. Bolt yourself in, and for three hours now, read the Lord's Prayer backwards."

Poor Annie was only too glad to escape, upon these conditions; and the Counsellor told her not to make her eyes red, because they were much too sweet and pretty. She dropped them at this, with a sob and a courtesy, and ran away to her bedroom.

Meanwhile the Counsellor was gone. He bade our mother adieu, with so much dignity of bearing, and such warmth and gratitude that when he was gone, dear mother fell back on the chair which he had used last night; as if it would teach her the graces.

"Oh the wickedness of the world! Oh the lies that are told of people because a man is better born, and has better manners! Oh Lizzie, you have read me beautiful things about Sir Gallyhead, and the rest; but nothing to equal Sir Counsellor."

"You had better marry him, madam," said I, coming in very sternly; "he can repay your adoration. He has stolen a hundred thousand pounds."

"John," cried my mother, "you are mad!" And yet she turned as pale as death.

"Of course, I am, mother; mad about the marvels of Sir Galahad. He has gone off with my Lorna's necklace. Fifty farms like ours can never make it good to Lorna."

Hereupon ensued grim silence. Then Lorna went up to my mother, who was still in the chair of elegance; and she took her by both hands, and said, "Dearest mother, I shall fret so, if I see you fretting."

Poor mother bent on Lorna's shoulder, and sobbed till Lizzie was jealous, and came with two pocket handkerchiefs. But who shall tell of Annie's grief? The poor little thing would have staked her life upon finding the trinket, in all its beauty, lying under the pannikin. She proudly challenged me to lift it. But when we raised the pannikin, and there was nothing under it, poor Annie fell against the wall, which had been whitened lately; and her face put all the white to scorn.

That same night Master Jeremy Stickles (of whose absence the Counsellor must have known) came back, with all equipment ready for the grand attack. Jeremy Stickles laughed heartily about Annie's new manner of charming the cream; but he looked very grave at the loss of the jewels, so soon as he knew their value.

"My son," he exclaimed, "this is very heavy. It will go ill with all of you to make good this loss, as I fear that you will have to do."

"What!" cried I, with my blood running cold. "We make good the loss, Master Stickles! Every farthing we have in the world, and the labour of our lives to boot, will never make good the tenth of it. Let me know the worst of it."

"Very well," replied Master Stickles, seeing that both the doors were closed. "Likely enough I am quite wrong; and God send that I be so. But what I guessed at some time back seems more than a guess, now that you have told me about those wondrous jewels. Now will you keep as close as death every word I tell you?"

"By my honour, I will. Until you yourself release me."

"My son," said Jeremy Stickles, with a good pull at his pipe, because he was going to talk so much, and putting his legs well along in the settle; "it may be six months ago, or it may be seven, when I was riding one afternoon from Dulverton to Watchett——"

"Dulverton to Watchett!" I cried. "Now what does that remind me of? I am sure, I remember something——"

"Remember this, John, that another word from thee, and thou hast no more of mine. I was riding on from Dulverton, and it was late in the afternoon, and I was growing weary. Watchett town was not to be seen, on account of a little foreland, a mile or more upon my course, and standing to the right of me. But close at hand, drawn above the yellow sands and long eyebrows of wrack-weed, as snug a little house blinked on me as ever I saw.

"I thought to myself how snug this same inn was, and how beautifully I could sleep there. And so I struck the door of the hostelry. Some one came, and peeped at me through the lattice overhead, which was full of bulls' eyes; and then the bolt was drawn back, and a woman met me very courteously. A dark and foreign-looking woman, very hot of blood, I doubt.

"'Can I rest here for the night?' I asked, with a lift of my hat to her; 'my horse is weary from the sloughs, and myself but little better: besides that, we both are famished.'

"'Yes, sir, you can rest and welcome. But of food, I fear, there is but little, unless of the common order. However, we have— what you call it? I never can remember, it is so hard to say—the flesh of the hog salted.'

"'Bacon!' said I; 'what can be better? And half-a-dozen eggs with it, and a quart of fresh-drawn ale. You make me rage with hunger, madam.'

"'Ah, good!' she replied with a merry smile, full of southern sunshine: 'you are not of the men round here: you can think, and you can laugh!' She laughed aloud, and swung her shoulders, as your natives cannot do; and then she called a little maid, to lead my horse to stable. However I preferred to see that matter done myself, and told her to send the little maid for the frying pan and the egg-box. Whether it were my London freedom and know-ledge of the world; or my ready and permanent appetite, an appreciation of garlic—I leave you to decide, John: but perhaps all combined to recommend me to my charming hostess.

"However, not to dwell too much upon our little pleasantries, I became reasonably desirous to know, by what strange hap or hazard a clever and a handsome woman, as she must have been some day, could have settled here in this lonely inn, with only the waves for company, and a boorish husband who slaved all day in turning a potter's wheel at Watchett. And what was the meaning of the emblem set above her doorway, a very unattrac-tive cat sitting in a ruined tree?

"When she found out who I was, and how I held the King's commission, her desire to tell me all was more than equal to mine of hearing it. By birth she was an Italian, from the mountains of Apulia, who had gone to Rome to seek her fortunes, after being badly treated in some love affair. Her Christian name was Benita. Being a quick and active girl, she found employment in a large hotel; and rising gradually, began to send money to her parents. And here she might have thriven well, and married well under sunny skies, and been a happy woman, but that some black day sent thither a rich and noble English family, eager to behold the Pope. It was not however their fervent longing for the Holy Father which had brought them to St. Peter's roof; but rather their own bad luck in making their home too hot to hold them. Some bitter feud had been among them, Benita knew not how it was; and the sister of the nobleman who had died quite lately was married to the rival claimant, whom they all detested. It was something about dividing land. But this Benita did know, that they were all great people, and rich, and very liberal; so that when they offered to take her, to attend to the children, and to speak the language for them, she was only too glad to go. Moreover she loved the children so, that it would have broken her heart almost never to see the dears again.

"And so, in a very evil hour, she accepted the service of the noble Englishman. At first all things went well. My Lord was as gay as gay could be: and never would come inside the carriage, when a decent horse could be got to ride. He would gallop in front, at a reckless pace, without a weapon of any kind, delighted with the pure blue air. And so they travelled through Northern Italy, and throughout the south of France, making their way; sometimes in coaches, sometimes in carts, sometimes upon mule-back, sometimes even a-foot and weary; but always as happy as could be. The children laughed, and grew, and throve (especially the young lady, the elder of the two).

"My lord, who was quite a young man still, rode on in front of his wife and friends, to catch the first of a famous view, on the French side of the Pyrenean hills. He kissed his hand to his wife, and said that he would save her the trouble of coming. For those two were so one in one, that they could make each other know, whatever he, or she, had felt. And so my Lord went round the corner, with a fine young horse leaping up at every step. They waited for him, long and long; but he never came again; and within a week, his mangled body lay in a little chapel-yard. My Lady dwelled for six months more, scarcely able to believe that all her fright was not a dream. She would not wear any mourning-clothes. She simply disbelieved the thing, and trusted God to right it.

"When the snow came down in autumn on the roots of the Pyrenees, many people told the lady that it was time for her to go. And the strongest plea of all was this, that now she bore another hope of repeating her husband's virtues. So at the end of October, when wolves came down to the farm-lands, the little English family went home towards their England. They landed somewhere on the Devonshire coast, ten or eleven years agone, and stayed some days at Exeter; and set out thence in a hired coach, for Watchett, in the north of Somerset. For the lady owned a quiet mansion in the neighbourhood of that town, and her one desire was to find refuge there, and to meet her lord, who was sure to come (she said) when he heard of his new infant. Therefore, the party set forth and lay the first night at Bampton. On the following morn they started bravely, with earnest hope of arriving at their journey's end by daylight. But the roads were soft and very deep, and the heavy coach broke down in the axle, and needed mending at Dulverton; and so they lost three hours or more, and would have been wiser to sleep there. But her ladyship would not hear of it; she must be home that night, she said, and her husband would be waiting.

"Therefore, although it was afternoon, and the year now come to December, the horses were put to again, and the heavy coach went up the hill, with the lady and her two children, and Benita, sitting inside of it; the other maid, and two serving men (each man with a great blunderbuss) mounted upon the outside; and upon the horses three Exeter postilions. Through the fog, and through the muck, the coach went on, as best it might; sometimes foundering in a slough. However, they went on till dark, but when they came to the pitch and slope of the sea-bank, leading on towards Watchett town, there they met their fate.

"Although it was past the dusk of day, the silver light from the sea showed them a troop of horsemen, waiting under a rock hard by, and ready to dash upon them. The postilions lashed towards the sea, and the horses strove in the depth of sand, and the serving-men cocked their blunderbusses, and cowered away behind them; but the lady stood up in the carriage bravely, and neither screamed nor spoke, but hid her son behind her. Meanwhile the drivers drove into the sea, till the leading horses were swimming. But before the waves came into the coach, a score of fierce men were round it. Then, while the carriage was heeling over, and well-nigh upset in the water, the lady exclaimed, 'I know that man! He is our ancient enemy,' and Benita (foreseeing that all their boxes would be turned inside out, or carried away) snatched the most valuable of the jewels, a magnificent necklace of diamonds, and cast it over the little girl's head, and buried it under her travelling-cloak, hoping so to save it. What followed Benita knew not, herself being stunned by a blow on the head. But when she recovered her senses, she found herself upon the sand, the robbers were out of sight, and one of the serving-men was bathing her forehead with sea water. Her mistress was sitting upright on a little rock, with her dead boy's face to her bosom, sometimes gazing on him, and sometimes questing round for the other one. Before the light of the morning came along the tide to Watchett my Lady had met her husband. The lady, whom all people loved, lies in Watchett little churchyard, with son and heir at her right hand, and a little babe, of sex unknown, sleeping on her bosom.

"This is a miserable tale," said Jeremy Stickles brightly; "hand me over the schnapps, my boy. What fools we are to spoil our eyes for other people's troubles!"

"And what was the lady's name?" I asked. "And what became of the little girl? And why did the woman stay there?"

"Well!" cried Jeremy Stickles, only too glad to be cheerful again. "Talk of a woman after that! But to begin, last first, my John: Benita stayed in that blessed place, because she could not get away from it. The Doones—if Doones indeed they were, about which you of course know best—took every stiver out of the carriage. And Benita could never get her wages; for the whole affair is in Chancery, and they have appointed a receiver. So the poor thing was compelled to settle down on the brink of Exmoor. She married a man who turned a wheel for making the blue Watchett ware. There they are, and have three children; and there you may go and visit them."

"I understand all that, Jeremy, though you do tell things too quickly. Now for my second question. What became of the little maid?"

"You great oaf!" cried Jeremy Stickles. "You are rather more likely to know, I should think, than any one else in all the king-doms. As certain sure as I stand here, that little maid is Lorna Doone."

Jeremy's tale would have moved me greatly, both with sorrow and anger, even without my guess at first, and now my firm belief, that the child of those unlucky parents was indeed my Lorna. For when he described the heavy coach, and the persons in and upon it, and the breaking down at Dulverton, and the place of their destination, my heart began to burn within me, and my mind replaced the pictures, first of the foreign lady's-maid by the pump caressing me, and then of the coach struggling up the hill, and the beautiful dame, and the fine little boy, with the white cockade in his hat; but most of all the little girl, dark-haired and very lovely, and having even in those days the rich soft look of Lorna. But when he spoke of the necklace thrown over the head of the little maiden, and of her disappearance, before my eyes arose at once the flashing of the beacon-fire, the lonely moors, the tramp of the outlaw cavalcade, and the helpless child head downward lying across the robber's saddle-bow.

14. Lorna Knows her Nurse

JEREMY STICKLES was quite decided that not a word of all these things must be imparted to Lorna herself, or even to my mother, or anyone whatever. "Keep it tight as wax, my lad," he cried, with a wink of great expression. "It would have taken you fifty years to put two and two together so, as I did, like a clap of thunder. Ah, God has given some men brains; and others have good farms and money, and a certain skill in the lower beasts. You work your farm: I work my brains. Now no more of that, my boy; a cigarro after schnapps, and go to meet my yellow boys."

His "yellow boys," as he called the Somerset trained bands, were even now coming down the valley. There was one good point about these men, that having no discipline at all, they made pretence to none whatever. On the other hand, Master Stickles' troopers looked down on these native fellows. Now these fine natives came along, singing for their very lives, a song the like of which set down here would oust my book from modest people, and make everybody say, "this man never can have loved Lorna." Having finished their canticle, they drew themselves up, in a sort of way supposed by them to be military, and saluted the King's Commissioner.

"Why, where are your officers?" asked Master Stickles.

Upon this a knowing look passed along their faces. "Plaise zur," said one little fellow at last, "hus tould Harfizers, as a wor no nade of un, now King's man hiszel wor coom, a puppose vor to command us laike."

"Well!" said poor Jeremy, turning to me; "a pretty state of things, John! Threescore cobblers, and farming men, plaisterers, tailors, and kettles-to-mend; and not a man to keep order among them, except my blessed self, John! The Doones will make riddles of all of us."

However, he had better hopes, when the sons of Devon appeared, as they did in about an hour's time; fine fellows, and eager to prove themselves. These had not discarded their officers, but marched in good obedience to them. The yellows and the reds together numbered a hundred and twenty men, most of whom slept in our barns and stacks; and besides these we had fifteen troopers of the regular army. You may suppose that all the country was turned upside down about it; and the folk who came to see them drill—by no means a needless exercise—were a greater plague than the soldiers.

Therefore all of us were right glad when Jeremy Stickles gave orders to march, and we began to try to do it. The culverins were laid on bark; and all our horses pulling them. They pulled their very best and the culverins went up the hill, without smack of whip, or swearing. It had been arranged, very justly no doubt, but as it proved not too wisely, that either body of men should act in its own county only. So when we reached the top of the hill, the sons of Devon marched on, and across the track leading into Doone-gate, so as to fetch round the western side, and attack with their culverin from the cliffs. Meanwhile the yellow lads were to stay upon the eastern highland. And here they were not to show themselves; but keep their culverin in the woods, until their cousins of Devon appeared on the opposite parapet of the glen. The third culverin was entrusted to the fifteen troopers; who with ten picked soldiers from either trained band, making in all five-and-thirty men, were to assault the Doone-gate itself, while the outlaws were placed between two fires from the eastern cliff and the western. And with this force went Jeremy Stickles, and with it went myself, as knowing more about the passage than any other stranger did. Therefore the Doones must repulse at once three simultaneous attacks, from an army numbering in the whole one hundred and thirty-five men, not including the Devonshire officers; fifty men on each side I mean, and thirty-five at the head of the valley.

I wish I could only tell what happened, in the battle of that day. But in truth, I cannot tell, exactly, even the part in which I helped; how then can I be expected, time by time, to lay before you, all the little ins and outs of places, where I myself was not? Now we five-and-thirty men lay back, a little way round the corner, in the hollow of the track which leads to the strong Doone-gate. Our culverin was in amongst us, loaded now to the muzzle. Although the yeomanry were not come (according to arrangement), some of us had horses there; besides the horses who dragged the cannon, and now were sniffing at it.

At last, we heard the loud bang-bang, which proved that Devon and Somerset were pouring their indignation hot into the den of malefactors, or at least so we supposed; therefore at double quick march we advanced round the bend of the cliff, hoping to find the gate undefended, and to blow down all barriers with the fire of our cannon. We shouted a loud hurrah, as for an easy victory. But while the sound of our cheer rang back among the crags above us, a shrill clear whistle cleft the air for a single moment, and then a dozen carbines bellowed, and all among us flew murderous lead. Several of our men rolled over, but the rest rushed on like Britons, Jeremy and myself in front, while we heard the horses plunging at the loaded gun behind us. "Now, my lads," cried Jeremy, "one dash, and we are beyond them!" For he saw that the foe was overhead in the gallery of brush-wood.

Our men with a brave shout answered him, for his courage was fine example; and we leaped in under the feet of the foe, before they could load their guns again. But here, when the foremost among us were past, an awful crash rang behind us, with the shrieks of men, and the din of metal, and the horrible screaming of horses. The trunk of the tree had been launched overhead, and crashed into the very midst of us. Our cannon was under it, so were two men and a horse with his poor back broken. Another horse vainly struggled to rise with his thigh-bone smashed and protruding. Now I lost all presence of mind at this, for I loved both those good horses, and shouting for any to follow me, dashed headlong into the cavern. Some five or six men came after me, the foremost of whom was Jeremy, when a storm of shots whistled and pattered around me, with a blaze of light and a thunderous roar. On I leaped, like a madman, and pounced on one gunner, and hurled him across his culverin; but the others had fled, and a heavy oak door fell to with a bang behind them. So utterly were my senses gone, and nought but strength remaining, that I caught up the Doone cannon with both hands, and dashed it, breech-first, at the doorway. The solid oak burst with the blow, and the gun stuck fast.

But here I looked round in vain, for any to come and follow up my success. Only a heavy groan or two went to my heart, and chilled it. So I hurried back to seek Jeremy, fearing that he must be smitten down. And so indeed I found him, as well as three other poor fellows, struck by the charge of the culverin. Two of the four were as dead as stones, and growing cold already, but Jeremy and the other could manage to groan. Having so many wounded men, and so many dead among us, we loitered at the cavern's mouth, and looked at one another, wishing only for somebody to come and take command of us. But no one came; and I was grieved so much about poor Jeremy, besides being wholly unused to any violence of bloodshed, that I could only keep his head up, and try to stop him from bleeding. The shot had taken him in the mouth; about that no doubt could be, for two of his teeth were in his beard, and one of his lips was wanting. I laid his shattered face on my breast, and nursed him, as a woman might. While here we stayed, a boy who had no business there came round the corner upon us.

"Got the worst of it!" cried the boy. "Better be off all of you. Zomerzett and Devon a vighting; and the Doones have drashed 'em both."

We few, who yet remained of the force which was to have won the Doone-gate, gazed at one another, like so many fools. We could not understand at all how Devonshire and Somerset should be fighting with one another. We laid poor Master Stickles and two more of the wounded upon the carriage of bark and hurdles, whereon our gun had laid; and we rolled the gun into the river, and harnessed the horses yet alive, and put the others out of their pain, and sadly wended homewards.

Now this enterprise having failed so, I prefer not to dwell too long upon it; only just to show the mischief which lay at the root of the failure. And this mischief was the vile jealousy betwixt red and yellow uniform. The men of Devon, who bore red facings, had a long way to go round the hills, before they could get into due position on the western side of the Doone Glen. And knowing that their cousins in yellow would claim the whole of the glory, if allowed to be first with the firing, these worthy fellows waited not to take good aim with their cannon, seeing the others about to shoot; but fettled it anyhow on the slope, pointing in a general direction, laid the rope to the breech, and fired. The shot, which was a casual mixture of anything considered hard—for instance jug-bottoms and knobs of doors—came scattering and shattering among the unfortunate yellow men upon the opposite cliff, killing one and wounding two. Now what did the men of Somerset do, but train their gun full mouth upon them, and with a vicious meaning shoot? Nor only this, but they loudly cheered, when they saw four or five red coats lie low. Now I need not tell the rest of it. Enough that both sides waxed hotter and hotter with the fire of destruction.

At last the Doones (who must have laughed at the thunder passing over head) recalling their men from the gallery, issued out of Gwenny's gate (which had been wholly overlooked) and fell on the rear of the Somerset men, and slew four beside their cannon. Then while the survivors ran away, the outlaws took the hot culverin, and rolled it down into their valley.

This was a melancholy end of our brave setting out: and everybody blamed every one else. Jeremy Stickles lay and tossed, and thrust up his feet in agony, and bit with his lipless mouth the clothes. He looked at us many times, as much as to say, "Fools, let me die; then I shall have some comfort." Colonel Stickles' illness was a grievous thing to us, in that we had no one now to command the troopers. Ten of these were still alive, and so well approved to us, that they could never fancy aught, whether for dinner or supper, without its being forthcoming. If they wanted trout, they should have it; if colloped venison, or broiled ham, or salmon from Lynmouth and Trentisoe, or truffles from the woodside; all these were at the warriors' service.

Be that as it might, we knew that if they once resolved to go, all our house, and all our goods, ay, and our own precious lives, would and must be at the mercy of embittered enemies. For now the Doones were in such feather all round the country, that nothing was too good for them. Offerings poured in at the Doonegate, faster than Doones could away with them; and the sympathy both of Devon and Somerset became almost oppressive.

But yet another cause arose, and this the strongest one of all, to prove the need of Stickles' aid, and calamity of his illness. For two men appeared at our gate one day, stripped to their shirts, and void of horses, and looking very sorrowful. We took them in, and fed, and left them to tell their business. And this they were glad enough to do; as men who have been maltreated almost always are. These two very worthy fellows were come from the Court of Chancery, sitting for everybody's good, and boldly redressing evil. This Court has a power of scent unknown to the Common-law practitioners, and slowly, yet surely, tracks its game. Now, as it fell on a very black day, His Majesty's Court of Chancery gained scent of poor Lorna's life, and of all that might be made of it. Chancery had heard of Lorna, and then had seen how rich she was.

The Doones had welcomed the two apparitors (if that be the proper name for them) and led them kindly down the valley, and told them then to serve their writ. And they stripped and lashed them out of the valley; only bidding them come to us, if they wanted Lorna Doone: and to us they came accordingly. We comforted and cheered them so considerably that, in gratitude, they showed their writs. And these were twofold: one addressed to Mistress Lorna Doone and bidding her keep in readiness to travel whenever called upon; while the other was addressed to all subjects of His Majesty, having custody of Lorna Doone.

I took the slip of brown parchment, and went to seek my darling. Lorna was in her favourite place, the little garden which she tended with such care and diligence.

"Darling," I said, "are your spirits good? Are you strong enough to-day, to bear a tale of cruel sorrow; but which perhaps, when your tears are shed, will leave you all the happier?"

"What can you mean?" she answered trembling.

"Now, Lorna," said I, as she hung on my arm, willing to trust me anywhere, "come with me, and hear my moving story. It is of your poor mother, darling. Lorna, you are of an ill-starred race."

"Better that than a wicked race," she answered with her usual quickness, leaping at conclusion: "tell me I am not a Doone, and I will—but I cannot love you more."

"You are not a Doone, my Lorna."

"And my father—your father—what I mean is"——

"Your father and mine never met one another. Your father was killed by an accident in the Pyrenean mountains, and your mother by the Doones; or at least they caused her death, and carried you away from her."

When at last my tale was done, she turned away, and wept bitterly for the sad fate of her parents.

"Lorna, darling," I said at length, "do you not even wish to know what your proper name is?"

"How can it matter to me, John?" she answered, with a depth of grief which made me seem a trifler. "Dearest, I have you. Having you, I want no other. All my life is one with yours."

So I led her into the house, and she fell into my mother's arms; and I left them to have a good cry of it.

If Master Stickles should not mend enough to gain his speech a little, and declare to us all he knew, I was to set out for Watchett, riding upon horseback, and there to hire a cart with wheels, such as we had not begun as yet to use on Exmoor. For all our work went on broad wood, with runners and with earth boards; and many of us still looked upon wheels as the invention of the Evil One. Now instead of getting better, Colonel Stickles grew worse and worse, in spite of all our tendance of him, with simples and with nourishment, and no poisonous medicines, such as doctors would have given him. For he roused himself up to a perfect fever, when through Lizzie's giddiness he learned the very thing which mother and Annie were hiding from him with the utmost care: namely, that Serjeant Bloxham had taken upon himself to send direct to London, by the Chancery officers, a full report of what had happened, and of the illness of his chief, together with an urgent prayer for a full battalion of King's troops, and a plenary commander. This Serjeant Bloxham had succeeded to the captaincy upon his master's disablement. Then, with desire to serve his country and show his education, he sat up most part of three nights, and wrote this wonderful report by the aid of our stable lanthorn. And all might have gone well with it, if the author could only have held his tongue, when near the ears of women. For having heard that our Lizzie was a famous judge of literature he must have her opinion upon his work. Lizzie sat on a log of wood, and listened with all her ears up. And she put in a syllable here and there, and many a time she took out one and then she declared the result so good that the Serjeant broke his pipe in three, and fell in love with her on the spot.

That great despatch was sent to London by the Chancery officers. Having done their business, and served both citations, these two good men had a pannier of victuals put up by dear Annie, and borrowing two of our horses, rode to Dunster, where they left them, and hired on towards London.

Jeremy lay between life and death, for at least a fortnight. At last I prevailed upon him, by argument, that he must get better, to save himself from being ignobly and unjustly superseded; and hereupon I reviled Serjeant Bloxham more fiercely than Jeremy's self could have done, and indeed to such a pitch that Jeremy almost forgave him, and became much milder. And after that his fever, and the inflammation of his wound, diminished very rapidly. However, not knowing what might happen, or even how soon poor Lorna might be taken from our power, I set forth one day for Watchett, taking advantage of the visit of some troopers from an outpost, who would make our house quite safe. Riding along, I meditated upon Lorna's history; how many things were now beginning to unfold themselves, which had been obscure and dark! For instance, Sir Ensor Doone's consent, or to say the least his indifference, to her marriage with a yeoman; which in a man so proud (though dying) had greatly puzzled both of us. But now, if she not only proved to be no grandchild of the Doone, but even descended from his enemy, it was natural enough that he should feel no great repugnance to her humiliation. And that Lorna's father had been a foe to the house of Doone I gathered from her mother's cry when she beheld their leader. Moreover that fact would supply their motive in carrying off the unfortunate little creature, and rearing her among them, and as one of their own family; yet hiding her true birth from her.

When I knocked at the little door, whose sill was gritty and grimed with sand, no one came for a very long time to answer me, or to let me in. After a good while a voice came through the key-hole, "Who is it that wishes to enter?"

"The boy who was at the pump," said I, "when the carriage broke down at Dulverton."

"Oh yes, I remember certainly. My leetle boy, with the fair white skin. I have desired to see him, oh many, yes, many times."

She was opening the door, while saying this; and then she started back in affright, that the little boy should have grown so.

"You cannot be that little boy. It is quite impossible."

"Not only am I that little boy, but also I am come to tell you all about your little girl."

"Come in, you very great leetle boy," she answered, with her dark eyes brightened. And I went in, and looked at her. She was altered by time, as much as I was. The slight and graceful shape was gone. Yet her face was comely still, and full of strong intelligence. Madame Benita Odam—for the name of the man who turned the wheel proved to be John Odam—showed me into a little room containing two chairs and a fir-wood table, and sat down on a three-legged seat and studied me very steadfastly.

Not wanting to talk about myself I drew her gradually to recollection of Lorna, and then of the little boy who died, and the poor mother buried with him. And her strong hot nature kindled, as she dwelled upon these things: and my wrath waxed within me; and we forgot reserve and prudence under the sense of so vile a wrong. She told me the very same story which she had told to Master Jeremy Stickles; only she dwelled upon it more, because of my knowing the outset.

"If I sleep in your good hostel to-night, after going to Watchett town, will you come with me to Oare to-morrow, and see your little maiden?"

"I would like—and yet I fear. This country is so barbarous. And I am good to eat—my God, there is much picking on my bones!"

At last I made her promise to come with me on the morrow, presuming that Master Odam could by any means be persuaded to keep her company in the cart, as propriety demanded. Having little doubt that Master Odam was entirely at his wife's command, I set off for Watchett, to see the grave of Lorna's poor mother, and to hire a cart for the morrow.

When I heard that Lorna's father was the Earl of Dugal, then I never thought but that everybody in Watchett town must know all about the tombstone of the Countess of Dugal. This however proved otherwise. For Lord Dugal had never lived at Watchett Grange, as their place was called; neither had his name become familiar as its owner. And upon news of his death, John Jones, a rich gentleman from Llandaff, had taken possession, as next of right, and hushed up all the story. And as the poor thing never spoke, and several of her servants and her baggage looked so foreign, and she herself died in a collar of lace unlike any made in England, all Watchett, without hesitation, pronounced her to be a foreigner. So the poor Countess of Dugal, almost in sight of her own grand house, was buried in an unknown grave, together with her pair of infants, without a plate, without a tombstone (worse than all), without a tear, except from the hired Italian woman.

Having obtained from Benita Odam a very close and full description of the place where her poor mistress lay, and the marks whereby to know it, I hastened to Watchett the following morning, before the sun was up, or any people were about. And so, without interruption, I was in the churchyard at sunrise. In the furthest and darkest nook, a little bank of earth betokened the rounding off of a hapless life. There was nothing to tell of rank, or wealth, of love, or even pity. Only some unskilful hand, probably Master Odam's under his wife's teaching, had carved a rude L., and a ruder D., upon a large pebble from the beach, and set it up as a headstone.

I gathered a little grass for Lorna, and then returned to the "Forest Cat," as Benita's lonely inn was called. For the way is long from Watchett to Oare. Therefore we set out pretty early, three of us, and a baby, who could not well be left behind. The wife of the man who owned the cart had undertaken to mind the business and the other babies, upon condition of having the keys of all the taps left with her. We all arrived, before dusk of the summer's day, safe at Plover's Barrows. Mistress Benita was delighted with the change from her dull hard life.

As luck would have it, the first who came to meet us at the gate was Lorna, her beautiful hair shed round her; and wearing a sweet white frock tucked in, and showing her figure perfectly. In her joy she ran straight up to the cart; and then stopped and gazed at Benita. At one glance her old nurse knew her. "Oh the eyes, the eyes!" she cried, and was over the rail of the cart in a moment, in spite of all her substance. Lorna, on the other hand, looked at her with some doubt and wonder. But when the foreign woman said something in Roman language, the young maid cried "Oh, Nita, Nita!" and fell upon her breast, and wept. This being so, there could be no doubt as to the power of proving Lady Lorna's birth, and rights, both by evidence and token. For though we had not the necklace now we had the ring of heavy gold, a very ancient relic. And Benita knew this ring as well as she knew her own fingers, having heard a long history about it; and the effigy on it of the wild cat was the bearing of the house of Lorne.

For though Lorna's father was a nobleman of high and goodly lineage, her mother was of yet more ancient and renowned descent, being the last in line direct from the great and kingly chiefs of Lorne. A wild and headstrong race they were, and must have everything their own way. And it was of a piece with this, that the Doones (who were an offset, by the mother's side) should fall out with the Earl of Lorne. Knowing Lorna to be direct in heirship to vast property, the Doones had brought her up with full intention of lawful marriage; and had carefully secluded her from the wildest of their young gallants.

While we were full of all these things, another very important matter called for our attention. This was no less than Annie's marriage to the Squire, Faggus. We had tried to put it off again; for in spite of all advantages, neither my mother, nor myself, had any real heart for it. When the time for the wedding came, there was such a stir and commotion as had never been known in the parish of Oare since my father's marriage. For Annie's beauty and kindliness had made her the pride of the neighbourhood; and the presents sent her were enough to stock a shop with.

And now my Lorna came to me, with a spring of tears in appealing eyes. "What is it, little darling?" I asked.

"You don't think, John, you don't think, dear, that you could lend me any money?"

"All I have got," I answered. "But I must know the purport."

"Then that you never shall know, John. I am very sorry for asking you. It is not of the smallest consequence. Oh dear, no!"

"Oh dear, yes!" I replied; "it is of very great consequence; and I understand the whole of it. You want to give that stupid Annie, who has lost you a hundred thousand pounds, and who is going to be married before us, dear—God only can tell why, being my younger sister—you want to give her a wedding present. And you shall do it, darling; because it is so good of you."

"Then perhaps you would lend me twenty pounds, dear John."

To this I agreed, upon condition that I should make the purchase myself, whatever it might be. For this end, and for many others, I set off to Dulverton, bearing more commissions, more messages, and more questions, than a man of thrice my memory might carry so far as the corner where the saw-pit is. To my dear mother, the most important matter seemed to ensure Uncle Reuben's countenance and presence at the marriage.

Uncle Reuben was not at home; but Ruth, who received me very kindly, was sure of his return in the afternoon, and persuaded me to wait for him. And by the time that I had finished all I could recollect of my orders, even with paper to help me, the old gentleman rode into the yard, and was more surprised than pleased to see me. But if he was surprised, I was more than that— I was utterly astonished at the change in his appearance since the last time I had seen him. From a hale, and rather heavy man, grey-haired, but plump, and ruddy, he was altered to a shrunken, wizened, trembling, and almost descrepit figure.

"Come inside, John Ridd," he said: "I will have a talk with you. It is cold out here: and it is too light. Come inside, John Ridd."

I followed him into a little dark room. It was closed from the shop by an old division of boarding, hung with tanned canvas;

and the smell was very close and faint. Here there was a ledger-desk, and a couple of chairs, and a long-legged stool.

"Take the stool," said Uncle Reuben, showing me in very quietly, "it is fitter for your height, John. My boy, do you wish me to die?" he asked, coming up close to my stool, and regarding me with a shrewd, though blear-eyed gaze. "Many do. Do you, John?"

"Come," said I, "don't ask such nonsense. You know better than that, Uncle Ben. Or else, I am sorry for you. I want you to live as long as possible, for the sake of—" Here I stopped.

"For the sake of what, John? I know it is not for my own sake. For the sake of what, my boy?"

"For the sake of Ruth," I answered; "if you must have all the truth. Who is to mind her when you are gone?"

"But if you knew that I had gold, or a manner of getting gold, far more than ever was heard of; and the secret was to be yours, John; then you would wish me dead, John."

"You are wrong, Uncle Ben; altogether wrong."

Presently he sent little Ruth for a bottle of wine. As I had but little time to spare (although the days were long and light), we were forced to take our wine with promptitude and rapidity; and whether this loosened my uncle's tongue, or whether he meant beforehand to speak, is now almost uncertain. But true it is that he brought his chair very near to mine, after three or four glasses, and sent Ruth away upon some errand.

"Come, Jack," he said, "here's your health, young fellow."

"Well, sir," cried I, in my sprightliest manner, which rouses up most people, "here's to your health and dear little Ruth's."

"Come now, John," said Uncle Ben, laying his wrinkled hand on my knee, when he saw that none could heed us, "I know that you have a sneaking fondness for my grandchild Ruth."

"I do like Ruth, sir," I said boldly, for fear of misunderstanding; "but I do not love her."

"Very well; that makes no difference. I do not attempt to lead you into any engagement with little Ruth; neither will I blame you (though I may be disappointed) if no such engagement should ever be. But whether you will have my grandchild, or whether you will not, I have at least resolved to let you know my secret. You are my next of kin, except among the womenkind; and you are just the man I want to help me in my enterprise."

"And I will help you, sir," I answered, fearing some conspiracy, "in anything that is loyal, and according to the laws of the realm."

"Ha, ha!" cried the old man, laughing until his eyes ran over, and spreading out his skinny hands upon his shining breeches, "thou hast gone the same fool's track as the rest; even as spy Stickles went, and all his precious troopers. Landing of arms at Glenthorne and Lynmouth, waggons escorted across the moor, sounds of metal, and booming noises! Ah, but we managed it cleverly, to cheat even those so near to us. We set it all abroad, right well. And not even you to suspect our work; though we thought at one time that you watched us. Now who, do you suppose, is at the bottom of all this Exmoor insurgency, all this western rebellion—not that I say there is none, mind—but who is at the bottom of it? Uncle Reuben!" Saying this, Master Huckaback cast back his coat, and stood up, and made the most of himself.

"Well!" cried I, being now quite come to the limits of my intellect, "then after all Captain Stickles was right in calling you a rebel, sir!"

"Of course he was: could so keen a man be wrong, about an old fool like me? But come, and see our rebellion, John. I will trust you now with everything. You shall come into partnership with me: your strength will save us two horses. Come and see our rebellion, my boy; you are a made man from to-night."

"But where am I to come and see it? Where am I to find it, sir?"

"Meet me," he answered, "come alone, of course; and meet me at the Wizard's Slough, at ten to-morrow morning."

15. Master Huckaback's Secret

KNOWING Master Huckaback to be a man of his word, as well
as one who would have others so, I was careful to be in good time
the next morning, by the side of the Wizard's Slough; and starting
about eight o'clock, without mentioning my business, arrived at
the mouth of the deep descent, such as John Fry described it. I
went boldly down the steep gorge of rock.

When I came to the foot of this ravine, a man on horseback appeared as suddenly as if he had risen out of the earth, on the other
side of the great black slough. At first I was a little scared, but
presently the white hair showed me that it was Uncle Reuben
come to look for me, that way. Then I waved my hat, and shouted
to him, and the sound of my voice among the crags and lonely
corners frightened me. Old Master Huckaback made no answer,
but beckoned me to come to him. There was just room between
the fringe of reed and the belt of rock around it, for a man going
very carefully to escape that horrible pit-hole.

"Now fasten up my horse, John Ridd, and not too near the
slough, lad. Ah, we have chosen our entrance wisely. Two good
horsemen, and their horses, coming hither to spy us out, are gone

mining on their own account (and their last account it is) down this good wizard's boghole."

With these words, Uncle Reuben clutched the mane of his horse, and came down, as a man does when his legs are old.

"Now follow me, step for step," he said, when I had tethered his horse to a tree; "many parts are treacherous."

Without any more ado, he led me, in and out of the marshy places, to a great round hole of shaft, bratticed up with timber. I never had seen the like before, and wondered how they could want a well, with so much water on every side. Around the mouth were a few little heaps of stuff unused to the daylight; and I thought at once of the tales I had heard concerning mines in Cornwall. He signed to me to lift a heavy wooden corb, with an iron loop across it, and sunk in a little pit of earth, a yard or so from the mouth of the shaft. I raised it, and by his direction dropped it into the throat of the shaft, where it hung and shook from a great cross-beam laid at the level of the earth. A very stout thick rope was fastened to the handle of the corb, and ran across a pulley hanging from the centre of the beam.

"I will first descend," he said; "your weight is too great for safety. When the bucket comes up again, follow me."

Then he whistled down, with a quick sharp noise, and a whistle from below replied: and he clomb into the vehicle, and the rope ran through the pulley, and Uncle Ben went merrily down, and was out of sight before I had time to think of him.

At last up came the bucket; and, with a short sad prayer, I went into whatever might happen. The scoopings of the side grew black, and the patch of sky above more blue, as a long way underground I sank. Then I was fetched up at the bottom, with a jerk and rattle. Two great torches of bale-resin showed me all the darkness, one being held by Uncle Ben and the other by a short square man with a face which seemed well known to me.

"Hail to the world of gold, John Ridd," said Master Huckaback, smiling in the old dry manner: "bigger coward never came down the shaft, now did he, Carfax?"

"They all be alike," said Carfax, "fust time as they doos it."

For my part, I had nought to do except to look about me, so far as the dullness of light would help.

"You seem to be disappointed, John," said Uncle Reuben; "did you expect to see the roof of gold, and the sides of gold, and the floor of gold?"

"You are wrong," I replied: "but I did expect to see something better than dirt and darkness."

"Come on then, my lad; and we will show you something better. We want your great arm on here, for a job that has beaten the whole of us."

With these words, Uncle Ben led the way along a narrow passage, roofed with rock, and floored with slate-coloured shale and shingle, until we stopped at a great stone block lying across the floor, and as large as my mother's best oaken wardrobe. Beside it were several sledge-hammers, some battered, and some with broken helves.

"Thou great villain!" cried Uncle Ben, giving the boulder a little kick; "I believe thy time has come at last. Now, John, give us a sample of the things they tell of thee. Take the biggest of them sledge-hammers and crack this rogue in two for us. We have tried at him for a fortnight, and he is a nut worth cracking. But we have no man who can swing that hammer."

"I will do my very best," said I, pulling off my coat and waistcoat, as if I were going to wrestle; "but I fear he will prove too tough for me."

"Ay, that her wull," grunted Master Carfax. "There be no man outside Carnwall, as can crack that boolder."

Nevertheless I took up the hammer, and swinging it far behind my head, fetched it down, with all my power, upon the middle of the rock. The roof above rang mightily, and the echo went down delven galleries, so that all the miners flocked to know what might be doing. But the stone was still unbroken.

"This little tool is too light," I cried; "one of you give me a piece of strong cord."

Then I took two more of the weightiest hammers, and lashed them fast to the back of mine, to burden the fall. Having made this firm, I smiled at Uncle Ben, and whirled the mighty implement round my head, just to try whether I could manage it. Then I swung me on high, and with all my power descending delivered the ponderous onset. Crashing and crushed the great stone fell over, and threads of sparkling gold appeared in the jagged sides of the breakage.

"How now, Simon Carfax," cried Uncle Ben triumphantly; "wilt thou find a man in Cornwall can do the like of that?"

"Ay, and more," he answered: "however, it be pretty fair for a lad of these outlandish parts. Get your rollers, my lads, and lead it to the crushing engine."

"Thou has done us a good turn, my lad," said Uncle Reuben, as the others passed out of sight at the corner; "and now I will show thee the bottom of a very wondrous mystery. But we must not do it more than once, for the time of day is wrong."

The whole affair being a mystery to me, I followed him without a word. He led me to a hollow place near the descending-shaft, where I saw a most extraordinary monster fitted up. In form it was like a great coffee-mill, only a thousand times larger, and with a heavy windlass to work it.

"Put in a barrow-load of the smoulder," said Uncle Ben to Carfax; "and let them work the crank."

"At this time of day!" cried Simon Carfax; "and the watching as has been o'late!"

However, he did it without more remonstrance; pouring into the scuttle at the top of the machine about a basketful of broken rock; and then a dozen men went to the wheel, and forced it round, as sailors do. Upon that such a hideous noise arose, as I never should have believed any creature capable of making.

"Enough, enough!" shouted Uncle Ben, by the time I was nearly deafened. "Now, John, not a word about what you have learned: but henceforth you will not be frightened by the noise we make at dusk."

160

I could not deny but what this was very clever management. The wisest plan was to open their valves during the evening; when folk would rather be driven away, than drawn into the wilds and quagmires, by a sound so deep and awful coming through the darkness. Although there are very ancient tales of gold being found upon Exmoor, in lumps and solid hummocks, this deep digging and great labour seemed to me a dangerous and unholy enterprise. And Master Huckaback confessed that, up to the present time, his two partners and himself had put into the earth more gold than they had taken out of it. Nevertheless he felt quite sure that it must in a very short time succeed, and pay them back a hundredfold; and he pressed me with great earnestness to join them, and work there as much as I could.

Now I had enough of that underground work, to last me for a year to come; neither would I, for sake of gold, have ever stepped into that bucket, of my own good will again. But when I told Lorna all about my great descent, then Lorna's chief desire was to know more about Simon Carfax.

"It must be our Gwenny's father," she cried; "the man who disappeared underground, and whom she has ever been seeking."

I begged my Lorna to say not a word of this matter to the handmaiden, until I had further searched it out. And to carry out this resolve I went again to the place of business. Having now true right of entrance, and being known to the watchman, I found the corb sent up for me rather sooner than I wished it. At the bottom Master Carfax met me, being captain of the mine, and desirous to know my business. He wore a loose sack round his shoulders, and his beard was two feet long.

"My business is to speak with you," I answered rather sternly.

"Coom into the muck-hole, then," was his gracious answer; and he led me into a filthy cell, where the miners changed their jackets.

"Simon Carfax," I began, with a manner to discourage him; "I fear you are a shallow fellow, and not worth my trouble."

"Then don't take it," he replied; "I want no man's trouble."

"For your sake I would not," I answered; "but for your daughter's sake I will: the daughter whom you left to starve so pitifully in the wilderness."

The man stared at me with his pale grey eyes, and his voice as well as his body shook, while he cried, "It is a lie, man. No daughter and no son have I. Nor was ever child of mine left to starve in the wilderness."

"Perhaps I have wronged you, Simon," I answered very softly; for the sweat upon his forehead shone in the smoky torch-light: "if I have, I crave your pardon. But did you not bring up from Cornwall a little maid named 'Gwenny,' and supposed to be your daughter?"

"Ay, and she was my daughter, my last and only child of five; and for her I would give this mine, and all the gold will ever come from it."

"You shall have her, without either mine or gold; if you only prove to me that you did not abandon her."

"Abandon her! I abandon Gwenny!" he cried, with such a rage of scorn, that I at once believed him. "They told me she was dead, and crushed, and buried in the drift here; and half my heart died with her. The Almighty blast their mining-work, if the scoundrels lied to me!"

"The scoundrels must have lied to you," I answered, with a spirit fired by his heat of fury: "the maid is living, and with us. Come up; and you shall see her."

"Rig the bucket," he shouted out along the echoing gallery. Without another word, we rose to the level of the moors and mires; neither would Master Carfax speak, as I led him across the barrows. I put him in the cow-house (not to frighten the little maid), and the folding shutters over him. Not to make long tale of it I went and fetched his Gwenny forth from the back kitchen, where she was fighting, as usual, with our Betty.

"Come along, you little Vick," I said, for so we called her; "Come, and see who is in the cow-house."

Gwenny knew; she knew in a moment. "Oh, Jan, you are too

good to cheat me. Is it a joke then you are putting upon me?"

I answered her with a gaze alone; and she tucked up her clothes and followed me, because the road was dirty. Then I opened the door just wide enough for the child to go to her father; and left those two to have it out, as might be most natural. And they took a long time about it. Meanwhile I needs must go and tell my Lorna all the matter.

Carfax was full as angry at the trick played on him, as he was happy in discovering the falsehood and the fraud of it. Nor could I help agreeing with him, when he told me all of it, as with tears in his eyes he did. I could not forbear from owning that it was a low and heartless trick. For when this poor man left his daughter, he meant to return in an hour or so, and settle about her sustenance in some house of the neighbourhood. But this was the very thing of all things which the leaders of the enterprise, who had brought him up from Cornwall, for his noted skill in metals, were determined, whether by fair means or foul, to stop at the very outset. Secrecy being their main object, what chance could be there of it, if the miners were allowed to keep their children in the neighbourhood? Hence, they kept him drunk for three days and three nights, assuring him that his daughter was as well as could be, and enjoying herself with the children. Not wishing the maid to see him tipsy, he pressed the matter no further. However, after three days of this, he became quite sober; with a certain lowness of heart he sought for Gwenny high and low. The other men combined to swear that Gwenny had come to seek for her father down the shaft-hole, and peering too eagerly into the dark, had toppled forward, and gone down, and lain at the bottom dead.

Simon Carfax swore that drink had lost him his wife, and now had lost him the last of his five children, and would lose him his own soul, if further he went on with it; and from that day to his death he never touched strong drink again.

16. Lorna Gone Away

As for me, I had no ambition to become a miner. Moreover, I was led from home, between the hay and corn harvests by a call there was no resisting; unless I gave up all regard for wrestling, and for my county. For a mighty giant had arisen in a part of Cornwall; and his calf was twenty-five inches round, and the breadth of his shoulders two feet and a quarter; and his stature seven feet and three quarters. Round the chest he was seventy inches, and his hand a foot across, and there were no scales strong enough to judge of his weight in the market-place. Now this man—or I should say, his backers and his boasters, for the giant himself was modest—sent me a brave and haughty challenge, to meet him in the ring at Bodmin-town, on the first day of August, or else to return my champion's belt to them by the messenger. It is no use to deny that I was greatly dashed and scared at first. For my part, I was only, when measured without clothes on, sixty inches round the breast, and round the calf scarce twenty-one, only two feet across the shoulders, and in height not six and three quarters. However, I resolved to go and try him, as they would pay all expenses, and a hundred pounds, if I conquered him.

Now this story is too well-known for me to go through it again and again. Enough that I had found the giant quite as big as they had described him, and enough to terrify any one. But trusting in my practice and study of the art, I resolved to try a back with him; and when my arms were round him once, the giant was but a farthingale put into the vice of a blacksmith. The man had no bones; his frame sank in, and I was afraid of crushing him. He lay on his back, and smiled at me; and I begged his pardon. Now this affair made a noise at the time, and redounded so much to my credit, that I was deeply grieved at it, because deserving none. For I do like a good strife and struggle. However, I got my hundred pounds, and made up my mind to spend every farthing in presents for mother and Lorna.

For Annie was married by this time, and long before I went away. The wedding was quiet enough, except for everybody's good wishes; and I desire not to dwell upon it, because it grieved me in many ways. But now that I had tried to hope the very best for dear Annie, a deeper blow than could have come, even through her, awaited me. For after that visit to Cornwall, and with my prize-money, I came on foot from Okehampton to Oare.

Now coming into the kitchen, with all my cash in my breeches pocket (golden guineas, with an elephant on them), I found dear mother most heartily glad to see me safe and sound again. Lizzie also was softer, especially when she saw me pour guineas, like pepper-corns into the pudding-basin. But by the way they hung about, I knew that something was gone wrong.

"Where is Lorna?" I asked at length, after trying not to ask it: "I want her to come, and see my money."

"Alas!" said mother, with a heavy sigh; "she will see a great deal more, I fear; and a deal more than is good for her. Whether you ever see her again will depend upon her nature, John."

"What do you mean, mother? Have you quarrelled? Why does not Lorna come to me! Am I never to know? Lizzie, you have a little sense; will you tell me where is Lorna?"

"The Lady Lorna Dugal," said Lizzie, screwing up her lips, as if the title were too grand, "is gone to London, brother John; and not likely to come back again. The Lady Lorna Dugal is gone, because she could not help herself; and she wept enough to break ten hearts—if hearts ever are broken, John. And Gwenny is gone with her. But she left a letter for 'poor John.' How grand she looked, with the fine clothes on that were come for her!"

"Where is the letter, you utter vixen?"

"The letter is in the little cupboard, near the head of Lady Lorna's bed, where she used to keep the diamond necklace, which we contrived to get stolen."

Without another word, I rushed (so that every board in the house shook) up to my lost Lorna's room, and tore the little wall-niche open, and espied my treasure. It was as simple, and as homely, and loving, as even I could wish. Part of it ran as follows —the other parts it behoves me not to open out to strangers—"My own love, and sometime lord, Take it not amiss of me, that even without farewell, I go; for I cannot persuade the men to wait, your return being doubtful. My great uncle, some grand lord, is awaiting me at Dunster, having fear of venturing too near this Exmoor country. I, who have been the child of outlaws, am now to atone for this, it seems, by living in a court of law, and under special surveillance of His Majesty's Court of Chancery. My uncle is appointed my guardian and master; and I must live beneath his care, until I am twenty-one years old. Although it pierced my heart not to say one 'Good-bye, John,' I was glad upon the whole that you were not here to dispute it. For I am almost certain that you would not, without force to yourself, have let your Lorna go to people who never, never can care for her."

Here my darling had wept again, by the tokens on the paper; and then there followed some sweet words, too sweet for me to chatter them. But she finished with these noble lines, which I do no harm, but rather help all true love, by repeating: "Of one thing rest you well assured: no difference of rank, or fortune, or of life itself, shall ever make me swerve from truth to you. Though they tell you I am false, though your own mind harbours it, yet take counsel of your heart, and cast such thoughts away from you; for they must be unworthy of the one who dwells there: and that one is, and ever shall be, your own Lorna Dugal."

All our neighbourhood was surprised, that the Doones had not ere now attacked, and probably made an end of us. For we lay almost at their mercy now, having only Serjeant Bloxham, and three men, to protect us, Captain Stickles having been ordered southwards. The Serjeant, having now imbibed a taste for writing reports, reported weekly from Plover's Barrows, whenever he could find a messenger. We treated him so well, that he reported very highly of us. And indeed he could scarcely have done less, when Lizzie wrote great part of his reports.

Now the reason why the Doones did not attack us, was that they were preparing to meet another, and more powerful assault, upon their fortress. Positive orders had been issued, that these outlaws and malefactors should at any price be brought to justice; when the sudden death of King Charles the Second threw all things into confusion, and all minds into panic. Appointed at last as churchwarden by virtue of being best farmer in the parish, I kept on thinking how his death would act on me.

And here I saw it, many ways. In the first place, troubles must break out; and we had eight-and-twenty ricks; counting grain, and straw, and hay. In the next place, much rebellion was whispering, and making signs, among us. And the terror of the Doones helped greatly; as a fruitful tree of lawlessness, and a good excuse for everybody. And after this—or rather before it—arose on me the thought of Lorna, and how these things would affect her fate. It had occurred to me sometimes, or been suggested by others, that the Lady Lorna had not behaved altogether kindly, since her departure from among us. For no message whatever had reached us; neither any token even of her safety in London. As to this last, however, we had no misgivings, having learned from the orderlies more than once, that the wealth, and beauty, and adventures of young Lady Lorna Dugal, were greatly talked of both at court, and among the common people.

Almost before we had put off the mourning, which as loyal subjects we kept for King Charles the Second three months and a week, rumours of disturbances, of plottings, and of outbreak began to stir among us. We heard of fighting in Scotland, and buying of ships on the continent, and of arms in Dorset and Somerset. For we had trustworthy reports that the new King, King James the Second, had been to high mass himself in the Abbey of Westminster, making all the bishops go with him, and all the guards in London, and then tortured all the Protestants who dared to wait outside. We of the moderate party having no love for this sour James, were ready to wait for what might happen, rather than care about stopping it. In our part, things went on as usual, until the middle of June was nigh. We ploughed the ground, and sowed the corn, and tended the cattle; and the only thing that moved us much was that Annie had a baby—this being a very fine child with blue eyes, and christened "John" in compliment to me.

But when I was down, on Saturday the thirteenth of June, at the blacksmith's forge by Brendon town, where the Lynn-stream runs so close that he dips his horse-shoes in it, round the corner came a man upon a pie-bald horse, looking flagged and weary. But seeing half-a-dozen of us, young, and brisk, and hearty, he made a flourish with his horse, and waved a blue flag vehemently, shouting with great glory, "Monmouth, and the Protestant faith! Monmouth and no Popery! Monmouth, the good King's eldest son! Down with the poisoning murderer! Down with the black usurper, and to the devil with all papists!"

For the next fortnight, we were daily troubled with conflicting rumours. We were told that the Duke had been proclaimed King of England, in every town of Dorset and of Somerset; that he had won a great battle at Axminster, and another at Bridport. And then, on the other hand, we heard that the Duke had been vanquished, and put to flight. Even Serjeant Bloxham, much against his will, was gone, having left his heart with our Lizzie, and a collection of all his writings. All the soldiers had been ordered at full speed for Exeter, to join the Duke of Albemarle.

One day at the beginning of July, I came home from mowing about noon, or a little later, to fetch some cider for all of us. In the courtyard I saw a little cart, with iron breaks underneath it, such

as fastidious people use to deaden the jolting of the road; but few men under a lord or baronet would be so particular. Therefore I wondered who our noble visitor could be. But when I entered the kitchen-place, behold it was no one greater than our Annie, with my godson in her arms, and looking pale and tear-begone. And at first she could not speak to me. But presently she smiled, and found her tongue, as if she had never gone from us.

"How natural it all looks again! Oh, I love this old kitchen so! Baby dear, only look at it, wid him pitty, pitty eyes, and him tongue out of his mousy! But now, John, I am in such trouble. All this talk is make-believe. Tom has gone off with the rebels: and you must, oh, you must go after him."

Moved as I was by Annie's tears, I yet declared that I could not go, and leave our house and homestead, far less my dear mother and Lizzie, at the mercy of the merciless Doones.

"Is that all your objection, John?" asked Annie.

"Now," I said, "be in no such hurry; there are many things to be thought about, and many ways of viewing it. I will go seek your husband, but only upon condition that you ensure this house, and people, from the Doones meanwhile. Even for the sake of Tom, I cannot leave all helpless."

Annie thought for a little while, trying to gather her smooth clear brow into maternal wrinkles, and then she looked at her child, and said, "I will risk it, for daddy's sake, darling; you precious soul, for daddy's sake." I asked her what she was going to risk. She would not tell me. And I kissed the baby, and took my cans, and went back to my scythe again.

By the time I came home it was dark night, and pouring again with a foggy rain. Being soaked all through and with water quelching in my boots, I was only too glad to find Annie's bright face, and quick figure, flitting in and out the firelight, instead of Lizzie sitting grandly, with a feast of literature, and not a drop of gravy. Lizzie showed no jealousy: she truly loved our Annie, and she adored the baby. Therefore Annie was allowed to attend to me, as she used to do.

"Now, John, you must start the first thing in the morning," she said, when the others had left the room, but somehow she stuck to the baby, "to fetch me back my rebel, according to your promise."

"Not so," I replied, misliking the job; "all I promised was to go, if this house were assured against any onslaught of the Doones."

"Just so; and here is that assurance." With these words she drew forth a paper, and laid it on my knee with triumph, enjoying my amazement. In truth it was no less than a formal undertaking, on the part of the Doones, not to attack Plover's Barrows farm, or molest any of the inmates, or carry off any chattels, during the absence of John Ridd upon a special errand. This document was signed not only by the Counsellor, but by many other Doones.

In the face of such a deed as this, I could no longer refuse to go; and having received my promise, Annie told me how she had procured·that paper. The first thing Annie had done was this: she made herself look ugly. This was not an easy thing; but she had learned a great deal from her husband, upon the subject of dis-guises. And then she left her child asleep under Betty Muxworthy's tendance—and away she went in her own "spring-cart" without a word to any one, except the old man who had driven her from Molland parish that morning; and who coolly took one of our best horses, without "by your leave" to any one. Annie made the old man drive her within easy reach of the Doone-gate. And there she bade the old man stay, until she should return to him. Then with her comely figure hidden by a dirty old woman's cloak, and her fair young face defaced by patches and by liniments, she addressed the young men at the gate in a cracked and trembling voice. She said that she bore important tidings for Sir Counsellor himself, and must be conducted to him.

She found Sir Counsellor at home and when the rest were out of sight, threw off all disguise to him. She flung her patches on the floor, amid the old man's laughter, and let her tucked up hair come down; and then went up and kissed him.

"Worthy and reverend Counsellor, I have a favour to ask," she began. "You owe me some amends, you know, for the way in which you robbed me."

"I own my debt, having so fair a creditor."

"And do you remember how you slept, and how much we made of you, and would have seen you home, sir; only you did not wish it?"

"And for excellent reasons, child. My best escort was in my cloak, after we made the cream to rise. Ha ha! The unholy spell. My pretty child, has it injured you?"

"Yes, I fear it has," said Annie; "or whence can all my ill luck come?" And here she showed some signs of crying, knowing that the Counsellor hated it. "But what I wish to know is this, will you try to help me?"

The Counsellor answered that he would do so, if her needs were moderate; whereupon she told of all her anxieties. Considering that Lorna was gone, and her necklace in his possession, and that I would be out of the way all the while, the old man readily undertook that our house should not be assaulted, nor our property molested, until my return. Annie thanked him most heartily, and felt that he had earned the necklace; while he disclaimed all obligation, and sent her under an escort safe to her own cart again.

Now there was no excuse left for me, after the promise given. But when my poor mother heard that I was committed, by word of honour, to a wild-goose chase, among the rebels, after that runagate Tom Faggus, she simply stared, and would not believe it. At last, however, we convinced her that I was in earnest, and must be off in the early morning, and leave John Fry with the hay crop.

17. Slaughter in the Marshes

RIGHT early in the morning I was off, without word to any one; and being well charged both with bacon and powder, forth I set on my wild-goose chase. I had a little kettle, and a pound and a half of tobacco, and two dirty pipes and a clean one; also a bit of clothes for change, also a brisket of hung venison, and four loaves of farm-house bread, and of the upper side of bacon a stone and a half it might be. We went away in merry style; my horse, good Kickums, being ready for anything, and I only glad of a bit of change, after months of working and brooding.

I knew nothing of the country I was bound to, nor even in what part of it my business might be supposed to lie. For beside the uncertainty caused by the conflict of reports, it was likely that the Duke of Monmouth would be moving from place to place. But the manner in which I was bandied about, by false information, from pillar to post, may be known by the names of the following towns, to which I was sent in succession, Bath, Frome, Wells, Wincanton, Glastonbury, Shepton, Bradford, Axbridge, Somerton, and Bridgwater. This last place I reached on a Sunday night. My horse and myself were glad to come to a decent place, where meat, and corn, could be had for money; and being quite weary of wandering about we hoped to rest there a little.

Of this, however, we found no chance, for the town was full of the good Duke's soldiers. And it was rumoured among them, that the "popish army," as they called it, was to be attacked that very night, and with God's assistance beaten. Having sought vainly for Tom Faggus, among these poor rustic warriors, I took to my hostel, and went to bed, being as weary as weary can be.

Falling asleep immediately, I took heed of nothing; although the town was all alive. And so for several hours I lay, until I was awakened at last, by a pushing, and pulling, and pinching, and a plucking of hair out by the roots. And at length, being able to open mine eyes, I saw the old landlady, with a candle.

"Can't you let me alone?" I grumbled. "I have paid for my bed, mistress; and I won't get up, for any one."

"Would to God, young man," she answered, shaking me as hard as ever, "that the popish soldiers may sleep, this night, only half as strong as thou dost! Fie on thee, fie on thee! Get up, and go fight; we hear the battle already; and a man of thy size mought stop a cannon."

I was by this time wide awake, and through the open window heard the distant roll of musketry, and the beating of drums. Therefore I arose, and dressed myself, and woke Kickums (who was snoring), and set out to see the worst of it. The sleepy hostler scratched his poll, and could not tell me which way to take; what odds to him who was King, or Pope, so long as he paid his way, and got a bit of bacon on Sunday? Therefore I was guided mainly by the sound of guns and trumpets, in riding out of the narrow ways, and into the open marshes. And thus I might have found my road, in spite of all the spread of water, and the glaze of moonshine; but that, as I followed sound, fog met me. Now fog is a thing that I understand, and can do with well enough, where I know the country: but here I had never been before. Yet the gleam of water always makes a fog more difficult; like a curtain on a mirror; none can tell the boundaries.

At last, when I almost despaired of escaping from this tangle of spongy banks, and of hazy creeks, my horse heard the neigh of a fellow-horse, and was only too glad to answer it; upon which the other, having lost his rider, came up, and pricked his ears at us, and gazed through the fog very steadfastly. However he capered away with his tail set on high, and the stirrup-irons clashing under him. We followed him very carefully; and he led us to a little hamlet, called West Zuyland, or Zealand. Here the King's troops had been quite lately, and their fires were still burning; but the men themselves had been summoned away by the night attack of the rebels. Hence I procured for my guide a young man who knew the district thoroughly, and who led me by many intricate ways to the rear of the rebel army. We came upon a broad open moor. By this time it was four o'clock, and the summer sun, arising wanly, showed us all the ghastly scene.

Would that I had never been there! Often in the lonely hours, even now it haunts me. Flying men, mud-bedraggled, foul with slime, reeking both with sweat and blood, cursing every stick that hindered them, or gory puddle that slipped the step, scarcely able to leap over the corpses that had dragged to die. And to see how the corpses lay; some, as fair as death in sleep. But others were of different sort: simple fellows unused to pain, accustomed to the bill-hook, perhaps, or rasp of the knuckles in a quick-set hedge. Yet here lay these poor chaps, dead. Seeing me riding to the front the fugitives called out to me, in half-a-dozen dialects, to make no utter fool of myself; for the great guns were come, and the fight was over; all the rest was slaughter.

"Arl oop wi Moonmo'," shouted one big fellow, whose weapon was a pickaxe; "na oose to vaight na moor. Wend thee hame, young mon, agin." Upon this I stopped my horse, desiring not to be shot for nothing; and eager to aid some poor sick people, who tried to lift their arms to me. And this I did to the best of my power. While I was giving a drop of cordial from my flask to one poor fellow, I felt warm lips laid against my cheek quite softly, and then a little push; and behold it was a horse leaning over me! I arose in haste, and there stood Winnie, looking at me with beseeching eyes, enough to melt a heart of stone. If ever a horse tried hard to speak, it was Winnie at that moment. I went to her side and patted her; but that was not what she wanted. She turned round, and shook her mane, entreating me to follow her.

Upon this I mounted my own horse again, and to Winnie's great delight, professed myself at her service. With her ringing silvery neigh, such as no other horse of all I ever knew could equal, she at once proclaimed her triumph, and told her master that she was coming to his aid. Broad daylight, and upstanding sun, winnowing fog from the eastern hills, and spreading the moors with freshness; all along the dykes they shone, glistened on the willow-trunks, and touched the banks with a hoary grey. But alas! those banks were touched more deeply with a gory red, while howling, cursing, yelling, and the loathsome reek of carnage, drowned the scent of new-mown hay, and the carol of the lark.

Then the cavalry of the King, with their horses at full speed, dashed from either side upon the helpless mob of countrymen. A few pikes feebly levelled met them; but they shot the pike-men, drew swords, and helter-skelter leaped into the shattered and scattering mass. Right and left, they hacked and hewed. How it must end was plain enough. But Winnie led me away to the left; and as I found the cannon-bullets coming very rudely nigh me, I was only too glad to follow her. That faithful creature stopped in front of a low black shed, such as we call a "linhay." She entered; and I followed. There I found her sniffing gently, but with great emotion, at the body of Tom Faggus. A corpse poor Tom appeared to be. But the mare would not believe it. She reached her long neck forth, and felt him with her under lip, and then she looked up at me again; as much as to say, "He is all right."

Upon this I took courage, and handled poor Tom, which being young I had feared at first to do. He groaned very feebly, as I raised him up; and there was the wound, a great savage one, gaping and welling in his right side, from which a piece seemed to be torn away. I bound it up with some of my linen, just to stanch the flow of blood, until we could get a doctor. Then I gave him a little weak brandy and water, which he drank with the greatest eagerness. After that he seemed better, and a little colour came into his cheeks; and he looked at Winnie and knew her; and would have her nose in his hand, though I thought it not good for either of them. Then he managed to whisper, "Is Winnie hurt?"

"As sound as a roach," I answered. "Then so am I," said he; "put me upon her back, John; she and I die together."

I knew not what to do; for it seemed to me a murderous thing to set such a man on horseback; where he must surely bleed to death, even if he could keep the saddle. But he told me, with many breaks and pauses, that unless I obeyed his orders, he would tear off all my bandages, and accept no further aid from me. Seeing this strong bent of his mind, I even did what his feeble eyes commanded. With a strong sash, from his own hot neck, bound and twisted around his damaged waist, I set him upon Winnie's back, and placed his trembling feet in stirrups, with a band from one to other, under the good mare's body; so that no swerve could throw him out: and then I said, "Lean forward, Tom; it will stop your hurt from bleeding." He leaned almost on the neck of the mare, which, as I knew, must close the wound.

"God bless you, John; I am safe," he whispered, fearing to open his lungs much: "who can come near my Winnie mare? A mile of her gallop is ten years of life. Look out for yourself, John Ridd." He sucked his lips, and the mare went off, as easy and swift as a swallow.

I resolved to abide awhile, even where fate had thrown me. Moreover the linhay itself was full of very ancient cow-dung; than which there is no balmier and more maiden soporific. I may have slept three hours, or four, when a shaking, more rude than the old landlady's, brought me back to the world again. I looked up with a mighty yawn; and saw twenty, or so, of foot-soldiers.

"This linhay is not yours," I said, when they had quite aroused me, with tongue, and hand, and even sword-prick: "what business have you here, good fellows?"

"Business bad for you," said one, "and will lead you to the gallows."

"No rebel am I. My name is John Ridd. I belong to the side of the King: and I want some breakfast."

These fellows were truly hospitable; that much I will say for them. They could toss a grill, or fritter, or the inner meaning of an egg, into any form they pleased, comely and very good to eat. So I made the rarest breakfast any man might hope for, after all his troubles. While this was going on a superior officer rode up, with his sword drawn, and his face on fire.

"What," he cried, smiting with the flat of his sword; "is this how you waste my time, when you ought to be catching a hundred prisoners, worth ten pounds apiece to me? Who is this young fellow we have here? Speak up, sirrah; what are thou, and how much will thy good mother pay for thee?"

"My mother will pay naught for me," I answered; "so please your worship, I am no rebel; but an honest farmer, and well-proved of loyalty."

"Ha, ha! a farmer art thou? Those fellows always pay the best. Good farmer, come to yon barren tree; thou shalt make it fruitful."

Colonel Kirke made a sign to his men, and before I could think of resistance, stout new ropes were flung around me; and with three men on either side, I was led along very painfully. I beheld myself in a grievous case, and likely to get the worst of it. For the face of the Colonel was hard and stern as a block of bogwood oak; and though the men might pity me, and think me unjustly executed, yet they must obey their orders, or themselves be put to death. It is not in my power to tell half the thoughts that moved me, when we came to the fatal tree, and saw two men hanging there already, as innocent perhaps as I was. Though ordered by the Colonel to look steadfastly upon them, I could not bear to do so: upon which he called me a paltry coward.

Colonel Kirke, now black in the face with fury and vexation, gave orders for to shoot me, and cast me into the ditch hard by. The men raised their pieces, and pointed at me, waiting for the word to fire. And a cold sweat broke all over me, as the Colonel, prolonging his enjoyment, began slowly to say, "Fire." But while he was yet dwelling on the "F," the hoofs of a horse dashed out on the road, and horse and horseman flung themselves betwixt me and the gun-muzzles.

"How now, Captain Stickles?" cried Kirke. "Dare you, sir, to come betwixt me and my lawful prisoner?"

"Nay, hearken one moment, Colonel," replied my old friend Jeremy; and his damaged voice was the sweetest sound I had heard for many a day; "for your own sake hearken." He looked so full of momentous tidings, that Colonel Kirke made a sign to his men, not to shoot me till further orders; and then he went aside with Stickles, so that in spite of all my anxiety I could not catch what passed between them.

"Then I leave him in your hands, Captain Stickles," said Kirke at last, so that all might hear him; "and I shall hold you answerable for the custody of this prisoner."

"Colonel Kirke, I will answer for him," Master Stickles replied, with a grave bow, and one hand on his breast: "John Ridd, you are my prisoner. Follow me, John Ridd."

18. Lorna still is Lorna

JEREMY STICKLES assured me, as we took the road to Bridgwater, that the only chance for my life (if I refused to fly) was to
obtain an order forthwith for my dispatch to London, as a
suspected person. "For," said he, "in a few hours' time, you would
fall into the hands of Lord Feversham, who has won this fight,
without seeing it. Now he may not be quite so savage perhaps as
Colonel Kirke, but he is equally pitiless, and his price no doubt
would be higher."

"I will pay no price whatever," I answered, "neither will I
fly. An hour agone I would have fled, for the sake of my mother,
and the farm. But now that I have been taken prisoner, and my
name is known, if I fly, the farm is forfeited; and my mother and
sister must starve. Moreover, I have done no harm; I have borne
no weapons against the King, nor desired the success of his
enemies. If they have aught to try me for, I will stand my trial."

"Then to London thou must go, my son."

We set forth at once for London; and truly thankful may I be
that God in His mercy spared me the sight of the cruel and bloody
work, with which the whole country reeked and howled, during

the next fortnight. Enough, therefore, that we rode on as far as Wells, where we slept that night; and being joined in the morning by several troopers and orderlies, we made a slow but safe journey to London, by way of Bath, and Reading.

The sight of London warmed my heart with various emotions. But what moved me most, when I saw the noble oil and tallow of the London lights, and the dripping torches at almost every corner, and the handsome sign-boards, was the thought that here my Lorna lived, and walked, and took the air. Thinking thus, I went to bed in the centre of London town, and was bitten so grievously, by creatures whose name is "Legion," mad with the delight of getting a wholesome farmer among them, that verily I was ashamed to walk in the courtly parts of the town next day, having lumps upon my face the size of a pickling walnut. The landlord said that this was nothing; and that he expected, in two days at the utmost, a very fresh young Irishman, for whom they would all forsake me. Nevertheless, I declined to wait.

And so I came to the house of a worthy furrier at the sign of the Seal and Squirrel, abutting upon the Strand road, which leads from Temple Bar to Charing Cross. Here I did very well, having a mattress of good skin-dressings, and plenty to eat every day of my life. Being under parole to Master Stickles, I only went out betwixt certain hours during the session of the courts of law. Thereby the chance of ever beholding Lorna was greatly damaged, if not altogether done away with. For these were the very hours in which the people of fashion, and the high world, were wont to appear to the rest of mankind, so as to encourage them. And of course by this time, the Lady Lorna was high among people of fashion, and was not likely to be seen out of fashionable hours.

Hence, and from many other causes—part of which was my own pride—it happened that I abode in London betwixt a month and five weeks' time ere ever I saw Lorna. Nevertheless I heard of Lorna, from my worthy furrier, almost every day, and with a fine exaggeration. This honest man was one of those who, in virtue of their trade, are admitted into noble life, to take measurements, and show patterns. And while so doing, they contrive to acquire what is to the English mind at once the most important, and most interesting of all knowledge,—the science of being able to talk about the titled people. So my furrier (whose name was Ramsack) knew the great folk, sham or real, as well as he knew a fox, or skunk, from a wolverine skin. From Master Ramsack I discovered that the nobleman, to whose charge Lady Lorna had been committed, by the Court of Chancery, was Earl Brandir of Loch Awe, her poor mother's uncle. For the Countess of Dugal was daughter, and only child, of the last Lord Lorne, whose sister had married Sir Ensor Doone; while he himself had married the sister of Earl Brandir. This nobleman had a country house near the village of Kensington; and here his niece dwelled with him, when she was not in attendance on Her Majesty Queen Mary of Modena who had taken a liking to her. Now since the King had begun to attend the celebration of mass in the chapel at Whitehall, he had given order that the doors should be thrown open, so that all who could make interest to get into the antechamber, might see this form of worship. Master Ramsack told me that Lorna was there almost every Sunday. And the worthy furrier, having influence with the door keepers, kindly obtained admittance for me, one Sunday, into the antechamber.

You may suppose that my heart beat high, when King James the Second and the Queen appeared, and entered, followed by the Duke of Norfolk bearing the sword of state, and by several other noblemen, and people of repute. Then the doors of the chapel were thrown wide open; and though I could only see a little, I thought that it was beautiful. Bowers of rich silk were there, and plenty of metal shining, and polished wood with lovely carving, flowers too of the noblest kind, and candles made by somebody who had learned how to clarify tallow. When the King and Queen crossed the threshold, a mighty flourish of trumpets arose, and a waving of banners. The Knights of the Garter were to attend that day in state; and some went in, and some stayed out. A number of ladies, beautifully dressed, being of the Queen's retinue, began to enter, and were stared at three times as much as the men had been. And indeed they were worth looking at, but none was so well worth eye-service as my own beloved Lorna. She entered modestly and shyly, with her eyes upon the ground. Would she see me, or would she pass?

By some strange chance she saw me. She looked up, and her eyes met mine. As I gazed upon her, steadfastly, yearningly, the colour of her pure clear cheeks was nearly as deep as that of my own. And the shining of her eyes was owing to an unpaid debt of tears. The lovely form of Lorna went inside, and was no more seen. Nevertheless, I waited on; as my usual manner is. While I stored up, in my memory, enough to keep our parson going through six pipes on a Saturday night, a lean man with a yellow beard came up to me. Nothing had this man to say; but with many sighs, because I was not of the proper faith, he took my reprobate hand and winked with one eye.

Although the skin of my palms was thick, I felt a little suggestion there, as of a gentle leaf in spring. I paid the man, and he went happy. Then I lifted up my little billet; and in that dark corner read it, with a strong rainbow of colours coming from the angled light. In my heart I knew that I was with all heart loved—and beyond that, who may need? All of it was done in pencil; but as plain as plain could be. In my coffin it shall lie, with my ring, and something else. Therefore will I not expose it to every man who buys this book. Enough that my love told me, in her letter, just to come and see her.

I ran away, and could not stop. My brain was so amiss, that I must do something. Therefore to the river Thames, with all speed, I hurried; and keeping all my best clothes on, into the quiet stream I leaped, and swam as far as London Bridge.

I took the lane to Kensington upon the Monday evening. For although no time was given in my Lorna's letter, I was not inclined to wait any more than decency required. The lanes, and fields, between Charing Cross and the village of Kensington, are, or were at that time, more than reasonably infested with footpads,

183

and with highwaymen. However, my stature and holly club kept these fellows from doing more than casting sheep's eyes at me. For it was still broad daylight, and the view of the distant villages, Chelsea, Battersea, Tyburn, and others, made it seem less lonely. When I came to Earl Brandir's house, I went to the entrance for servants and retainers. Here, to my great surprise, who should come and let me in but little Gwenny Carfax. Her mistress, no doubt, had seen me coming, and sent her to save trouble. But when I offered to kiss Gwenny, in my joy and comfort to see a farm-house face again, she looked ashamed, and turned away, and would hardly speak to me.

I followed her to a little room, furnished very daintily; and there she ordered me to wait, in a most ungracious manner. Almost ere I hoped, the velvet hangings of the doorway parted. Lorna, in her perfect beauty, stood before the crimson folds. The hand she offered me I took, and raised it to my lips with fear, as a thing too good for me. "Is that all?" she whispered; and in another instant she was weeping on my breast.

Enough that we said nothing more than, "Oh, John, how glad I am!" and, "Lorna, Lorna, Lorna!" for about five minutes. Then my darling drew back proudly; with blushing cheeks, and tear-bright eyes, she began to cross-examine me.

"Master John Ridd, why have you never, for more than a twelvemonth, taken the smallest notice of your old friend, Mistress Lorna Doone?"

"Simply for this cause," I answered, "that my old friend, and true love, took not the smallest heed of me. Nor knew I where to find her." I told her, over and over again, that not a single syllable of any message from her, or tidings of her welfare, had reached me, or any one of us, since the letter she left behind; except by soldiers' gossip.

"Oh, you poor dear John!" said Lorna, sighing at thought of my misery. "And now for the head-traitor. I have often suspected it: but she looks me in the face, and wishes—fearful things, which I cannot repeat."

With these words, she moved an implement such as I had not seen before, and which made a ringing noise at a serious distance. And before I had ceased wondering little Gwenny Carfax came, with a grave and sullen face.

"Gwenny," began my Lorna, in a tone of high rank and dignity, "go and fetch the letters, which I gave you at various times for dispatch to Master Ridd."

"How can I fetch them, when they are gone? It be no use for him to tell no lies"——

"Now, Gwenny, can you look at me?" I asked very sternly; for the matter was no joke to me, after a year's unhappiness.

"I don't want to look at 'ee. What should I look at a young man for, although he did offer to kiss me?"

I saw the spite and impudence of this last remark; and so did Lorna, although she could not quite refrain from smiling.

"Now, Gwenny, not to speak of that," said Lorna very demurely, "if you thought it honest to keep the letters, was it honest to keep the money?"

At this the Cornish maiden broke into a rage of honesty: "A' putt the money by for 'ee. 'Ee shall have every farden of it." And so she flung out of the room.

"I trusted her so much," said Lorna, in her old ill-fortuned way; "and look how she has deceived me!"

Gwenny came back with a leathern bag, and tossed it upon the table. Not a word did she vouchsafe to us; but stood there, looking injured.

"Go, and get your letters, John," said Lorna very gravely. "As for Gwenny, much gratitude you have shown," said Lorna, "to Master Ridd, for all his kindness, and his goodness to you. Who was it that went down, at the peril of his life, and brought your father to you, when you had lost him for months and months? Who was it? Answer me, Gwenny?"

"Girt Jan Ridd," said the handmaid, very sulkily.

"What made you treat me so, little Gwenny?" I asked, for Lorna would not ask, lest the reply should vex me.

"Because 'ee be'est below her so. All her land, and all her birth—and who be you, I'd like to know?"

"Gwenny, you may go," said Lorna, reddening with quiet anger; "and remember that you come not near me for the next three days. It is the only way to punish her," she continued to me, when the maid was gone, in a storm of sobbing and weeping. "Now, for the next three days, she will scarcely touch a morsel of food, and scarcely do a thing but cry. Make up your mind to one thing, John; if you mean to take me, for better for worse, you will have to take Gwenny with me."

"I would take you with fifty Gwennies," said I, "although every one of them hated me; which I do not believe this little maid does, in the bottom of her heart."

After this, we spoke of ourselves, and the way people would regard us, supposing that when Lorna came to be her own free mistress she were to throw her rank aside, and refuse her title, and should shape her mind to its native bent, and to my perfect happiness. It was not my place to say much, lest I should appear to use an improper and selfish influence.

"Now, John," she cried; for she was so quick that she always had my thoughts beforehand; "why will you be backward, as if you cared not for me? My mind has been made up, good John, that you must be my husband, for—well, I will not say how long, lest you should laugh at my folly. But I believe it was ever since you came, with your stockings off, and the loaches. Now, after all this age of loving, shall a trifle sever us?"

I told her that it was no trifle, but a most important thing, to abandon wealth and honour, and the brilliance of high life, and be despised by every one for such abundant folly. Moreover that I should appear a knave for taking advantage of her youth.

"Now, will you allow me just to explain my own view of this matter, John?" said she, once more my darling. "It may be a very foolish view, but I shall never change it. Please not to interrupt me, until you have heard me to the end. In the first place, it is quite certain, that neither you nor I can be happy without the other. Then what stands between us? Wordly position, and nothing else. I have no more education than you have, John Ridd; nay, and not so much. My birth and ancestry are not one whit more pure than yours, although they may be better known. As for difference of religion, we allowed for one another, neither having been brought up in a bitterly pious manner."

Here I could not help a little laugh, at the notion of any bitter piety being found among the Doones, or even in mother, for that matter. Lorna smiled, in her slyest manner, and went on again, "Now, you see, I have proved my point; there is nothing between us but worldly position—if you can defend me against the Doones, for which, I trow, I may trust you. Oh, John, you must never forsake me, however cross I am to you. And now to put aside all nonsense; though I have talked none for a year, John, having been so unhappy; and now it is such a relief to me"—

"Then talk it for an hour," said I; "and let me sit and watch you. To me it is the very sweetest of all sweetest wisdom."

"Nay, there is no time," she answered, glancing at a jewelled timepiece, scarcely larger than an oyster, which she drew from near her waist-band; and then she pushed it away, in confusion, lest its wealth should startle me. "My uncle will come home in less than half an hour, dear: and you are not the one to take a side passage, and avoid him. I shall tell him that you have been here: and that I mean you to come again."

As Lorna said this, with a manner as confident as need be, I saw that she had learned in town the power of her beauty, and knew that she could do with most men aught she set her mind upon. Therefore I gave in and said, "Darling, do just what you please. Only make no rogue of me."

For that she gave me the sweetest of all kisses; and I went down the great stairs grandly, thinking of nothing else.

19. John is John no longer

IT would be hard for me to tell the state of mind in which I lived for a long time after this. I put away from me all torment and the thought of future cares, and the sight of difficulty; and to myself appeared, which means that I became the luckiest of lucky fellows, since the world itself began. My mother, having received from me a message containing my place of abode, contrived to send me, by the pack-horses, provisions, and money, and other comfort. Therein I found addressed to Colonel Jeremiah Stickles, in Lizzie's best handwriting, half a side of the dried deer's flesh, in which he rejoiced so greatly. Also, for Lorna, a fine green goose, with a little salt towards the tail, and new laid eggs inside it, as well as a bottle of brandied cherries, and seven, or it may have been eight pounds of fresh home-made butter. Moreover to myself there was a letter. I read all about the farm affairs, and that the Doones were quiet; the parishes round about having united to feed them well through the harvest time, so that after the day's hard work, the farmers might go to bed at night. But Lizzie thought that the Doones could hardly be expected much longer to put up with it, and probably would not have done so now, but for a little adversity; to wit, that the famous Colonel Kirke had, in the most outrageous manner, hanged no less than six of them, who were captured among the rebels. Moreover, I found from this same letter (which was pinned upon the knuckle of a leg of mutton, for fear of being lost in straw) that good Tom Faggus was at home again, and nearly cured of his dreadful wound.

Lorna was greatly pleased with the goose, and the butter, and the brandied cherries; and the Earl Brandir himself declared that he never tasted better than those last, and would beg the young man from the country to procure him instructions for making them. This nobleman, being as deaf as a post, could never be brought to understand the nature of my thoughts towards Lorna. He looked upon me as an excellent youth, who had rescued the maiden from the Doones, whom he cordially detested; he patted me on the back, and declared that his doors would ever be open to me, and that I could not come too often.

Lorna said to me one day, "I will tell him, John; I must tell him, John. It is mean of me to conceal it."

I thought that she meant all about our love, which we had endeavoured thrice to drill into his fine old ears; but could not make him comprehend, without the risk of bringing the house down: and so I said, "By all means, darling: have another try at it."

Lorna, however, looked at me as much as to say, "Well, you are a stupid! We agreed to let that subject rest." And then she saw that I was vexed at my own want of quickness; and so she spoke very kindly.—"I meant about this poor son, dearest; the son of his old age almost; whose loss threw him into that dreadful cold—for he went, without hat, to look for him—which ended in his losing the use of his dear old ears. And look at his age! he is not much over seventy, John, you know. My poor uncle still believes that his one beloved son will come to light and life again. He has made all arrangements accordingly: all his property is settled on that supposition. He knows that young Alan always was what he calls a 'feckless ne'er-do-weel;' but he loves him all the more for that. He cannot believe that he will die without his son coming back to him; and he always has a bedroom ready, and a bottle of Alan's favourite wine cool from out the cellar; he has made me work him a pair of slippers, from the size of a mouldy boot."

"It is a piteous thing," I said; for Lorna's eyes were full of tears.

"And he means me to marry him. It is the pet scheme of his life. I am to grow more beautiful, and more highly taught, and graceful; until it pleases Alan to come back, and demand me. It makes me very sorrowful. For I know that Alan Brandir came to rescue me and now lies below the sod in Doone-valley."

"And if you tell his father," I answered softly, but clearly, "in a few weeks he will lie below the sod in London."

"Perhaps you are right, John," she replied: "to lose hope must be a dreadful thing, when one is turned of seventy. Therefore I will never tell him."

The good Earl Brandir kept most of his money in a handsome pewter box, with his coat of arms upon it, and a double lid, and locks. Moreover, there was a heavy chain, fixed to a staple in the wall, so that none might carry off the pewter with the gold inside of it. Lorna told me the box was full, for she had seen him go to it. Now one evening towards September, when the days were drawing in, looking back at the house, to see whether Lorna were looking after me, I espied a pair of villainous fellows watching from the thicket-corner, some hundred yards or so behind the good Earl's dwelling. "There is a mischief a-foot," thought I.

Therefore I resolved to wait, and see what those two villains did, and save (if it were possible) the Earl Brandir's fine pewter box. When all the lights were quenched, and all the house was quiet, I heard a low wily whistle from a clump of trees close by; and then three figures passed between me and a whitewashed wall, and came to a window. This window was carefully raised by someone inside the house: and after a little whispering, and something which sounded like a kiss, all the three men entered.

"Oh, you villains!" I said to myself; "this is worse than any Doone job; because there is treachery in it." I crept along the wall, and entered very quietly after them; being rather uneasy about my life, because I bore no fire-arms. I went along very delicately (as a man who has learned to wrestle can do, although he may weigh twenty stone), following carefully the light, brought by the traitorous maid. I saw her lead the men into a little place called a pantry; and there she gave them cordials, and I could hear them boasting.

I followed them from this drinking-bout, by the aid of the light they bore, as far as Earl Brandir's bedroom. Now, keeping well away in the dark, I saw these fellows try the door of the good Earl Brandir, knowing from the maid, of course, that his lordship could hear nothing. They tried the lock, and pushed at it, and were forced to break it open; and at this the guilty maid, or woman, ran away. These three rogues—for rogues they were, and no charity may deny it—burst into Earl Brandir's room, with a light, and a crowbar, and firearms.

When I came to the door of the room, being myself in shadow, I beheld two bad men trying vainly to break open the pewter box, and the third with a pistol muzzle laid to the night-cap of his lordship. With foul face, and yet fouler words, this man was demanding the key of the box, which the other men could by no means open, neither drag it from the chain. "I tell you," said this aged Earl, beginning to understand at last what these rogues were up for; "I will give no key to you. It all belongs to my boy, Alan. No one else shall have a farthing."

"Then you may count your moments, lord. The key is in your old cramped hand. One, two; and at three, I shoot you."

The thief with the pistol began to count, as I crossed the floor very quietly, while the old Earl fearfully gazed at the muzzle, but clenched still tighter his wrinkled hand. The villain, with hair all over his eyes, and the great horse-pistol levelled, cried, "three," and pulled the trigger; but luckily, at that very moment, I struck up the barrel with my staff, and then with a spin and a thwack, I brought the good holly down upon the rascal's head, in a manner which stretched him upon the floor. Meanwhile the other two robbers had taken the alarm, and rushed at me, one with a pistol, which forced me to be very lively. Fearing the pistol, I flung the heavy velvet curtain of the bed across, that he might not see where to aim at me, and then stooping very quickly, I caught up the senseless robber, and set him up for a shield and target; whereupon he was shot immediately, without having the pain of knowing it; and a happy thing it was for him. Now the other two were at my mercy, being men below the average strength.

So I took these two rogues, and bound them together; and leaving them under charge of the butler (a worthy and shrewd Scotchman), I myself went in search of the constables. In the morning, these two men were brought before the Justices of the Peace: and now my wonderful luck appeared; for the merit of having caught them, would never have raised me one step in the State, or in public consideration, if they had only been common robbers, or even notorious murderers. But these fellows were recognised as Protestant witnesses out of employment, companions and understrappers to Oates, and Bedloe, and Carstairs, and hand-in-glove with Dangerfield, Turberville, and Dugdale— in a word, the very men against whom His Majesty the King bore the bitterest rancour, but whom he had hitherto failed to catch. When this was laid before the public (with emphasis, and admiration), at least a dozen men came up, whom I had never seen before, and prayed me to accept their congratulations, and to be sure to remember them.

In the course of that same afternoon, I was sent for by His Majesty. In great alarm and flurry, I put on my best clothes, and hired a fashionable hairdresser, and drank half-a-gallon of ale, because both my hands were shaking. Then forth I set, with my holly staff, wishing myself well out of it. I was shown at once into His Majesty's presence, and there I stood most humbly and made the best bow I could think of. As I could not advance any further—for I saw that the Queen, Mary of Modena, was present, which frightened me tenfold—His Majesty, in the most gracious manner, came down the room to encourage me.

"I have seen thee before, young man," he said; "thy form is not one to be forgotten. Where was it? Thou art most likely to know."

"May it please Your Most Gracious Majesty the King," I answered, finding my voice in a manner which surprised myself; "it was in the Royal Chapel."

"I am well-pleased," said His Majesty, with a smile which almost made his dark and stubborn face look pleasant, "to find that our greatest subject, greatest I mean in the bodily form, is a good Catholic. Thou needest not say otherwise. The time shall be, and that right soon, when men shall be proud of the one true faith."

"This is that great Johann Reed," said Her Majesty, coming forward; "for whom I have so much heard, from the dear, dear, Lorna."

"Now, John Ridd," said the King, recovering from his thoughts about the true Church, and thinking that his wife was not to take the lead upon me; "thou hast done great service to the realm, and to religion. It was good to save Earl Brandir, a loyal and Catholic nobleman; but it was great service to catch two of the vilest bloodhounds ever laid on by heretics. And to make them shoot another: it was rare; it was rare, my lad. Now ask us anything in reason; thou canst carry any honours, on thy club, like Hercules. What is thy chief ambition, lad?"

"Well," said I, after thinking a little, "my mother always used to think that having been schooled at Tiverton, with thirty marks a year to pay, I was worthy of a coat of arms. And that is what she longs for."

"A good lad! A very good lad;" said the King, and he looked at the Queen, as if almost in joke; "but what is thy condition in life?"

"I am a freeholder," I answered in my confusion, "ever since the time of King Alfred. We have had three very good harvests running, and might support a coat of arms."

"Thou shalt have a coat, my lad," said the King, smiling at his own humour; "but it must be a large one to fit thee. And more than that shalt thou have, John Ridd, being of such loyal breed, and having done such service."

194

And while I wondered what he meant, he called to some of the people in waiting at the farther end of the room, and they brought him a little sword. Then he signified to me to kneel, which I did (after dusting the board, for the sake of my best breeches), and then he gave me a little tap very nicely upon my shoulder, before I knew what he was up to; and said, "Arise, Sir John Ridd!"

This astonished and amazed me to such extent of loss of mind, that I said to the King, without forms of speech, "Sir, I am very much obliged. But what be I to do with it?"

The coat of arms, devised for me by the Royal heralds, was of great size, and rich colours, and full of bright imaginings. They did me the honour to consult me first, and to take no notice of my advice. The gentlemen inquired strictly into the annals of our family. I told them, of course, all about King Alfred; upon which they settled that one quarter should be three cakes on a bar, with a lion regardant, done upon a field of gold. Without any weak misgiving, they charged my growing escutcheon with a black raven on a ground of red. My third quarter was made at once, by a two-headed boar with noble tusks, sable upon silver. All this was very fierce and fine; and so I pressed for a peaceful corner in the lower dexter, and obtained a wheat-sheaf set upright, gold upon a field of green.

Here I was inclined to pause, and admire the effect. But the heralds said that it looked a mere sign-board, without a good motto under it; and the motto must have my name in it. They gave me, "Ridd never be ridden," and I let them inscribe it in bronze upon blue. The heralds thought that the King would pay for this noble achievement; but his Majesty declined in the most decided manner to pay a farthing towards it; and as I had no money left, the heralds became as blue as azure, and as red as gules; until Her Majesty the Queen came forward very kindly, and herself did so quite handsomely.

Beginning to be short of money, and growing anxious about the farm, longing also to show myself and my noble escutcheon to mother, I took advantage of Lady Lorna's interest with the

Queen, to obtain my acquittance and full discharge from even nominal custody. I then was sure that I was fully pardoned and free, and no longer a prisoner to Jeremy Stickles. When the brisk air of the autumn cleared its way to Ludgate Hill, then such a yearning seized me for moory crag, and for dewy blade, and even the grunting of our sheep, that nothing could have held me in London town. Lorna cried, when I came away, and she sent a whole trunkful of things for mother, and Annie, and even Lizzie.

All the parishes round about united in a sumptuous dinner, to which I was invited, so that it was as good as a summons. And if my health was no better next day, it was not from want of good wishes, any more than from stint of the liquor.

As the winter passed, the Doones were not keeping themselves at home, as in honour they were bound to do. Twenty sheep a week, and one fat ox, and two stout red deer (for wholesome change of diet), as well as threescore bushels of flour, and two hogsheads and a half of cider, and a hundredweight of candles, not to mention other things of almost every variety, which they got by insisting upon it—surely these might have sufficed to keep the robbers happy in their place, with no outburst of wantonness. Nevertheless, it was not so; they had made complaint about something—too much ewe-mutton, I think it was—and in spite of all the pledges given, they had ridden forth, and carried away two maidens of our neighbourhood. Before we had finished meditating upon this loose outrage we had news of a thing far worse, which turned the hearts of our women sick.

Mistress Margery Badcock, a healthy and upright young woman, with a good rich colour, and one of the finest hen-roosts anywhere round our neighbourhood, was nursing her child about six of the clock, and looking out for her husband. Christopher Badcock was a tenant farmer, in the parish of Martinhoe, renting some fifty acres of land, with a right of common attached to them: and at this particular time, being now the month of February, and fine open weather, he was hard at work ploughing, and preparing for the spring corn. His wife was surprised, nay astonished, when by the light of the kitchen fire she saw six or seven great armed men burst into the room upon her. Two of the strongest and fiercest men at once seized poor young Margery. In spite of tears and shrieks and struggles, they tore the babe from the mother's arms, and cast it on the lime-ash floor; then they bore her away to their horses and telling the others to sack the house, rode off with their prize to the valley. And from the description of one of those two, who carried off the poor woman, I knew beyond all doubt that it was Carver Doone himself.

The other Doones being left behind, set to with a will to scour the house, and to bring away all that was good to eat. And being a little vexed herein (for the Badcocks were not a rich couple), and finding no more than bacon, and eggs, and cheese, and little items, and nothing to drink but water, they came back to the kitchen, and stamped; and there was the baby lying. By evil luck, this child began to squeal about his mother; the maid (who had stolen to look at him, when the rough men were swearing upstairs) kissed him, and left him, as the fierce men came downstairs. And being alarmed by their power of language (because they had found no silver), she crept away.

While this good maid was in the oven, by side of back-kitchen fire-place, with a faggot of wood drawn over her, and lying so that her own heart beat worse than if she were baking, the men (as I said before) came downstairs, and stamped around the baby.

"Rowland, is the bacon good?" one of them asked, with an oath or two. "What was farmer to have for supper?"

"Nought but an onion or two, and a loaf, and a rasher of rusty bacon. These poor devils live so badly, they are not worth robbing."

"No game! Then let us have a game of loriot with the baby! It will be the best thing that could befall a lusty infant heretic. Ride a cock-horse to Banbury Cross. Bye, bye, baby Bunting; toss him up, and let me see if my wrist be steady."

The cruelty of this man is a thing it makes me sick to speak of; enough that when the poor baby fell (without attempt at cry or scream, thinking it part of his usual play, when they tossed him up, to come down again), the maid in the oven of the back-kitchen, not being any door between, heard them say as follows:—

> "If any man asketh who killed thee,
> Say 'twas the Doones of Bagworthy."

Now I think that when we heard this story, and poor Kit Badcock came all around, in a sort of half-crazy manner, our gorge was risen, and our hearts in tumult. What could a man dare to call his own, while he left his wife and children at the pleasure of any stranger? The people all agreed that I was bound to take command and management. I bade them go to the magistrates, but they said they had been too often. All they said was, "Try to lead us; and we will try not to run away."

Being pressed still harder and harder, as day by day the excitement grew and no one else coming forward to undertake the business, I agreed at last to take command of the honest men, who were burning to punish, ay and destroy, those outlaws, as now beyond all bearing. One condition however I made, namely, that the Counsellor should be spared, if possible: not because he was less a villain than any of the others, but that he seemed less violent: and above all, had been good to Annie. We arranged that all our men should come, and fall into order with pike and musket, over against our dunghill; and we settled, early in the day, that their wives might come and look at them. And all these women pressed their rights upon their precious husbands, and brought so many children with them, and made such a fuss, and hugging, and racing after little legs, that our farm-yard might be taken for an out-door school for babies, rather than a review-ground.

I myself was to and fro among the children continually; for if I love anything in the world, foremost I love children. Nevertheless, I must confess, that the children were a plague sometimes. They never could have enough of me, but I had more than enough of them. However, the children proved also of some use to me; for their mothers were so pleased, by the exertions of the "great Gee-gee"—as all the small ones entitled me—that they gave me unlimited power and authority over their husbands; moreover, they did their utmost among their relatives round about, to fetch recruits for our little band. And by such means, several of the yeomanry from Barnstaple, and from Tiverton, were added to our number; and inasmuch as these were armed with heavy swords, and short carabines, their appearance was truly formidable.

Tom Faggus also joined us heartily, being now quite healed of his wound, except at times when the wind was easterly. He was made second in command to me. Also Uncle Ben came over to help us with his advice and presence, as well as with a band of stout warehousemen, whom he brought from Dulverton. For he had never forgiven the old outrage put upon him; and though it had been to his interest to keep quiet during the last attack, under Commander Stickles—for the sake of his secret gold mine—yet now he was in a position to give full vent to his feelings. For he, and his partners, had obtained from the Crown a licence to adventure in search of minerals, by payment of a yearly royalty. Therefore they had now no longer any cause for secrecy, neither for dread of the outlaws; having so added to their force as to be a match for them. And although Uncle Ben was not the man to keep his miners idle, he promised that when we had fixed the moment for an assault on the valley, a score of them should come to aid us, headed by Simon Carfax, and armed with the guns which they always kept for the protection of their gold.

20. Blood upon the Altar

HAVING resolved on a night-assault (as our undisciplined men, three-fourths of whom had never been shot at, could not fairly be expected to march up to visible musket-mouths), we cared not much about drilling our forces, only to teach them to hold a musket, so far as we could supply that weapon to those with the cleverest eyes; and to give them familiarity with the noise it made in exploding. And we fixed upon Friday night for our venture, because the moon would be at the full; and our powder was coming from Dulverton, on the Friday afternoon.

Uncle Reuben did not mean to expose himself to shooting, his time of life for risk of life being now well over. But his counsels, and his influence, and above all his warehousemen, well practised in beating carpets, were of true service to us. His miners also did great wonders, having a grudge against the Doones; as indeed who had not for thirty miles round their valley?

We were to fall to, ostensibly at the Doone gate (which was impregnable now), but in reality upon their rear, by means of my old water slide. For I had chosen twenty young fellows, all to be relied upon for spirit and power of climbing. The moon was lifting well above the shoulder of the uplands, when we, the chosen band, set forth, having the short cut along the valleys to foot of the Bagworthy water; and therefore, having allowed the rest an hour to fetch round the moors and hills. We were not to begin our climbing until we heard a masket fired from the heights, on the left hand side, where John Fry himself was stationed, upon his own and his wife's request, to keep him out of combat. And John Fry was to fire his gun, with a ball of wool inside it, so soon as he heard the hurly-burly at the Doone-gate beginning; which we, by reason of waterfall, could not hear, down in the meadows there.

We waited a very long time, with the moon marching up heaven steadfastly, and yet there was no sound of either John Fry, or his blunderbuss. I began to think that the worthy John must veritably have gone to sleep. But suddenly the most awful noise that anything short of thunder could make, came down among the rocks, and went and hung upon the corners.

"The signal, my lads!" I cried, leaping up. "Now hold on by the rope, and lay your quarter-staffs across, my lads; and keep your guns pointing to heaven, lest haply we shoot one another."

My chief alarm in this steep ascent was neither of the water, nor of the rocks, but of the loaded guns we bore. If any man slipped, off might go his gun. However, thank God, though a gun went off, no one was any the worse for it, neither did the Doones notice it, in the thick of the firing in front of them. For the order to those of the sham attack, conducted by Tom Faggus, was to make the greatest possible noise, without exposure of themselves; until we, in the rear, had fallen to; which John Fry was again to give signal of.

Therefore we, of the chosen band, stole up the meadow quietly, keeping in the hollow of the watercourse. And the earliest notice the Counsellor had of our presence, was the blazing of the log-wood house, where lived that villain Carver. It was my especial privilege to set this house on fire. And I must confess that I rubbed my hands, with a strong delight and comfort, when I saw the home of that man, who had fired so many houses, having its turn of smoke, and blaze, and of crackling fury. We took good care, however, to burn no innocent women, or children, in that most righteous destruction. For we brought them all out beforehand; some were glad, and some were sorry; according to their dispositions. For Carver had ten or a dozen wives; and perhaps that had something to do with his taking the loss of Lorna so easily. One child I noticed, as I saved him; a fair and handsome little fellow, beloved by Carver Doone. The boy climbed on my back. Leaving these poor injured people to behold their burning home, we drew aside, by my directions, into the covert beneath the cliff. But not before we had laid our brands to three other houses, after calling the women forth, and bidding them go for their husbands, to come and fight a hundred of us. In the smoke, and rush, and fire, they believed that we were a hundred; and away they ran, in consternation, to the battle at the Doone gate.

"All Doone-town is on fire, on fire!" we heard them shrieking as they went; "a hundred soldiers are burning it, with a dreadful great man at the head of them!"

Presently, just as I expected, back came the warriors of the Doones; leaving but two or three at the gate, and burning with wrath to crush under foot the presumptuous clowns in their valley. Just then, the waxing fire leaped above the red crest of the cliffs, and danced on the pillars of the forest, and lapped like a tide on the stones of the slope. But the finest sight of all was to see those haughty men striding down the causeway darkly, reckless of their end, but resolute to have two lives for every one. A finer dozen of young men could not have been found in the world perhaps, nor a braver, nor a viler one. Seeing how few there were of them, I was very loth to fire. But my followers waited for no word: they saw a fair shot at the men they abhorred, the men who had robbed them of home or of love; and the chance was too much for their charity. A dozen muskets were discharged, and half of the Doones dropped lifeless, like so many logs of firewood, or chopping-blocks rolled over.

While the valley was filled with howling, and with shrieks of women, all the rest of the Doones leaped at us, like so many

202

demons. They fired wildly, not seeing us well among the hazel bushes; and then they clubbed their muskets, or drew their swords, as might be; and furiously drove at us. I like not to tell of slaughter, though it might be of wolves, and tigers: and that was a night of fire, and slaughter, and of very long-harboured revenge. Enough that ere the daylight broke, upon that wan March morning, the only Doones still left alive were the Counsellor, and Carver. And of all the dwellings of the Doones (inhabited with luxury, and luscious taste, and licentiousness) not even one was left, but all made potash in the river.

We returned on the following day, almost as full of anxiety, as we were of triumph. What could we frugally do with all these women and children, thrown on our hands, as one might say, with none to protect and care for them? We did our very best at the farm, and so did many others, to provide for them, until they should manage about their own subsistence. And after a while, this trouble went, as nearly all troubles go with time. Some of the women were taken back by their parents, or their husbands, or it may be their old sweethearts; and those who failed of this, went forth, some upon their own account to the New World plantations, where the fairer sex is valuable; and some to English cities; and the plainer ones to field-work. And most of the children went with their mothers, or were bound apprentices; only Carver Doone's handsome child had lost his mother, and stayed with me.

This boy went about with me everywhere, and I, perceiving his noble courage, scorn of lies, and high spirit, became almost as fond of Ensie, as he was of me. He told us that his name was "Ensie," meant for "Ensor," I suppose, from his father's grandfather, the old Sir Ensor Doone. And this boy appeared to be Carver's heir, having been born in wedlock, contrary to the general manner and custom of the Doones. However, although I loved the poor child, I could not help feeling very uneasy about the escape of his father, the savage and brutal Carver. This man now roamed the country, homeless, and desperate, with his giant strength, and great skill in arms, and the whole world to be revenged upon.

After the desperate charge of young Doones had been met by us, and broken, I had happened to descry a patch of white on the grass of the meadow. I ran up at full speed; and lo, it was the flowing silvery hair of that sage the Counsellor, who was scuttling away upon all fours; but now rose, and confronted me.

"John," he said, "Sir John, I look to you to protect me, John."

"Honoured sir, you are right," I replied. "It is my intention to let you go free. But upon two conditions," I added: "the first is, that you tell me truly who it was that slew my father."

"I will tell you, truly and frankly, John; however painful to me to confess it. It was my son, Carver. If I had been there, it would not have happened. I am always opposed to violence. Therefore, let me haste away: this scene is against my nature."

"You shall go directly, Sir Counsellor, after meeting my other condition; which is, that you place in my hands Lady Lorna's diamond necklace."

"Alas, John, the thing is not in my possession. Carver, my son, who slew your father, upon him you will find the necklace. What are jewels to me, young man, at my time of life? Ah! ah! Let me go. I have made my peace with God."

I thrust my hand inside his waistcoat, and drew forth Lorna's necklace, purely sparkling in the moonlight, like the dancing of new stars. The old man made a stab at me, with a knife which I had not espied; but the vicious onset failed; and then he knelt, and clasped his hands.

"Oh, for God's sake, John, my son, rob me not, in that manner. They belong to me; I would give almost my life for them. There is one jewel there I can look at for hours, and see all the lights of heaven in it. All my wretched, wicked life—oh, John, I am a sad hypocrite—but give me back my jewels."

As his beautiful white hair fell away from his noble forehead, and his powerful face, for once, was moved with real emotion, I was so amazed and overcome by the grand contradictions of nature, that verily I was on the point of giving him back the necklace. But I said, without more haste than might be expected, "Sir

205

Counsellor, I cannot give you what does not belong to me. But if you will show me that particular diamond, which is heaven to you, I will take upon myself the risk of cutting it out for you. And with that you must go contented."

Seeing no hope of better terms, he showed me his pet love of a jewel; and I thought of what Lorna was to me, as I cut it out (with the hinge of my knife severing the snakes of gold) and placed it in his careful hand. Another moment, and he was gone; and God knows what became of him.

It cost no more than sixteen lives to be rid of nearly forty Doones, each of whom would most likely have killed three men, in the course of a year or two. The thing which next betided me was a most glorious rise to the summit of all fortune. For in good truth it was no less than the return of Lorna—my Lorna, my own darling; in wonderful health and spirits, and as glad as a bird to get back again. It would have done any one good for a twelvemonth to behold her face and doings, and her beaming eyes and smile when this Queen of every heart ran about our rooms again. All the house was full of brightness. My mother sat in an ancient chair, and wiped her cheeks, and gazed at her; and even Lizzie's eyes must dance to the freshness and joy of her beauty.

What a quantity of things Lorna had to tell us!

"Oh, I do love it all so much," said Lorna, now for the fiftieth time, "the scent of the gorse on the moors drove me wild, and the primroses under the hedges. And now, since you will not ask me, dear mother, in the excellence of your manners, and even John has not the impudence, in spite of all his coat of arms, I must tell you a thing, which I vowed to keep until to-morrow morning; but my resolution fails me. I am my own mistress; what think you of that, mother? I am my own mistress!"

"Then you shall not be so long," cried I; "darling, you shall be mistress of me; and I will be your master."

With tears springing out of smiles, she fell on my breast, and cried a bit. In the morning, Lorna was ready to tell her story, and we to hearken. Earl Brandir's ancient steward, in whose charge she had travelled, looked upon her as a lovely maniac; and the mixture of pity, and admiration, wherewith he regarded her was a strange thing to observe; especially after he had seen our simple house and manners. On the other hand, Lorna considered him a worthy but foolish old gentleman; to whom true happiness meant no more than money and high position. These two last she had been ready to abandon wholly, and had in part escaped from them, as the enemies of her happiness. And she took advantage of the times in a truly clever manner. For that happened to be a time when everybody was only too glad to take money for doing anything. And the greatest money-taker in the kingdom was generally acknowledged to be the Lord Chief Justice Jeffreys.

Upon his return from the Bloody Assizes, with triumph and great glory, after hanging every man who was too poor to help it, he pleased His Gracious Majesty so purely with the description of their delightful agonies, that the King exclaimed, "This man alone is worthy to be at the head of the law." Accordingly in his hand was placed the Great Seal of England.

So it came to pass that Lorna's destiny hung upon Lord Jeffreys; for at this time Earl Brandir died, being taken with gout in the heart, soon after I left London. Lorna grieved for him, as we ought to grieve for any good man going. Now the Lady Lorna Dugal appeared, to Lord Chancellor Jeffreys, so exceeding wealthy a ward, that the lock would pay for turning. Therefore he came, of his own accord, to visit her, and to treat with her; having heard that this wealthy and beautiful maiden would not listen to any young lord, having pledged her faith to the plain John Ridd.

Thereupon, the Lord High Chancellor saw his way to a heap of money. And there and then upon surety of a certain round sum he gave to his fair ward permission, under sign and seal, to marry that loyal knight, John Ridd. Lorna told me, with the sweetest smile, that if I were minded to take her at all, I must take her without anything; inasmuch as she meant, upon coming of age, to make over the residue of her estate to the next of kin, as being unfit for a farmer's wife. And I replied, with the greatest warmth, and a readiness to worship her, that this was exactly what I longed for.

Everything was settled smoothly, and without any fear or fuss, that Lorna might find end of troubles, and myself of eager waiting, with the help of Parson Bowden, and the good wishes of two counties. I could scarce believe my fortune, when I looked upon her beauty, gentleness, and sweetness.

But this was far too bright to last, without bitter break, and the plunging of happiness in horror, and of passionate joy in agony. I could not be regardless of some hidden evil; and my dark misgivings deepened as the time drew nearer. I kept a steadfast watch on Lorna, neglecting a field of beans entirely, as well as a litter of young pigs, and a cow somewhat given to jaundice. However humble I might be, no one, knowing anything of our part of the country, would for a moment doubt that now here was a great to-do, and talk of John Ridd, and his wedding. We heard that people meant to come from more than thirty miles around, upon excuse of seeing my stature and Lorna's beauty; but in good truth out of sheer curiosity, and the love of meddling.

Dear mother arranged all the ins and outs of the way in which it was to be done; and Annie, and Lizzie, and all the Snowes, and even Ruth Huckaback made such a sweeping of dresses, that I scarcely knew where to place my feet, and longed for a staff, to put by their gowns. Then Lorna came out of a pew half-way, in a manner which quite astonished me, and took my left hand in her right, and I prayed God that it were done with. Lorna's dress was of pure white, clouded with faint lavender and as simple as need be, except for perfect loveliness. I was afraid to look at her, as I said before, except when each of us said, "I will;" and then each dwelled upon the other.

It is impossible for any, who have not loved as I have, to conceive my joy and pride, when after ring and all was done, and the parson had blessed us, Lorna turned to look at me. Her eyes told me such a tale of hope, and faith, and heart's devotion, that I was almost amazed, thoroughly as I knew them.

The sound of a shot rang through the church, and those eyes

were dim with death. Lorna fell across my knees; a flood of blood came out upon the yellow wood of the altar steps; and at my feet lay Lorna, trying to tell me some last message. I lifted her up, and petted her, and coaxed her, but it was no good; the only sign of life remaining was a drip of bright red blood. To me comes back as a hazy dream, what I did, or felt, or thought, with my wife's arms flagging, flagging, around my neck, as I raised her up, and softly put them there. She sighed a long sigh on my breast, for her last farewell to life, and then she grew cold.

I laid my wife in my mother's arms, and went forth for my revenge.

Of course, I knew who had done it. There was but one man upon earth, who could have done such a thing. I used no harsher word about it, while I leaped upon our best horse, with bridle but no saddle, and set the head of Kickums towards the course now pointed out to me.

Weapons of no sort had I. Unarmed, and wondering at my strange attire (with a bridal vest, wrought by our Annie, and red with the blood of the bride), I went forth just to find out this: whether in this world there be, or be not, God of justice. With my vicious horse at a furious speed, I came upon Black Barrow Down, directed by some shout of men, which seemed to me but a whisper. And there, about a furlong before me, rode a man on a great black horse; and I knew that the man was Carver Doone.

"Thy life, or mine," I said to myself; "as the will of God may be. But we two live not upon this earth, one more hour, together." I knew the strength of this great man; and I knew that he was armed with a gun—if he had time to load again, after shooting my Lorna—or at any rate with pistols, and a horseman's sword as well. Nevertheless, I had no more doubt of killing the man before me, then a cook has of spitting a headless fowl. Although he was so far before me, and riding as hard as ride he might, I saw that he had something on the horse in front of him; something which needed care, and stopped him from looking backward.

The man turned up the gully leading from the moor to Cloven

Rocks. But as Carver entered it, he turned round, and beheld me not a hundred yards behind; and I saw that he was bearing his child, little Ensie, before him. Ensie also descried me, and stretched his hands, and cried to me; for the face of his father frightened him.

Carver Doone, with a vile oath, thrust spurs into his flagging horse, and laid one hand on a pistol-stock. And a cry of triumph rose from the black depths of my heart. What cared I for pistols? I had no spurs, neither was my horse one to need the rowel; I rather held him in that urged him, for he was fresh as ever; and I knew that the black steed in front, if he breasted the steep ascent, where the track divided, must be in our reach at once.

His rider knew this; and, having no room in the rocky channel to turn and fire, drew rein at the crossways sharply, and plunged into the black ravine leading to the Wizard's Slough. I followed my enemy carefully, steadily, even leisurely; for I had him, as in a pitfall, whence no escape might be.

A gnarled and half-starved oak, as stubborn as my own resolve, and smitten by some storm of old, hung from the crag above me. Rising from my horse's back, although I had no stirrups, I caught a limb, and tore it from the socket. Men show the rent even now, with wonder; none with more wonder than myself.

Carver Doone turned the corner suddenly, on the black and bottomless bog; with a start of fear he reined back his horse, and I thought he would have rushed upon me. But instead of that, he again rode on; hoping to find a way round the side. Now there is a way between cliff and slough, for those who know the ground thoroughly, or have time enough to search it; but for him there was no road, and he lost some time in seeking it. Upon this he made up his mind; and wheeling, fired, and then rode at me.

His bullet struck me somewhere, but I took no heed of that. Fearing only his escape, I laid my horse across the way, and with the limb of the oak struck full on the forehead his charging steed. Ere the slash of the sword came nigh me, man and horse rolled over, and well-nigh bore my own horse down, with the power of their onset.

Carver Doone was somewhat stunned, and could not rise for a moment. Meanwhile I leaped on the ground, and waited, smoothing my hair back and baring my arms, as though in the ring for wrestling. Then the little boy ran to me, clasped my leg, and looked up at me: and the terror in his eyes made me almost fear myself.

"Ensie, dear," I said quite gently, grieving that he should see his wicked father killed, "run up yonder round the corner, and try to find a bunch of bluebells for the pretty lady." The child obeyed me, hanging back, and looking back, and then laughing, while I prepared for business. There and then, I might have killed mine enemy, with a single blow, while he lay unconscious; but it would have been foul play.

With a sullen and black scowl, the Carver gathered his mighty limbs, and arose, and looked round for his weapons; but I had put them well away. Then he came to me, and gazed, being wont to frighten thus young men.

"I would not harm you, lad," he said, with a lofty style of sneering: "I have punished you enough, for most of your impertinence. For the rest I forgive you; because you have been good, and gracious, to my little son. Go, and be contented."

For answer, I smote him on the cheek, lightly, and not to hurt him: but to make his blood leap up. There was a level space of sward, between us and the slough. To this place I led him. I think he felt that his time was come. At any rate a paleness came, an ashy paleness on his cheeks, and the vast calves of his legs bowed in, as if he were out of training. Seeing this, villain as he was, I offered him first chance. I stretched forth my left hand, as I do to a weaker antagonist, and I let him have the hug of me. But in this I was too generous having forgotten my pistol-wound, and the cracking of one of my short lower ribs. Carver Doone caught me round the waist, with such a grip as never yet had been laid upon me.

I heard my rib go; I grasped his arm, and tore the muscle out of it (as the string comes out of an orange); then I took him by the throat, which is not allowed in wrestling; but he had snatched at mine; and now was no time of dalliance. In vain he tugged, and strained, and writhed, dashed his bleeding fist into my face, and flung himself on me, with gnashing jaws. Beneath the iron of my strength, I had him helpless in two minutes, and his blazing eyes lolled out.

"I will not harm thee any more," I cried, so far as I could for panting, the work being very furious; "Carver Doone, thou art beaten; own it, and thank God for it; and go thy way, and repent thyself."

It was all too late.

The black bog had him by the feet; the sucking of the ground drew on him, like the thirsty lips of death. In our fury, we had heeded neither wet nor dry, nor thought of earth beneath us. I myself might scarcely leap from the engulfing grave of slime. He fell back, with his swarthy breast like a hummock of bog-oak, standing out the quagmire; and then he tossed his arms to heaven, and they were black to the elbow, and the glare of his eyes was ghastly. I could only gaze and pant: for my strength was no more than an infant's, from the fury and the horror. Scarcely could I turn away, while, joint by joint, he sank from sight.

21. Give away the Grandeur

WHEN the little boy came back with the bluebells, which he had managed to find—as children always do find flowers, when older eyes see none—the only sign of his father left was a dark brown bubble, upon a new-formed patch of blackness. But to the centre of its pulpy gorge, the greedy slough was heaving, and sullenly grinding its weltering jaws, among the flags, and the sedges. With pain, and ache, both of mind and body, and shame at my own fury, I heavily mounted my horse again, and looked down at the innocent Ensie.

"Don"—for he never could say "John"—"oh Don, I am so glad, that nasty naughty man is gone away. Take me home, Don. Take me home."

I had spent a great deal of blood, and was rather faint and weary. And it was lucky for me that Kickums had lost spirit, like his master, and went home as mildly as a lamb. For, when we came towards the farm. I seemed to be riding in a dream almost. Only the thought of Lorna's death, like a heavy knell, was tolling in the belfry of my brain.

When we came to the stable door, I rather fell from my horse than got off; and John Fry, with a look of wonder, took Kickums' head, and led him in. Into the old farm-house I tottered.

"I have killed him," was all I said; "even as he killed Lorna. Now let me see my wife, mother. She belongs to me none the less, though dead."

"You cannot see her now, dear John," said Ruth Huckaback, coming forward; since no one else had the courage. "Annie is with her now, John."

"What has that to do with it? Let me see my dead one; and then die."

All the women fell away, and whispered, and looked at me, with side-glances, and some sobbing; for my face was hard as flint. Ruth alone stood by me, and whispered, "John, she is not your dead one. She may even be your living one yet, your wife, your home, and your happiness. But you must not see her now. The sight of you, in this sad plight, would be certain death to her. Now come first, and be healed yourself."

If it had not been for this little maid, Lorna must have died at once, as in my arms she lay for dead, from the dastard and murder-our cruelty. But the moment I left her Ruth came forward, and took the command of every one. She made them bear her home at once upon the door of the pulpit, with the cushion under the drooping head. With her own little hands she cut off the bridal-dress so steeped and stained, and then she probed the vile wound in the side, and fetched the reeking bullet forth; and then with the coldest water staunched the flowing of the lifeblood. All this while, my darling lay insensible, and white as death; and the rest declared that she was dead, and needed nothing but her maiden shroud.

But Ruth bade them fetch her Spanish wine. Then she parted the pearly teeth and poured in wine from a christening spoon, and waited; and then poured in a little more. Annie all the while looked on, with horror and amazement, counting herself no second-rate nurse, and this as against all theory. And at the very moment, when all the rest had settled that Ruth was a simple idiot, but could not harm the dead much, a little flutter in the throat, followed by a short low sigh, made them pause, and hope.

214

For hours, however, and days, she lay at the very verge of death, kept alive by nothing but the care, the skill, the tenderness, and perpetual watchfulness of Ruth. Luckily Annie was not there very often, so as to meddle; for kind and clever nurse as she was, she must have done more harm than good. But my broken rib, which was set by a doctor, who chanced to be at the wedding, was allotted to Annie's care; and great inflammation ensuing, it was quite enough to content her. This doctor had pronounced poor Lorna dead; wherefore Ruth refused most firmly to have aught to do with him. She took the whole case on herself; and with God's help, she bore it through.

Lorna recovered long ere I did. Slowly came back my former strength, with a darling wife, and good victuals. As for Lorna, she never tired of sitting and watching me eat and eat.

There is no need for my farming harder than becomes a man of weight. Lorna has great stores of money, though we never draw it out, except for some poor neighbour; unless I find her a sumptuous dress, out of her own perquisites. And this she always looks upon as a wondrous gift from me; and kisses me much when she puts it on, and walks like the noble woman she is. And yet I may never behold it again; for she gets back to her simple clothes and I love her the better in them. I believe that she gives half the grandeur away, and keeps the other half for the children.

As for poor Tom Faggus, the good and respectable Tom lived a godly and righteous (though not always sober) life; and brought up his children to honesty, as the first of all qualifications.

My dear mother was as happy as possibly need be with us; having no cause for jealousy, as other arose round her. And everybody was well pleased, when Lizzie came in one day and tossed her book-shelf over, and declared that she would have Captain Bloxham, and nobody should prevent her. For that he alone, of all the men she had ever met with, knew good writing when he saw it, and could spell a word when told. As he had now succeeded to Captain Stickles' position there was nothing to be said against it; and we hoped that he would pay her out.

I sent little Ensie to Blundell's school, at my own cost and charges, having changed his name, for fear of what any one might do to him. I called him "Ensie Jones;" and I hope that he will be a credit to us. He looks upon me as his father; and without my leave, will not lay claim to the heritage, and title of the Doones, which clearly belong to him.

Ruth Huckaback is not married yet: although upon Uncle Reuben's death she came into all his property; except, indeed, £2000, which Uncle Ben, in his driest manner, bequeathed "to Sir John Ridd, the worshipful knight, for greasing of the testator's boots." And he left almost a mint of money, not from the mine, but from the shop, and the good use of usury. For the mine had brought in just what it cost, when the vein of gold ended suddenly; leaving all concerned much older, and some, I fear, much poorer; but no one utterly ruined, as in the case with most of them. Ruth herself was his true mine, as upon death-bed he found. I know a man even worthy of her: and though she is not very young, he loves her, as I love Lorna. More and more I hope, and think, that in the end he will win her; and I do not mean to dance again, except at dear Ruth's wedding; if a floor can be found strong enough.

Of Lorna, of my lifelong darling, I will not talk. Year by year, her beauty grows, with the growth of goodness, kindness, and true happiness—above all with loving. And if I wish to pay her out for something very dreadful—as may happen once or twice, when we become too gladsome—I bring her to forgotten sadness, and to me for cure of it, by the two words, "Lorna Doone."

Lifetime Library

Favorite Stories For Young Readers